RALPH COMPTON
WEST OF PECOS

**Also by David Robbins
in Large Print:**

The Return of the Virginian
Ralph Compton: Nowhere, TX

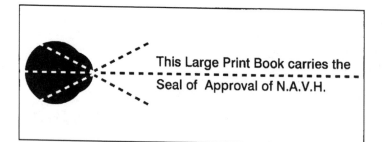

RALPH COMPTON
WEST OF PECOS

A Ralph Compton Novel
DAVID ROBBINS

Thorndike Press • Waterville, Maine

Published in 2006 by arrangement with NAL Signet, a division of Penguin Group (USA) Inc.

Thorndike Press® Large Print Western.

The tree indicium is a trademark of Thorndike Press.

The text of this Large Print edition is unabridged.
Other aspects of the book may vary from the original edition.

Set in 16 pt. Plantin.

Printed in the United States on permanent paper.

Library of Congress Cataloging-in-Publication Data

Robbins, David, 1950–
    West of Pecos : a Ralph Compton novel / by David
  Robbins.
      p. cm. — (Thorndike Press large print westerns)
    At head of title: Ralph Compton.
    ISBN 0-7862-8339-4 (lg. print : hc : alk. paper)
    1. United States — History — Civil War, 1861–1865 —
  Veterans — Fiction.   2. Guadalupe Mountains (N.M. and
  Tex.) — Fiction.   3. Large type books.   I. Title: Ralph
  Compton, West of Pecos.   II. Compton, Ralph.   III. Title.
  IV. Thorndike Press large print Western series.
  PS3568.O22288W47 2006
    813′.6—dc22
                                                    2005031016

RALPH COMPTON
WEST OF PECOS

As the Founder/CEO of NAVH, the only national health agency solely devoted to those who, although not totally blind, have an eye disease which could lead to serious visual impairment, I am pleased to recognize Thorndike Press* as one of the leading publishers in the large print field.

Founded in 1954 in San Francisco to prepare large print textbooks for partially seeing children, NAVH became the pioneer and standard setting agency in the preparation of large type.

Today, those publishers who meet our standards carry the prestigious "Seal of Approval" indicating high quality large print. We are delighted that Thorndike Press is one of the publishers whose titles meet these standards. We are also pleased to recognize the significant contribution Thorndike Press is making in this important and growing field.

Lorraine H. Marchi, L.H.D.
Founder/CEO
NAVH

* Thorndike Press encompasses the following imprints: Thorndike, Wheeler, Walker and Large Print Press.

THE IMMORTAL COWBOY

This is respectfully dedicated to the "American Cowboy." His was the saga sparked by the turmoil that followed the Civil War, and the passing of more than a century has by no means diminished the flame.

True, the old days and the old ways are but treasured memories, and the old trails have grown dim with the ravages of time, but the spirit of the cowboy lives on.

In my travels — to Texas, Oklahoma, Kansas, Nebraska, Colorado, Wyoming, New Mexico, and Arizona — I always find something that reminds me of the Old West. While I am walking these plains and mountains for the first time, there is this feeling that a part of me is eternal, that I have known these old trails before. I believe it is the undying spirit of the frontier calling, allowing me, through the mind's eye, to step back into time. What is the appeal of the Old West of the American frontier?

It has been epitomized by some as the dark and bloody period in American history.

Its heroes — Crockett, Bowie, Hickok, Earp — have been reviled and criticized. Yet the Old West lives on, larger than life.

It has become a symbol of freedom, when there was always another mountain to climb and another river to cross; when a dispute between two men was settled not with expensive lawyers, but with fists, knives, or guns. Barbaric? Maybe. But some things never change. When the cowboy rode into the pages of American history, he left behind a legacy that lives within the hearts of us all.

— *Ralph Compton*

I

"Are we going to die?" young Sally Waldron asked.

"Don't talk nonsense, child," Constance Waldron said. But she had to admit there had been times during their long journey when she thought they might. They had come so far — so very, very far. Day after day, week after week, of lumbering along in their prairie schooner. Of blistering heat and choking dust and the god-awful flies. She dearly wished they had never left their home in Ohio, dearly wished her husband had never heard of Texas.

Tom Waldron was perched on the edge of the seat, his brown eyes fixed straight ahead, his face almost grim. He did not seem to feel it when she put a hand on his arm and gently squeezed.

"Are you all right?" Constance was worried. He had been like this ever since they crossed the Pecos River.

"I'm fine," Tom said absently.

"Are you sure?"

Tom Waldron turned his gaze from the

hazy horizon and looked at his wife. Despite the sheen of sweat on her brow and the stray wisps of sandy hair that had come loose from the bun at the back of her head and the splotches of dirt on her dress, she was as lovely to him as the day he married her. She had made the dress herself, just as she made all their clothes. "Of course I'm sure. What kind of silly question is that?"

Constance's green eyes flared with fire and she retorted, "Is it silly of a woman to worry about her husband?" Her tone warned Tom he had overstepped himself. She was a feisty woman, his wife, and never afraid to speak her mind.

"Of course not. I have a lot to think about, is all." It was no excuse and he knew it, and he knew that she knew he knew it, but she had the tact not to dwell on it as some wives were wont to do.

"You still think we'll find our slice of paradise?"

"As God is my witness," Tom vowed. But even he could not say where. All he had to go on was a yearning, a sense that somewhere out there was a place they were meant to be. A place where they would set down roots and live out the rest of their days. "I'll know it when I see it."

Constance smiled. He had been saying

the same thing ever since that night almost a year ago when he shocked her by suggesting they sell their small farm and head west into the vast unknown.

"We're close," Tom said. "I can feel us getting closer every day." He resumed staring straight ahead, a big man with broad shoulders and a blue cap on his head, his brown hair a lot longer than it had been when they started.

Constance wished she could feel what he felt. All she felt was tired and worn. More tired and more worn than anytime in her life. Their daily grind was to blame. Every morning they were up at the crack of dawn, and she and the girls prepared breakfast while Tom hitched the team. Then off they went, hour after hour of eating dust and being baked alive by the burning sun. At midday they rested, but only for a short while, long enough for her to slap the dust from her dress and serve something that would tide them over until supper. The afternoon was spent in more monotonous plodding westward. At twilight, Tom would search for a suitable spot to stop for the night. Sometimes there was water; more often there was not, which was why they had to severely ration the water in the barrel on the side of their wagon, to the point where they couldn't do more than dab at the dirt and the grime. Constance hated it, hated it more than anything, but she endured it for her husband's sake, and for her family's.

Tom Waldron felt his wife put her hand on his knee and was spiked by a twinge of conscience. He would never admit as much, but for all his confident talk, he was worried, deeply worried, that he had dragged his loved ones off across the frontier for nothing. He was sure he'd have found a spot he liked by now. A place so special, it would justify uprooting them.

Tom was aware his wife had not approved. She had liked their little farm. Liked her flower garden and the chickens and the few cows they owned, and thought that a hundred acres was plenty enough, thank you very much.

Tom disagreed. He envisioned something better, something greater. He had read of land beyond the Mississippi River, there for the taking. The government offered acreage to anyone who settled, but it was a paltry amount. He had bigger plans. He had some money socked away, enough to make his dream come true.

Tom wasn't one of those who pined after a million dollars, or a mansion with servants to wait on him hand and foot. His dream was not that grand. All he wanted was a ranch. A sizable ranch of his very own, with enough cattle, so that he and his would never want for the necessities and maybe more than a few luxuries.

His friends thought he was crazy. Fred Dimple down to the feed store told him to his face that he was a damned fool. He was a farmer, not a rancher, and he was taking his family west to get them killed at the hands of marauding hostiles or to have them starve, sacrifices on the altar of his ignorance. Fred always had a way with words, but Tom refused to listen. He had a dream, and he would follow his dream wherever it led him, and at whatever cost.

"What's that?" Constance asked, pointing.

Tom blinked, and saw a figure ahead on the baked plain. At first he did not quite know what to make of it. The figure was short and squat and seemed to be some sort of deformed buffalo, but Tom remembered hearing that few buffalo came this far south. Besides, he soon realized the figure had two legs, not four, and that it wasn't as wide as he thought it was. The heat haze was playing tricks on him.

"It's a man!" Sally exclaimed. She was ten

and the spitting image of her mother, with the same sandy hair and the same green eyes.

"And he's on foot," said Heather, their other daughter. At sixteen, she had Tom's brown hair and brown eyes and a cute cherub face with a button nose. "But what's that he's carrying?"

"A saddle," Tom said. "His horse must have gone lame or died on him."

"What's he doing way out here?" Sally wondered.

Tom was tempted to veer wide and avoid him, but the stranger had heard them and stopped and turned. Love thy neighbor, the Good Book said, so Tom kept straight on and soon they were close enough to see him clearly.

Not much over five feet tall, and dressed all in black, the man wore a flat-crowned black hat and black boots with silver spurs. His black saddle was decorated with silver, too, and had a large silver horn, or apple, as Tom believed it was called. But it was not the strange preference for black or the flashy silver that caught Tom's eye; it was the pearl-handled revolver in a holster high on the man's right hip. There was something about it, something about the way it was worn, that told Tom the man was not a run-of-the-mill Texan.

The man had set the heavy saddle down and was waiting for them, his face invisible in the shadow of his hat's wide brim. He did not smile or raise a hand in greeting.

"Is he a cowboy?" Sally asked.

"I don't think so," Constance said, and glanced meaningfully at Tom. "Maybe we shouldn't stop."

"It wouldn't be polite." Tom hauled on the reins. He smiled and looked down into the most piercing gray eyes he had ever seen, eyes so intense, they startled him. "Howdy there, stranger."

The man's intent gaze flicked from Tom to his wife to the two girls, who were peeking out behind them. "A rattler got my claybank," he said.

"What's a claybank?" Sally asked Tom, but it was the man with the pearl-handled pistol who answered her.

"A horse, girl. Mine was a fine animal. He could go all day and all night. I didn't like havin' to blow his brains out."

"There's no reason to talk about that," Constance said stiffly.

The small man in black stared at her a moment, then said, "My apologies, ma'am. I tend to forget how it is with young ones around."

Tom introduced himself and his family.

"You're lucky we came along when we did. I'd wager there isn't a town within a hundred miles of here."

"Vinegar Flats is only ten miles yonder," the man in black said, with a nod to the west. "I'll make it by the day after tomorrow, I reckon."

"Sooner if you go with us," Tom offered, and was conscious of his wife stiffening beside him. "Throw your saddle in the back and climb on." He paused. "I didn't catch your name?"

The man's gray eyes were fixed on Constance. "I'm obliged. It's neighborly of you. I hope I'm not imposin'."

Constance avoided looking at him. "Nonsense," she said. "We're happy to extend a helping hand, Mr. — ?"

"Folks hereabouts call me Vantine, ma'am."

"Is that your first or your last name?" Constance asked.

"It's just how I'm called," Vantine said, tilting his head. The late-afternoon sun lit a hard face with high cheekbones and thin lips framed by curly hair the color of ripe corn. "You don't sound happy, ma'am."

Constance smoothed her dress but she still would not look at him. There was something about those eyes. "My husband has invited you. Mr. Vantine. It would be rude not to accept."

"It's just Vantine, ma'am. And I've been called a heap of things but never rude to females." Vantine carried his saddle around to the rear of the prairie schooner and swung it up and in. Then he sauntered to the front, his spurs jangling, and lithely climbed onto the seat.

"I meant you could ride in the back," Tom said. He was uneasy having the man so close to his wife.

"I like it here better," Vantine said. "I can see who's comin'."

"Who are you expecting way out here in the middle of nowhere?" Constance scoffed. "We haven't seen a soul in weeks."

"You've been lucky, ma'am," Vantine said. "Comanches, Kiowas, outlaws, renegades — this country is plumb crawlin' with curly wolves who would as soon buck you out in gore as look at you." He nodded at the team. "You've been lucky, too, those horses have made it this far. Most folks would use oxen or mules."

"I picked them on purpose," Tom said, a trifle defensively. "I'll need all the horses I can get my hands on when I start my ranch." He flicked the reins and shouted, "Get along, there!"

17

The schooner creaked into motion. One of the front axles was in dire need of grease and squeaked like a mouse.

"Homesteaders," the man in black remarked.

"You make it sound like a disease, Mr. Vantine," Constance said. "Do you have something against us?"

"Again, it's just Vantine, ma'am." He stared at her from under his hat until she looked away; then he said, "I have nothin' against settlers. It's just that you're being damned foolish."

Sally gasped and Heather laughed and Constance said sharply, "I'll thank you not to use that kind of language in the presence of a lady and her children. I don't let my husband do it. I certainly will not let a complete stranger."

Tom saw Vantine flush red. With anger, he assumed, and he quickly asked, "Why do you think we're fools? Is it wrong of me to want a better life for my family?"

Vantine sighed. "It's not wrong at all. But a lot of folks come out here thinkin' it's the Promised Land and all they get for their trouble are shallow graves."

"You're trying to scare us," Constance said.

"Yes, ma'am, I am," Vantine admitted.

"If you had any sense, you would talk this husband of yours into turnin' around and headin' back to wherever you came from. You'll live longer."

Constance did not like this little man with his scornful attitude, and she was not one to be belittled. "Who are you to criticize? What have you ever done that entitles you to think we're idiots?"

"I'm alive," Vantine said, "and in these parts, that's sayin' a lot." He contemplated his scuffed boots, then said slowly, "It's nothin' personal, ma'am. But you don't belong here. In case you haven't heard, there's no law west of the Pecos."

Tom construed that as a slight. "I can take care of my own, thank you very much. I fought in the war."

Vantine glanced at the blue cap. "This isn't Gettysburg or Bull Run. When an hombre's out to make coyote bait of you, he won't come marchin' into your gun sights. He'll kill you any way he can."

"Enough talk about killing," Constance said sternly. She was sorry they had let Vantine ride with them.

For a while, no one said a word. Then Tom cleared his throat and asked, "What was the name of that town you mentioned?"

"Vinegar Flats. But callin' it a town is a

19

mite much. There's a saloon and store, and that's all."

"A store in the middle of nowhere?" Tom was amazed. "How does the man who owns it make ends meet?"

For some reason Vantine's mouth quirked upward. "The owner isn't out to get rich. Maybe two or three times a month travelers like yourselves stop by. I've been there before, and it's a right fine establishment."

"Are you a cowboy?" Sally piped up from inside the wagon. "A man in Kansas told us there are a lot of cowboys in Texas."

Vantine chuckled. "Missy, you couldn't pay me enough to nursemaid a bunch of smelly cows. It would bore me to drink."

Heather asked, "Then what do you do?"

"Enough," Constance said, smoothing her dress. "It's not polite to pry into someone's personal affairs, girls." No matter how often she reminded them, they couldn't seem to mind their manners.

"That's all right, ma'am," Vantine said. "Fact is, you could say I'm a hunter, of sorts."

Tom looked at him. "What is there to hunt out here? I haven't seen any sign of wildlife in days."

"It's not game I hunt, Mr. Waldron," Vantine said. "It's men."

2

The rim of the world was devouring the sun and they still had six miles to go. Tom Waldron was tempted to push on until they reached Vinegar Flats but the team was flagging and badly needed rest, and he could not afford to lose one of his horses. In that respect he sympathized with the flint-faced man in black.

"We can make it by midnight, can't we? Maybe sooner?" Constance objected when Tom announced they would stop. She refrained from glancing at the man to her left, for fear he would see the reason in her eyes. She had never been very good at hiding her feelings.

"Look at the team," Tom said. "Do you really want to push them until they keel over?"

Constance bit her lower lip and did not answer. Yes, the horses were lathered with sweat, and yes, they were hanging their heads with fatigue as was usually the case along about this time of the day, but she still did not like the idea of spending the night on the prairie with the man wearing the pearl-handled revolver.

"Tomorrow we can stock up on supplies and refill the water barrel and find out about the country ahead." Tom always liked to have things worked out in advance, which made his decision to sell the farm and strike off into the heart of the unknown as puzzling to him as it was to everyone else. He had never been impulsive by nature, yet there he was, dragging his family off across the wilds of Texas as the result of a yearning he could not define or describe beyond calling it an "urge." "We'll make camp right here," he announced. He didn't see where it made much of a difference; the arid prairie was flat for leagues around.

"I know a better spot," Vantine said and pointed north. "It's only a couple of hundred yards, and you'll be safer."

"Safer from what, Mr. Vantine?" Constance asked. It occurred to her that the man might be up to something, that perhaps her family was in danger. "The rattlesnake that bit your claybank?"

"You sure are a caution, ma'am."

"Am I?" Constance had noticed he didn't answer her question. She looked at Tom to try to warn him by her expression not to do anything hasty but he was already turning the prairie schooner. Now if she said something, Vantine might take offense.

Soon they came to a dry wash. Its high sides promised shelter from the wind, but Tom did not see how he could get their heavy wagon down to the bottom until Vantine pointed out a forty-foot gap where the bank had crumbled long ago, forming a natural ramp. He brought the team to a halt and clambered down to unhitch them.

Constance went to slide after him, then saw that Vantine had jumped down on the other side and was holding his hands up, waiting to help her. Against her better judgment, she let him, marveling at the corded muscles on his arms and shoulders. He was short but he was immensely powerful. "Thank you."

Vantine touched a finger to his hat brim and walked toward the team.

"Isn't he something?" Heather whispered as she alighted. A tall, winsome girl, she was just coming into the bloom of womanhood. "So handsome and mysterious."

"That is quite enough," Constance said, aghast at her offspring's lack of modesty. "We know nothing about the man. He could be fixing to murder us in our sleep and then rob us, for all you know."

Sally was about to hop down, and she tittered. "He would never do that. He's a nice man. I can tell."

Constance had a sharp retort on the tip of her tongue but she reminded herself that ten-year-old girls could hardly be blamed for being poor judges of character. "Never take anything for granted, child," she warned. "Suppose you two help me with supper so we can take your minds off the mystery man."

Tom was grateful when Vantine, without being asked, came forward to help. He smiled at Constance as she led the girls around to the rear of the wagon.

The moment they were out of earshot, Vantine said, "I lied about the rattler."

About to unhitch a horse, Tom wasn't quite sure he understood. "Why would you do a thing like that?"

"Did you kill in the war, Mr. Waldron?"

Tom turned and placed his hands on his hips. "That's not something I care to talk about, if you don't mind."

"I just hoped, you mentionin' Gettysburg, and all."

"What difference does it make whether I did or I didn't?" Tom didn't see the point, and it was a touchy subject with him.

"It would help if you're not the yellow

sort when the Comanches hit us tonight," Vantine said.

A tingle of apprehension ran down Tom's spine clear to his toes. "Comanches?" His secret fear since striking Texas had been of running into a roving war party and having his family wiped out — or worse.

"They shot my horse out from under me with an arrow two days ago," Vantine casually mentioned while continuing to unfasten the traces. "They'd have overrun me but they didn't have a gun. I held them off with my rifle until they pretended to give up and made a show of ridin' off. Then I stripped my saddle and started walkin'. They've been doggin' my tracks ever since, bidin' their time."

"Why didn't you tell me this sooner?" Tom asked, horrified by the implications. "You've put my whole family in peril, damn it!"

"I could have let you go your merry way," Vantine said. "The Comanches wouldn't mind. They lost interest in me the moment you showed up."

"You're just saying that," Tom said angrily.

Vantine stopped working and stared. "Put yourself in their moccasins. If you had a choice between a gent who had already killed three of your war party or a wagon filled with three females and a white man who doesn't have the sense to wear a revolver or have a rifle by his side at all times, which would you pick?"

The barb stung, but it was not nearly as upsetting as the thought that unseen eyes might be on them at that very instant. Tom cupped a hand to his mouth to call out to Constance and warn her.

"Don't," Vantine said.

"I beg your pardon?"

"Give a holler, and the Comanches might hit us now, before you can get to your wagon and that Sharps I saw in the bed. Let them think we don't know they're out there and they'll wait until we're bedded down for the night before they try to part us from our hair."

"I've never fought Indians," Tom said, his mouth abruptly dry. "There aren't any hostiles back in Ohio." Nor had they seen a single red man the whole trek. He had begun to think all those tales of savage hordes roaming the wilds were so many lies.

"They're tricky devils," Vantine said. "They usually like an edge before they attack, so we'll give them one."

"We will?"

"We want to lure them in and finish it or the next family that comes along might not be as lucky as you."

Tom thought to ask, "How many are we up against?"

"There are five left," Vantine said while continuing to work. "Sometimes when you kill one, the rest will break off and take the body back to their village. Not this time."

"You took on eight Comanches alone and you're still alive?" To Tom it seemed an incredible feat but the small man in black did not regard it as anything extraordinary.

"Like I said, I had a rifle and they didn't. They'd love to get their hands on it, and my pistol, both. A Comanche rates a gun almost as high as slittin' a white throat."

Tom resumed unhitching the team, then was jolted by a thought. "I still say you should have told me sooner. I could have pushed on to Vinegar Flats and we would be safe. You've needlessly put my family at risk." He was mad, and it took every iota of self-control he had not to sock the shorter man on the jaw.

"Do you really reckon the Comanches would let you get there?" Vantine shook his head. "And in your wagon on the open prairie, your family wouldn't stand a prayer. The Comanches would drop your lead horses with arrows. All you could do is wait around for them to do whatever they had in mind."

Tom imagined his wife and daughters huddled in the wagon bed with barbed shafts raining down, and shuddered. They would be skewered like meat on a spit. "I'm sorry. I shouldn't have snapped at you like that."

Vantine shrugged. "A gent doesn't always think straight when people he cares about are in danger."

Something in the way the man in black said it gave Tom food for musing. He had the impression Vantine was speaking from experience, and he was tempted to pry but he had the decency not to. It gave him something to ponder, though.

"We'd best hurry and hobble these horses so we can let your family know what they're in for."

"I'd rather not tell them just yet," Tom said. They would be scared enough as it was, and he saw no point in having them endure hours of uncertainty and fear.

"What if I'm wrong and the Comanches don't wait until we've bedded down?" Vantine brought up. "Or what if they decide they would rather help themselves than kill us outright?"

"Help themselves how?" Tom asked, and felt his cheeks grow warm as the obvious seared him like a red-hot fireplace poker.

"Takin' your wife and those cute girls captive. They're fond of white women. Which is strange, since they say white women make terrible wives. But unless you like the notion of your loved ones spendin' the rest of their days in a Comanche lodge, I would let them know what's at stake so they can defend themselves, if it comes to that."

"You're right." Tom's gut had twisted into a knot. If the worst did come to pass, it would be his fault. He was the one who had dragged his family to Texas.

"Go ahead and get it done. I'll finish with the team," Vantine offered.

"Thank you." Tom walked to the rear of the prairie schooner. Constance had lowered the gate and was handing pots and plates to Heather and Sally. "We need to talk," he informed them, and told them everything Vantine had told him except the part about Comanches being fond of white women.

Constance was stunned speechless. She had dreaded something like this would happen, and now that it had, she couldn't quite accept it. "Maybe he's wrong. Maybe

Comanches aren't really out there."

"I wouldn't count on it," Tom said. "Vantine seems to know what he's doing. He's our best hope of making it through the night alive."

"Aren't you putting just a bit too much trust in a perfect stranger?" Constance chided. "For all you know, he's up to no good himself. Maybe he intends to rob us and kill us and blame it on the Comanches."

"You're being silly," Tom said.

"Me? I'm not the one who —" Constance did not finish what she was going to say. But she could not keep the accusation out of her voice or her features.

Tom remembered the few times his wife had voiced objections to his brainstorms. But never until this moment had he realized how deeply she resented it, and how much more deeply she would resent him if things went wrong.

There was a low cough, and Vantine stepped past the end of the wagon. "The horses are hobbled," he reported. "Now we need to get a fire going and supper on so the Comanches will think we're as stupid as most whites."

"Not so fast," Constance said, facing him. "Can we trust you, Mr. Vantine? You're asking us to put our lives in your hands, after all." When he did not say anything, she demanded, "Well? I'm waiting for an answer."

A slow smile split Vantine's sun-bronzed face. "You have grit, ma'am. I'll give you that. But whether you trust me or not isn't up to me, is it? I can give you my solemn promise I'd never hurt you in a million years, but it would only be words."

"I see," Constance said, although she did not truly see what he was getting at, unless he was saying she had to rely on her judgment and intuition, which, come to think of it, were all she had to judge him by.

"I trust him, mother," Heather said.

"Me, too," Sally chimed in.

Constance ignored them. They were children and they did not know any better. "Fair enough, Mr. Vantine. But heed me. If this is a ruse, if you have an ulterior motive, if you harm a hair on any of our heads, I will kill you."

"Connie!" Tom exclaimed.

Vantine was not the least bit offended. In fact, he smiled and nodded. "As you say, fair enough, ma'am. And if you don't mind my sayin' so, maybe you can make a go of it in this country, after all."

Constance was not used to a man other than her husband flattering her, and to cover her embarrassment she had Heather and Sally help her kindle a fire using dry brush Tom collected from the edge of the wash. She rigged a tripod over the flames and hung their big cooking pot from it. They were low on provisions, so the best she could do was stew using the few strips of jerked venison they had left, and almost the last of her flour. She made the girls sit near her at all times.

The wagon creaked, and Tom climbed down, holding the Sharps he had brought home from the war. On his right hip in a flapped holster was his revolver.

"May I?" Vantine asked, holding out his hand.

"This?" Tom said, following the other's gaze. He gave Vantine the revolver to examine. "I have a box of cartridges to go with it."

"A Starr Army revolver," Vantine said. "Not the best, not the worst. Have you used this much?"

"In the war a few times. But I'm not very good with it, if that's what you're asking." Tom accepted the revolver back from Vantine, and could not resist nodding at the pearl-handled model the other man wore. "What about yours?"

Vantine's hand moved and, just like that,

twirled his pistol up and out. "I'm partial to Colts. I've tried others, but a Colt fits my hand best and has never let me down when I needed it most."

Tom admired the shiny pearl grips and the finely engraved barrel and cylinder. It was a regular work of art. He did not know a lot about guns but he did know enough to tell that this particular pistol had cost a lot of money. He gave it a tentative twirl, as Vantine had done, and found it to be superbly balanced. "What caliber is it?"

Before Vantine could answer, the night was rent by bloodcurdling yips.

3

"Was that a wolf, Pa?" Pitney Adams asked. Only twelve years old, he wore a hand-me-down shirt in need of stitching and tattered pants but no shoes. Pitney hated shoes. He preferred to go barefoot everywhere, summer or winter, he didn't care. He even rode barefoot.

"There aren't any wolves in these parts, son," Jed Adams answered. "Most likely it was a coyote. I thought I'd taught you better," he teased, and grinned. He wore a gray shirt and gray pants and a gray cap that had once been the uniform of the Army of the Confederacy. It was the same uniform he wore when Lee surrendered, and the only clothes he owned.

"There's another coyote, Pa," said Jed's older son, Bret, who at seventeen was a lanky bundle of bones in a shirt he had outgrown two years ago and pants in no better condition than Pitney's. All three had the same black hair and jutting chins; all three had sky blue eyes.

"There sure are a lot of them critters out

tonight," Jed commented.

"Too bad Ma ain't here to hear them," Pitney said. "I sure do miss her."

"We all do, boy," Jed Adams said, his grip tightening on the lead rope to the three packhorses strung out behind him. He glanced sadly at his sons, riding on either side of him, Pitney on a dun that was getting on in years but had lasted the long, long ride from South Carolina, and Bret on a buttermilk their Ma had favored until her passing over a year ago.

"There's another coyote, Pa," the older boy mentioned.

Jed heard it, too, but now he gave a start and drew rein and listened more intently to the fading cry. Three coyotes in three minutes were not unusual in certain parts of the country, but it was there, in that dry, nigh-lifeless land barely fit for lizards and snakes. His boys followed his example.

"Is somethin' wrong, Pa?" Pitney asked.

"Could be Injuns," Jed said. "I've heard tell they pretend to be critters now and then." He had never fought redskins, thank God. All the tribes in his neck of the woods had been wiped out or driven off before he came of age to carry a gun. "We'd best be careful." He bent and shucked his carbine from the saddle scabbard.

35

The boys were unlimbering their own rifles. Pitney, his eyes as wide around as walnuts, was glancing right and left as if he feared they would be set upon at any second.

"Nice and slow now," Jed said, and kneed his sorrel on at a walk. He braced the stock of the Morse carbine against his thigh and curled his thumb around the hammer and his finger lightly around the trigger.

"Do you reckon they're after us?" Pitney whispered.

"I can't rightly say," Jed admitted, "but they're a ways off yet. If they are Injuns, they might not even know we're here."

"What kind of Injuns?" Bret voiced the pertinent question.

"Well, I ain't familiar with all the ones hereabouts," Jed said, "but likely as not they'd be Comanches or maybe some of those Kiowas we've heard so much about."

Pitney's eyes grew wider. "I sure don't want to be killed after comin' all this way, Pa."

"That makes two of us, son," Jed said lightheartedly and smiled to put his younger boy at ease. It didn't work. Pitney took more after his ma, and Melanie had been the biggest worrywart this side of creation.

Bret was peering into the night to the west. "Where about do you reckon we are?"

Again Jed had to confess, "I don't rightly know. We crossed the Pecos days ago. I doubt we've gone far enough to strike New Mexico yet, so I figure we're in west Texas somewhere."

"Are there any towns hereabouts?" Bret asked. "We'd be safer there than out in the open like this."

"Not that I'm aware of, no." Jess always admired his oldest's logical bent. It made him proud that one of his family used his head for something other than a hat rack. His own thinker wasn't anything to brag about. "There might be a settlement or two but they're few and far between."

"Then if it is Injuns," Bret said, "we're pretty much up the creek without a paddle, aren't we?"

"Let's just say we shouldn't go tanglin' with anybody wearin' feathers if we can help it." Jed rose in the stirrups to peer into the darkness but he did not see anyone or anything.

"At least we're not in Apache country," Bret said. "They're supposed to be the worst of the bunch. A jasper at that tradin' post told me they like to tie folks upside down to wagon wheels and bake their brains."

"For real?" Pitney asked.

"For real," Bret confirmed. "He was sayin' as how a freight train of greasers was jumped by Apaches in a mountain pass a while back. They butchered and raped and roasted everybody."

Jed stopped straining his eyes to say, "Maybe we shouldn't be talkin' about rapin' and such. Your ma wouldn't like it."

"I don't mind, Pa," Pitney said. "Shucks, I like to hear about stuff like that. Haven't you always said that the more a man learns, the better man he is?"

"That's the general idea," Jed conceded, "or so my grandpa told me when I was your age. But I can't say as it's helped me much. I'm still not worth a shovelful of chicken tracks when it comes to knowin' what to do and what not to."

Bret shifted in his saddle. "That not true and you know it. I wish to blazes you would stop puttin' yourself down so much."

"Yeah, Pa," Pitney said.

"I'm right sorry, boys," Jed responded. "But when a man has lost his dignity and his wife and his home and doesn't have much more in this world than the clothes on his back, it ain't as if he can brag he's a success."

"How did you lose your dignity?" Pitney wanted to know. "And what exactly is it, anyhow?"

"Dignity is what a man needs if he's to hold his head up high," Jed explained, "and I lost any I had in the war. Remind me when you're a lot older and maybe I'll tell you about it."

"That danged war again," Bret said. "I wish it never happened. Ma died, and we've lost almost all we had because of it. What good did it do anybody but those stinkin' Yankees?"

"Now, now," Jed said, only because Melanie would have said the same thing. "You can't judge the whole world by a few bad apples."

Bret saw right through him. "You sound just like Ma, Pa. But she wouldn't cotton to those carpetbaggers any more than we did. They stole our home out from under us, didn't they?"

"That they did," Jed said, grimacing at the memory. "I suppose I should have shot that banker dead for doing what he did. But then Yankee soldiers would have come for me, and I'd be behind bars right now, or they'd have put me on trial and hung me for sure."

39

"Consarn all Yankees!" Pitney said. It was the strongest oath he was allowed to use.

"They ain't all bad," Jed stressed, although he would be hard pressed to think of one who had ever treated him half decent.

"I hope to God I never set eyes on another Yankee as long as I live!" Bret declared.

"There has to be a place somewhere," Jed voiced his innermost hope. "A place where there aren't any. Where we can start over and make a new life for ourselves and I can forget that damn war and all it did to us."

"Amen," Bret said.

"Why did you go off to fight in it, anyway, Pa?" Pitney inquired. "I wouldn't have — that's for sure."

Jed shrugged. "I thought it was the right thing to do at the time. A lot my age were signin' up. We couldn't let those Yankee know-it-alls tell us how we could and couldn't live. I never owned a slave, myself, but I reckoned anyone who did had the right to if they wanted."

"So slavery ain't all bad like the Yankees claim?"

Jed chose his next words with care. "I never much thought about it until the Yankees started kickin' up a fuss and all the newspapers were talkin' about how the government was goin' to make the South abolish it whether the South wanted to or not. I just sort of took it for granted. I mean, slavery had been around since before I was born. Lots of folks had slaves, not just the big plantations. Your mother's pa had a couple of slaves for years to help with his farm. And he always treated them decent that I could see."

"Yankees are natural-born liars," Bret said.

"I'm not done, boy. When I got to thinkin' about it later, it didn't sit as well with me, one person lordin' it over another. But that wasn't why I went to war. I went to stop the Yankees from shovin' their ways down our throats."

Bret snorted like an angry bull. "And they sure shoved, didn't they? Now there ain't any slaves and there ain't any South and if we're not careful, there won't be any of us, either."

They had been riding slowly, the dull clomp of hooves the only sound other than an occasional sigh of the breeze.

"Those coyotes have gone quiet," Bret said. "Maybe it really was the four-legged kind and they've gone elsewhere."

"Pa?" Pitney said.

Jed was tugging on the lead rope. The

41

last packhorse liked to balk when it was tired, as it always was after twelve hours on the go. "What is it, son?"

"Will there be other folks where we settle or will it be just us?"

His younger son was forever asking things that gave Jed pause. When Melanie was alive, the boy was a continual font of questions, but ever since she died, much of the spirit and a lot of the curiosity had gone out of him. "Why do you ask?"

Pitney gnawed on his lower lip, then said, "Well, the way you talk and all, sometimes I think you don't want anythin' to do with anyone else for the rest of your born days. I think maybe you would be happy if it was just the three of us way off in the mountains somewhere."

"I wouldn't mind that," Jed admitted, "would you?"

"Sort of. I mean, the Yankees are vermin and all, and I miss Ma as much as you do, but I miss my friends, too, an awful lot, and it would be nice if I had me some new ones. If you don't mind, that is."

"I miss Ruby Porter," Bret said. "Now that I'm gone, likely as not she'll take up with that Butler boy who has been hankerin' after her but afraid to say so because he knows I'd have whupped him."

Pushing his Confederate cap back on his head, Jed let out a sigh. "We talked this over before we left. I told you how things would be. That you would miss your kin and your friends. I didn't want any hard feelin's later."

"You explained everythin', sure," Bret said. "But hearin' it and livin' it ain't quite the same."

"Are you havin' second thoughts?" Jed prayed not. They had come too far to turn back now.

"We can't hardly help it, Pa," Bret said. "But you let us have a say in things and we agreed so we're not goin' to gripe. We'll take our medicine like men should, just like you always say to."

"I just hope there are other people," Pitney said. "It would get awful lonely with the three of us."

Jed reminded himself that they were at the age where it was natural for them to want to associate with other boys and, in Bret's case, with pretty girls. "To be honest, I hadn't given it much thought. But I will. I promise."

"Thanks, Pa," Bret said. "You've always been fair with us, and we're grateful. And we know how hard it's been for you since Ma died."

A flood of memories welled up. Jed tried to suppress them but they washed over him like waves on a shore. In his mind's eye he saw himself enlist and go marching off to war, proudly wearing his new uniform, while Melanie and other wives and sisters and cousins of the men in his company waved and smiled and called out to come back to them in one piece. He relived the battles and the blood and the gore. He saw the letter in his hand from Melanie, a letter that took three months to reach him, saying she was sick, powerful sick, and could he please come home right away. He saw the captain saying they had another engagement in the morning and he couldn't be spared. It was their last battle, for shortly afterward the war ended, and Jed rushed home to Chattooga Ridge, only to arrive too late. His beloved Melanie had gone to her reward a few hours before he got there. Old Doc Samuels told him she had clung to life for weeks, praying with all her heart he would make it, and telling the doctor over and over that Jed would never let her down, that he would get there in time to spend their last precious moments together. Samuels had been with her at the end, and her last words had been, "It's so unfair."

"Pa? Are you all right?" Bret asked.

Jed realized his boys were staring at him strangely and Bret had leaned over to place a hand on his arm. "I'm fine," he lied. He would never be fine again. He would never be the man he had been.

"Were you thinkin' of Ma?" Pitney asked.

"No," Jed lied. God help him, but he wished it were true. He wished he could stop thinking about her, wished he could shed the hurt and the misery. It had been worse in South Carolina. Everywhere he went he was reminded of her. The one-room school they attended. The willow tree they spent many an evening under. The church where they were wed. Their cabin, which he'd built with his own hands. He never told his boys, but he was almost glad when their farm was stolen out from under them by greedy carpetbaggers. It gave him an excuse to leave, to start a new home in a new place, somewhere he could make it through the day without having his heart torn apart by yet another painful reminder.

"These wagon tracks are fresh," Bret unexpectedly announced.

Jed blinked and looked down, and sure enough, a set of wagon ruts showed that they were not the only ones to cross that particular stretch of prairie that particular day.

"Whoever it is, if those coyotes were really Injuns, they could be in trouble," his older son said.

No sooner were the words uttered than the night stillness was shattered by a new sound: a woman's scream.

4

Constance Waldron had never thought of herself as especially brave. She was scared of spiders and snakes, she was uneasy in pitch-dark rooms, and in the woods at night, her stomach became queasy if a buckboard or wagon she was in went too fast, and she rarely rode a horse any faster than she absolutely had to. Her true courage, if she had any, had never been put to a true test. Until now.

When Vantine calmly informed them that the coyotes they heard were not coyotes at all but Comanches, Constance thought she would faint. But she didn't. Her heart leaped to her throat and her blood raced but she kept her wits about her, determined not to let anything happen to those she most cared for. At the man in black's suggestion, she had the girls huddle with her near the fire and she added more fuel.

"The Comanches won't come close so long as we keep it going," Vantine said.

Tom Waldron was impressed by his

wife's poise. She had not gone into hysterics. She had not screamed or railed at him for placing them in peril. In a way, it was too bad she hadn't, because he felt he deserved it. Guilt ate at him like a ravenous wolf at a deer carcass.

Worse was the fear. Tom was afraid, terribly afraid, in the grip of panic, not for himself but for Constance and his daughters. He sat near the fire, where Vantine told him to sit, and gritted his teeth to keep them from chattering. This was not like the war. Not like engaging the enemy in formation and with men from his company on either side, firing at the Rebs as slugs buzzed past. This was his family. This was much more personal. Instead of hundreds or thousands of bluebellies against hundreds of thousands of Sons of the South, it was the four of them against five savage Comanches. Five of them, counting Vantine.

The man in black was acting as if nothing were out of the ordinary, as if they were enjoying a Sunday picnic in a park instead of waiting for hostiles to jump them. Tom could not understand how Vantine could be so calm about it all.

"Why are they howling like that?" Sally whispered.

"It's a good sign, missy," Vantine said. "It means they're not ready to move in on us yet. We'll take every minute they give us."

Tom dipped his wooden spoon into his bowl and raised it to his lips but he did not swallow the soup. He was straining every sense he had into the night around them. Judging by the cries, Comanches were on both sides of the wash. Maybe fifty yards out. Or so the warriors wanted them to think. One or two might be much closer, watching them at that very moment.

Heather and Sally were holding up well, too, Tom was glad to see, although both were plainly nervous. He smiled to reassure them and said, "Don't you worry, girls. I won't let them harm you." He patted his Sharps rifle. "I'm a pretty fair shot with this cannon, if I say so myself."

Vantine was eating his soup with relish. "You're a fine cook, ma'am," he praised Constance.

"Oh, bosh," she said. "It's just something I whipped together."

"Even so, a man gets mighty tired of eatin' his own cookin'. To me this is as tasty as food gets." Vantine smacked his lips and flashed a smile, then shifted toward Tom. "If you're fixin' to make a go of it out here, you'd do better with a repeater than a single-shot." He patted the Henry rifle propped against his leg, which he had taken from his saddle scabbard. "Sixteen shots beats one all hollow when your skin is at stake."

Tom envied him the weapon. He had heard about Henry rifles. How a man could load one on Sunday and shoot it all week. How all a man had to do was work the lever to eject a spent cartridge and load a new one. But they were terribly pricey. Close to fifty dollars, he'd heard, with ammunition twice as much as most. He simply couldn't afford one.

Vantine picked the Henry up and held it out. "Take a look. Those Comanches would have had my hair if not for this lead chucker."

The rifle was a beauty. Henrys had long barrels with tubular magazines underneath and brass frames. This one had silver-plating and fine etching similar to the etching on the pearl-handled Colt that ran from the stock to the front sights. "You sure like fancy guns," Tom commented.

"You wouldn't plow a field with a rusty plow, would you?" Vantine responded.

Tom had mentioned that he was a farmer. Now, emboldened by the man in black's talkative manner, he asked, "What is it you do for a living, if you don't mind my asking? You mentioned something about hunting men."

Vantine's smile vanished and he took the Henry and leaned it against his leg. "Out here we call that pryin', and as a general rule it can get a man perforated."

"Mr. Vantine!" Constance declared. "Need I remind you we could have left you back on the plain? You are our guest, and guests do not threaten those kind enough to feed them."

Tom thought the man in black would take exception but Vantine surprised him by saying rather meekly, "My apologies again, ma'am. I tend to forget my manners. It's so rare I'm around a lady like yourself."

Sally had not appeared to be paying attention but now she stirred and asked, "What *do* you do, Mr. Vantine?"

"I gamble, mostly. When I'm not playin' poker for high stakes, I hire out my guns to them as can afford it."

"Hire it out how?" Sally asked.

"Let's just say that once I find whoever I'm after, they're breathin' days are over," Vantine responded.

In the tense silence that fell, Tom thought he heard a soft scrape from the south rim of the wash. Cold sweat broke out on his forehead and palms but he did as Vantine had told them to do and pretended he hadn't noticed.

In her youth and innocence, Sally did not know when to let a subject be. "You kill people for a living? Why would you do a thing like that?"

"Hush, child," Constance said.

"That's all right, Mrs. Waldron," Vantine said. "I was her age once." He placed his bowl on the ground. "I do it because I'm good at it, and I get paid a lot of money."

"By who?" Sally asked.

"That should be whom," Constance corrected her. Each day she spent a couple of hours teaching her girls grammar and arithmetic, and reading to them from a thick book on the history of the world.

Vantine did not answer, and Tom figured the matter had been dropped until the small man began speaking again.

"Texas is known for being wild and woolly. It's a big state, raw and untamed, with not much law to speak of except in the cities and bigger towns. Killin' goes on all the time, and the killers go free because there's no one to arrest them. No one to see justice is done." Vantine rested his hand on his Colt. "People pay me for the justice they can't get anywhere else."

"My word!" Constance exclaimed. "I've never heard of a such a thing! How can you earn a living off the blood of others? You seem so considerate, so" — she had to search for the right word — "reasonable."

"The men I go after have usually spilled blood themselves," Vantine said. "They've spilled it and got away with it. And they'll go on spillin' it unless they're stopped."

"How can you say that for sure?" Constance demanded. "You've set yourself up as judge, jury and hangman, all rolled into one."

"I never judge, ma'am. I do what I'm paid for, then go back to playin' cards until I'm paid to go out again."

Tom found himself asking, "How do people know where to find you to hire you?"

"I can usually be found at the Red Rose in San Antonio. Word gets to me one way or another."

It was a minute before Tom put two and two together. "Then you must be after someone now."

Vantine was pouring coffee and did not reply.

"I find this talk disturbing," Constance said. "Texas isn't the right kind of place to

raise a family, in my opinion."

Tom could not let the comment go un-challenged. "We went all through this be-fore we left Ohio. Sure, Texas is unstable right now, but there are a lot of decent people living here. People just like us, who came with the dream of starting over, of making a new and better life." He had used the same argument before, and it always soothed her worries, but this time someone else was involved.

"Dreams are fine," Vantine said, "but dreams can also plant you six feet under." He glanced at Constance and the girls as if trying to make up his mind about some-thing, then said, "Texas is a keg of powder waitin' to be lit. The Radicals are in power, Northern sympathizers who resent that Texas sided with the South during the war. There's a lot of bad blood all around. People on both sides are shot dead on the street and nothin' is ever done about it. The Klan is burnin' crosses and hangin' blacks in the middle of the night. The Co-manches are actin' up. Outlaws roam as free as birds." He looked Tom in the eyes. "If I had a family, I would never sit them on a powder keg and hope to heaven it never blows up in their faces."

In a flash of insight, Tom saw that there

was a lot more to the man called Vantine than he had imagined. He also saw that Vantine's comments had had an effect, and his wife and daughters were staring at him accusingly. "Thanks," he said, with no real bitterness.

"I'm only tellin' you how things are," Vantine said. "In a few years, after the bad feelin's have faded and Texas is readmitted to the Union, things will calm down. You're right that Texas is a place where dreams can come true. The trick is to live long enough for that to happen."

"Thank you for your advice," Constance said.

"You're welcome, ma'am." Vantine made a show of stretching and yawning. "Now why don't we all turn in and get a good night's rest?" He winked at Tom as he said it.

"It's a little early yet," Constance began, then caught herself. "Oh. Where do you think the girls and I should sleep?"

"In your wagon would be best." Vantine stood and hefted his Henry. "I'll check on the horses." He turned and the darkness claimed him.

Sally said, "He's sure a nice man."

Constance rose and gathered up their bowls. "Let's turn in like he wants. We'll leave the rest of the soup in the pot for breakfast." Since they were low on water, she had been cleaning their dishes by cutting strips from an old blanket and wiping them clean, then burying the strips afterward so they wouldn't smell up the wagon. But she had run out of old blanket, and the next best thing was to use brush or gravel. "Stay here," she told the girls, and walked to the south side of the wash. She felt safe enough. She was only a few yards from the wagon and she could see Tom sipping coffee and vaguely make out Vantine over by the team.

Bending, Constance pried at the dirt but it was hard packed. She moved several steps to the left and tried again. Then several more. Tom had told her that crops in Texas practically grew themselves, that the soil was rich and easy to till, but it just wasn't so. She wondered how much of what he had claimed would turn out to be false, and felt a burst of anger at letting herself be persuaded to leave a safe, civilized state like Ohio for a violent land like Texas.

Constance couldn't find any gravel. Frustrated, she moved a couple steps sideways, and suddenly the bank in front of her seemed to come alive and rise up and seize her by the arms. Shock hit her, shock so potent her vocal cords froze. She was staring into a swarthy visage painted for war.

A Comanche! Fear spiked through her, overcoming her shock, and as the warrior's hand rose to her mouth, she did what she should have done the instant he grabbed her; she threw back her head and screamed.

Tom Waldron dropped his tin cup and sprang to his feet, spilling hot coffee over his pants. "Constance!" Tingling with apprehension, he ran past their wagon. "Constance! Where are you?" A low sob drew him toward grappling figures. He snapped the Sharps to his shoulder but did not have a clear shot.

Suddenly the night erupted in a fierce screech and a figure came hurtling over the rim. A knife blade glinted in the starlight. Tom tried to bring the Sharps up but the Comanche slammed into him with the force of a cannonball, and the next thing he knew, he was flat on his back and the Sharps was gone and he had one hand locked on the Comanche's wrist and the Comanche had iron fingers clamped on his throat.

The night spat flame and lead. The warrior was flung back against the side of the wash and hung suspended for a moment, gaping at a dark hole in his chest. Shrieking in fury, he lunged at Tom. Again a rifle blasted, and the Comanche pitched to his knees and toppled forward.

As Tom scrambled up, a hand slid under his arm to give him an extra boost.

"Are you hurt?" Vantine asked.

"No, but one of them has my wife!" Tom cast about for the Sharps, snatched it up, and turned. Constance was nowhere to be seen. "Dear God!"

Twin screams rose to the stars. "The girls!" Vantine cried and raced back past the wagon.

Tom hesitated, torn by indecision. His children were in danger. But so was his wife. Counting on Vantine to take care of Heather and Sally, he ran to where Constance had been struggling with the Comanche. There was only one direction they could have gone without him seeing them, and that was up and out of the wash.

His legs pumping, Tom climbed the incline. Stones and loose dirt cascaded from under him, and then he was on flat ground at the top. A veil of darkness greeted him, a veil in which nothing moved. He was too late. The Comanches had carried Constance off. The world spun, the stars whirling around and around. "No! It can't be!"

"Tom! Help me!"

The frantic appeal galvanized Tom into racing toward where he believed her to be. Behind him in the wash, Vantine's rifle blasted once and then a second time. A whoop punctuated the gunshots, and from out of the gloom charged a Comanche brandishing a tomahawk. Tom barely brought the Sharps up in time to ward off the blow. More rained down, and suddenly a foot hooked his ankle and he tripped and fell on his back.

Sheer bloodlust lit the Comanche's face. The warrior loomed against the backdrop of stars, the tomahawk poised for a fatal swing.

Tom fired without bracing the stock against his shoulder and the recoil nearly tore the Sharps from his grasp. The muzzle was only inches from the Comanche's chest, and the heavy slug left a hole big enough to stick his fist through. Springing upright, Tom raced on, his ears ringing so that he could scarcely hear. "Constance!" he shouted. "Constance, where are you?"

There was no answer.

5

Jed Adams drew rein as the scream wavered on the wind. Bret and Pitney did likewise, and the three of them sat perfectly still, listening with bated breath for the scream to be repeated.

"Who was that?" Pitney broke the stillness by whispering.

"Hush." Jed was hoping to pinpoint where the woman might be. His patience was rewarded with a shriek, then the boom of guns, and anxious shouts, all from the northwest.

"Some folks are in trouble, Pa!" Bret said, and raised his reins. "We should help them!"

"Sit tight," Jed directed. Among the many lessons he had learned during the war was the importance of caution. Only reckless fools rushed in where wiser heads would not. He never rode to the sound of the guns unless he knew who was firing those guns and where they were.

"But, Pa!" Bret protested.

"You heard me." Jed had noticed that

the older Bret became, the more he sassed back. Jed seemed to recollect doing the same to his pa at that age but somehow he always thought his boys would be different.

The shooting had stopped, and someone was shouting what sounded like a name over and over again. Jed was about to ride on when hooves drummed and an apparition materialized out of the darkness. Instinctively, he jerked his carbine to his shoulder, but he held his fire.

"It's an Injun!" Pitney exclaimed.

An Indian, and someone else. Jed saw a fair-haired woman struggling mightily to free herself from the warrior's grasp. Since they were in the heart of Comanche country, Jed figured the warrior must be one of the scourges of Texas, as they were sometimes described, and suddenly all the ruckus made sense. A Comanche war party had attacked some whites, and now one of the warriors was making off with a captive. Neither had seen him or his boys. The warrior was distracted by the woman's effort to break free, and she was twisted partway around, beating at her captor with her fists.

"Let go of me! Do you hear? Let go!"

Jed lowered his carbine. Shooting at night was always a tricky proposition, and he could not be sure he would hit the Comanche and only the Comanche. Neglected instincts took over. Once again he was Jed Adams, Confederate cavalryman. A jab of his spurs, and he reined his horse to cut them off. The Comanche glanced up and saw him and attempted to veer aside but Jed's sorrel was well trained. Hickory, Jed called him, and he would as soon part with an arm or a leg as the mount that had saved his life more times than he could ever repay.

Hickory came up alongside the warhorse and turned broadside. The Comanche whisked a knife from a sheath but Jed was a shade faster; he slammed his carbine's stock against the warrior's head and the Comanche swayed and his arms sagged. Jed drew back the carbine to hit him again but the woman unexpectedly sprang free of the Comanche's grasp and leaped straight at him. Instantly, Jed looped an arm around her waist and clung on so she wouldn't fall.

Comanches were not renowned as the best horsemen of the plains for nothing. Even though dazed, the warrior reined smoothly to the north and bent low over his mount. Jed wanted to shoot but couldn't with the woman in his arms.

Then a rifle cracked, and another, and the Comanche's horse whinnied and went down in a forward roll. The Comanche jumped clear, or tried to, and was struck by a flying leg. The horse squealed and convulsed and sought to rise, then collapsed. The warrior lifted an arm, gasped, and was still.

"We did it!" Pitney hollered. "We stopped the varmint!"

Bret started to kneed the buttermilk toward the prone form.

"Hold on there, boy!" Jed warned and reined over beside them. "Watch this lady," he commanded, depositing the Comanche's captive between them. She was flustered and flushed but appeared to be unharmed, but he asked anyway, "Are you hurt, ma'am?"

"No, no, I'm fine," Constance Waldron said, astonished at her miraculous deliverance. "Who are you? Where did you come from?"

"First things first, ma'am," Jed said. Alighting, he walked warily toward the Comanche. Indians were notorious for their tricks, and he wasn't hankering for a knife in the belly. He stopped well short and thumbed back the hammer. "Are you alive, Injun?"

"Kill him, Pa!" Pitney yelled. "Finish him off!"

Once, Jed would have done just that. But he'd had his fill of killing in the war. He had seen enough men die horrible deaths to last him ten lifetimes, and he was no longer as eager to squeeze the trigger as he used be. Not even if the target at the other end of his carbine was a heathen Comanche. "Quiet down, boy."

The warrior as one lay dead. Jed recollected a time he was checking for wounded among the hundreds of bodies littering a battlefield, and a Yankee he mistook for dead lunged at him with a bayonet and nearly opened him up like a melon. That Yank had taken four bullets and had blood all over his uniform but he was alive enough to seek revenge on those who had killed him.

"Be careful!" Constance advised.

Jed edged nearer. He poked the Comanche's moccasin with the toe of his boot but the warrior just lay there. Jed nudged a leg with the same result. He would like to believe the Comanche was dead but there was no bullet hole and no blood. The man might be busted up inside or have a broken neck from the tumble but somehow Jed doubted it. "I think you're playin' possum,

Injun. Maybe I should just shoot you to be sure."

The Comanche's eyes snapped open, eyes filled with hatred the likes of which Jed had never seen, not even in the Yankees he fought. "White dog."

Hearing English startled Jed. "You speak our language?"

"Stupid white dog."

"I reckon you do." Jed pointed the carbine at the Comanche's forehead. "And I reckon I should splatter your brains for what you tried to do with that lady yonder."

"Shoot," the Comanche said. He was in pain, great pain, and trying hard not to show it.

"You'd like that, wouldn't you, Injun? Should I put you out of your misery like I would a dog?"

The Comanche did not respond. He did not need to. His eyes said it all.

Jed nearly squeezed the trigger. Then he lowered the carbine and looked closer. "I'll be damned. Your leg is busted. I can see the bone stickin' out." He grinned. "Tell you what, redskin. If you're so powerful eager to die, slit your own damn throat. You haven't harmed me or mine." He winked and backed slowly away, saying,

"Just lie there. Don't get up and don't lift a finger to stop us and you get to keep your hair." Chuckling at his little joke, he retraced his steps.

"Why didn't you kill him?" Bret asked.

"Why waste the bullet?" Jed rejoined.

"But he's an Injun!" Pitney declared.

"Who can't harm us none, son," Jed said. "Thanks to you and your brother."

Pitney beamed. "We did good, then?"

"Real good. I'm proud of you," Jed said, and he was. He had seen grown men do a lot worse, soldiers who froze in the heat of combat or turned tail and ran away screaming or blubbering like babies. "Proud of both of you."

"I wish I'd been old enough to fight in the war," Bret unexpectedly commented.

Jed was glad he hadn't been. Suddenly remembering the woman, he doffed his cap and bowed. "Jedidiah Nathan Adams, at your service, ma'am. I'm glad me and my boys were in the right place at the right time to lend you a hand."

"So am I," Constance said. Now that she had recovered somewhat from the shock of being abducted, she was flustered to discover her dress was askew and her hair was out of place. Introducing herself, she said, "If you would be so kind, our wagon isn't

66

far, and my family must be worried sick."

"We'd be happy to escort you, ma'am," Jed said. "Would you like to ride double with me or walk?"

Constance hesitated. She was still so rattled her legs felt weak, but it would not do for Tom to see her riding with a perfect stranger. He had a bit of a jealous streak, and this particular stranger was quite handsome. "We should walk, I guess."

Jed handed the lead rope to Bret, took Hickory's reins in hand, and gestured. "Lead the way, Mrs. Waldron. I believe you came from that way." He pointed in the direction the shots came from.

Smoothing her dress and fluffing her hair, Constance began walking. "I only pray my husband and my daughters have not been harmed."

"How many more Comanches are there?"

"Only four, I believe," Constance said, remembering what Vantine had told them.

"It's been quiet for a while now," Jed observed, "so maybe they drove the redskins off." To Bret and Pitney he said, "Keep your eyes skinned, boys, and holler if you see anythin'."

Constance had been so swept up in the rush of events that only now did she notice his uniform. "Oh my. You're a Confederate."

"Yes, ma'am," Jed grinned. "One of those awful Johnny Rebs. I take it by your accent that you and yours are Yankees?"

"We're from Ohio," Constance revealed. She thought of Tom, and how he might react.

"We sure lost a lot of good men on both sides, didn't we?" Jed said. His personal count tallied two brothers and four cousins and more friends and acquaintances than he would care to count.

Constance thought that a nice thing to say. "Yes. Yes, we did. My husband lost his best friend and he has never quite been the same." She hoped that would suffice as a subtle warning.

"If you don't mind my askin', what are you and yours doin' way out here in the wilds?"

"Looking to start over," Constance said. "Tom hopes to start up a ranch. He's heard marvelous account of this Texas country, but for the life of me, I can't help but wonder if they weren't exaggerated."

Jed chuckled. "The way I heard it, Texas is a land of milk and honey, and all a gent has to do is plant a corn seed in the mornin' and by supper he'll be eatin' corn on the cob."

Constance laughed heartily and felt much of her tension drain away. "I was told that eastern Texas is a lot prettier than here. There's a lot more water and a lot more grass and trees. But there are also a lot more people and my husband doesn't want much to do with people these days."

"He's not the only one."

Constance glanced at him. His face had darkened with anger just like Tom's did on occasion, and she could never quite understand why. Sure, Tom had had it rough in the war, but that was no excuse for despising people in general, in her estimation. She decided to change the subject. "Are you going to send for your wife once you're settled?" To her dismay, his features darkened even more.

"My wife went to her reward while I was off tryin' to get myself killed fightin' for a losin' cause."

"I'm sorry," Constance said. She wanted to add that he sounded awfully bitter but that might be too forward.

"I have no one to blame but myself, ma'am. It's easy to get caught up in the spirit of things when everyone is doin' the same. I was protectin' the South and the flower of Southern womanhood from all you Yankee monsters."

Again Constance glanced at him, unsure whether he was serious or joshing. "We heard a lot of terrible things about you Rebels, too. There was a lot of silliness on both sides, if you ask me."

"Silliness," Jed said. "That's just about right." He was thinking of Cemetery Ridge. Nearly fifteen thousand of his fellow Confederates, the cream of the Southern army, charged across more than a mile of open country straight into waiting Yankee guns and were cut to ribbons. It was slaughter, plain and simple. The Yankees let them think a heavy bombardment had silenced their cannons and scattered their troops, but it was a ruse. The Federals held their fire until the right moment and then blasted away with cannons and rifle and musket fire. Rebels fell in droves. Later, Jed learned that Longstreet hadn't wanted to make that charge but General Lee had insisted. All those men in the flower of life, all those valiant sons of the South, slain because a general was too stubborn to admit when he was wrong and too proud to rescind an order he never should have given.

"Pa, I heard somethin'," Bret suddenly said.

Jed stopped and raised his carbine. He

wanted to club himself with it for being so careless. Here they were, hostiles lurking about, and he was strolling along with Mrs. Waldron as if they were in the heart of Charleston. He would never have made a mistake like this during the war. If he had, he wouldn't be standing there. Motioning for her to get behind him in case they were attacked, he strained his ears into the night but heard nothing other than the ever-present wind.

After a while Bret said, "Maybe I was wrong. I'm a bit jumpy after tanglin' with that Injun."

"You did right to tell me," Jed said. They were such good sons. He was sorry his wife would never get to see them grow into manhood and one day bounce grandchildren on her knee as she always looked forward to doing. He resumed walking, but slowly.

"Can I say something?" Constance whispered. She was reluctant to disturb him when he was so intent on preserving her life.

"Sure." Jed glimpsed movement, or thought he did, way off in the darkness. The other Comanches might be closing in.

"I don't want any harm to come to your boys on my account. Lend me a pistol and I will go on alone."

Deeply touched, Jed placed a hand on her shoulder. "I couldn't claim to be any kind of a man if I let you do that. You'll stay with us, and we'll protect you with our lives, if need be."

"I just —" Constance said and stopped, aghast, as her husband came hurtling out of the night and raised his rifle to bash her rescuer over the head.

6

Tom Waldron was beside himself. He ran a dozen yards in one direction, then a dozen yards in another. Constance and her captor had disappeared. He hoped she would call out for help again so he would have some idea of which way to go. He started to bear in another direction but a sharp cry stopped him in his tracks, a cry from the wash, from one of his daughters.

Momentarily torn by indecision, Tom glared into the gloom, then wheeled and sprinted for the wash. But it was not where he thought it would be. He turned and tried another direction and this time nearly pitched over the bank when he came on it without warning. "Heather! Sally!"

"Over here!"

It sounded like his oldest. Tom leaped to the bottom and sprinted to a bend. From beyond it came a peculiar gurgling. He envisioned one of his daughters being strangled, and in a near panic he sprinted around the turn. Too late, Tom saw a sprawled figure in his path. He tried to stop but he was moving too fast. Tripping, he went down hard on his hands and knees and lost his hold on the Sharps. He glimpsed a swarthy face, grit in menace. Grabbing the rifle, he spun, only to remember he had neglected to reload. He stabbed for his revolver, instead, and fumbled at the flap to his holster. Then he saw it wasn't necessary.

A slug had caught the Comanche high in the chest and exited out his back and a pool of blood was spreading from under him. The Comanche's mouth was opening and closing but no sounds came out.

"Serves you right, damn you," Tom said.

The Comanche began to weakly grope about. A few feet away lay a knife he had dropped when he was shot.

"Looking for this?" Tom asked, helping himself. "Where are my daughters?" He could see the prairie schooner on down the wash, and the horses were there, but there was no sign of Heather and Sally. "Tell me, by God, or else!"

Crooking a finger, the warrior beckoned for him to bend closer.

Suspicious, Tom slowly leaned down. It occurred to him that the Comanche might not know English although a lot of Indians had picked up a smattering, but he tried again anyway. "What have you done with my girls?" The Comanche's features contorted with great effort. "What is it you're trying to say?"

The warrior spat on him.

Dumfounded, Tom felt the spittle dribble down his cheek. Before he quite knew what he was doing, he had buried the knife in the Comanche's ribs. Once, twice, three times. Amazingly, the Comanche smiled, then exhaled loudly and went limp. Tom quickly rose, looked down at the bloody blade in his hand, and threw the knife down.

"Father?"

Heather and Sally were by the prairie schooner. Tom flew to them and hugged them to him, so relieved they were alive, tears filled his eyes. "Thank God! I thought I was too late."

"Thank Mr. Vantine," Heather said, pointing. "They would have dragged us off if not for him."

Two dead Comanches lay nearby, one still clutching a lance, the other with his teeth bared in a feral snarl.

"One had my hair and was pulling me," Sally sniffled. "It hurt, and I couldn't make him let go."

"You're safe now. It's over," Tom said,

not wanting her to break down and start bawling.

That was when Vantine came silently around the front of the wagon. "Aren't you forgettin' someone?"

Annoyed, Tom straightened and snapped, "How could I forget my own wife? Watch over my girls while I go after her." He moved toward the horses but Sally gripped his sleeve.

"What happened to Mother? Where is she?" Sally asked.

"A Comanche took her," Tom said, and immediately regretted it. Both girls turned and went to run off up the wash and he grabbed at them to hold them there. "No! Stay put!" He caught hold of Sally but he had the Sharps in his other hand and couldn't stop Heather. She would have run off had Vantine not stepped in front of her, shaking his head.

"Listen to your pa, girl. Your mother wouldn't want you to get yourself killed. I'll go after her."

"Like hell!" Tom said. "She's *my* wife." He would have said more but just then the prairie resounded to the crack of two shots, each by a different gun, from the sound of it. "Keep them here!" he barked at Vantine, and pushed Sally at him. Then he was past the schooner and up the side of the wash and running as he had not run since he was a boy, in the direction the shots came from.

All Tom could think of was Constance. Of how much she meant to him. Of how crushed he would be if he lost her. She was his heart, his soul, his very life. All those years of the war, the one thought that sustained him was the thought of making it home to take her into his arms and feel her lips on his and her warm breath on his neck. At night he would lie awake with her face seeming to float in the air above him, smiling that loving smile of hers. He would softly say her name and yearn for her with a yearning that seared him to his core.

Tom had known she was the one for him the day he first set eyes on her. He was seventeen, she was fifteen, and her family had just moved to Ohio from Pennsylvania. He was passing by in a buckboard and saw her helping her parents unload their wagon, and he had an irresistible urge to stop. A strange tingle shot through him and he went over and introduced himself and asked if he could help.

He surprised himself. Usually, he was always so shy around girls, so tongue-tied, he couldn't string four words together to make a sentence. But Constance put him right at ease. It felt so natural being with her, after that first summer he couldn't imagine ever being without her. So he had spoken to her father and courted her for two years and eventually taken her for his wife, and it was the smartest thing he had ever done.

Now the thought of something happening to her filled him with fear so potent, Tom's insides churned. He remembered a buggy ride they had taken to a covered bridge, and a picnic in the shade of high maples trees. He remembered how delicious the chicken tasted, and how she had laughed and flirted and made him feel like he was the luckiest man alive. He remembered their first kiss, sitting there on that blanket with a shaft of sunlight streaming through the branches and falling on her upturned face, in such a way, she was breathtakingly beautiful. Their lips touched and the world stood still and he had never been the same.

Running pell-mell through the night in the wilds of west Texas, Tom felt his guilt return. He was the one who had persuaded her to move. He was the one who went on and on about how they could make a new and better life for themselves. But the truth was, he had grown tired of farming, tired of Ohio, tired of the same routine day in and day out. He craved something new, something different.

One bright morning a drummer stopped at the farm to try to sell them soaps and lotions. The drummer made it sound as if females everywhere were falling all over themselves to buy his products. Tom had sat off to one side in the parlor, inwardly laughing, until the drummer mentioned that he had peddled his wares from Texas to New England and never had any complaints. Afterward, Tom asked the man if he had really been to Texas and what it was like, and he had been treated to a discourse that made Texas seem like paradise.

Over the months that followed Tom did some asking around, and the more he learned, the more excited he became. He had still not made up his mind completely, when one evening at a tavern on the main highway, the bartender, who knew of his interest in all things Texan, pointed out a bone fide Texican on his way to New York on business. They had a wonderful talk.

"Cattle will be the next big boom," the Texan said at one point. "Wait and see. Easterners can't raise enough to keep beef on the table, and the demand will grow.

Out west there's plenty of wide-open space, prime grazin' land just there for the takin'. Gettin' the cows to market will take some doing but there's already talk of the railroads pushin' their lines clear to Kansas and beyond. A smart man could get rich in cattle, I tell you. Just think of it!"

Tom did. It was all he could think about for weeks. Fate had shown him how to fulfill his dream of a new life, and he presented the idea to his family with all the zeal of that drummer pitching soap.

And now look! A strangled groan passed Tom's lips at the thought of his folly costing his wife her life. For that is what it had been: folly. Texas was not anything like he thought it would be, and his dream might well be their ruin.

Suddenly figures moved in the darkness. Tom stopped and crouched, nearly out of breath, suspecting more Comanches. Then he saw Constance and he started forward with a shout of elation on his lips, only to freeze when he realized others were with her, a man and two boys, and the man was dressed in the uniform of a soldier of the Confederate States of America.

Tom was startled. He could not make sense of what he was seeing. Then he remembered the shots. The only explanation was that the Rebel had saved Constance from the Comanche. They were talking and Constance was smiling, and the Rebel turned to her and put a hand on her shoulder. A burning rage seized him. Raising his Sharps, he rushed at his former enemy.

"Tom, no!" Constance sprang between them and lifted her arms to stop the rifle's downward stroke, but it never came.

Her cry was like a bucket of cold water thrown in Tom's face. He stopped, appalled at what he had been about to do but unable to quell his simmering rage. Jerking the Sharps down, he demanded, "Who is this man? What's going on here?"

"He saved me," Constance confirmed Tom's hunch. "I'm not in any danger." But she knew that was not the reason Tom nearly assaulted Adams.

Tom knew he should have been grateful. He should have thanked the man and pumped his hand but instead he stared at the gray uniform and thought of all those who had died fighting other men wearing the same uniform and he said, "You're a long way from home, Reb."

Jed Adams glanced at the blue cap Waldron wore. He had not understood why the man attacked him. Now he did. "I could say the same thing about you, Yankee."

"I suppose I should be grateful."

"Don't put yourself out on my account," Jed said. "In the South we're brought up to always respect womanhood. Even Yankee womanhood." It was wrong to say but he had met men like Waldron before, men who despised anyone and anything connected to the Southern cause.

Stung by the veiled barb, Tom said, "How decent of you. But then, you Johnny Rebs always did think your manners were better than the manners of us Yanks."

Constance was in a quandary. She liked Jed Adams and she could not stand there and let her husband and Adams sling insults. "Enough about Rebs and Yanks and the like. The war is over, remember? We should try to get along."

"If you say so," Tom said with no enthusiasm.

Jed was not one to stick around where he wasn't wanted. Touching his cap, he said, "We'll be on our own way. It was a pleasure meetin' you, ma'am." He deliberately did not say it had been a pleasure meeting her husband, since it hadn't.

Constance waited for Tom to say something and when he didn't she quickly suggested, "Why not spend the night with us? There might be more Comanches around."

Tom blinked. He hadn't thought of that. Three more guns would come in handy. As much as he disliked Rebels, he had his family to think of. "She's right. As the old saying goes, there's strength in numbers."

Jed noticed that the Yankee hadn't apologized for nearly caving in his skull. He would just as soon go on but there were Bret and Pitney to consider. Shooting one Comanche did not make them a match for an entire war party. "I reckon we'll take you up on your offer."

"Fine." Tom clasped Constance's hand and walked briskly toward the wash. He did not look back.

"What on earth has gotten into you?" Constance whispered. "You're treating that poor man like he's scum."

"He's a Confederate," Tom said.

"And you're a Yankee? So what? You can't go on hating them for the rest of your life."

"You weren't there. You didn't see what I saw. You didn't sit by your best friend's side and hold his hand while he died a slow and agonizing death from a Confederate ball in his belly. You didn't see half

83

your regiment blown apart by cannon fire."

"Granted. But I wouldn't dwell on it if I had." Constance had been all through this with him before and she was tired of having to remind him. "You must learn to forget. You must shut your mind to the past and concentrate on the future."

Tom grit his teeth. She was asking the impossible. The memories were too vivid. Several nights a week he had nightmares, and would wake up in cold sweats. For that matter, he hadn't slept right since he enlisted. Back then, he could sleep for eight to ten hours a night and wake up refreshed. Nowadays, four hours was a luxury. More often it was two.

"Cat got your tongue?" Constance asked. Lord help her, but she resented his childishness, especially now, of all times.

"You ask a lot of me," Tom answered defensively.

"All I ask is common courtesy. What's so hard about that? Honestly. You men and your grudges. Is this how it will be ten years from now? Or twenty? Both sides still hating each other?"

"I'm sorry I'm not perfect but I never claimed to be. And it's more than a grudge. It's important we never forget what their side put us through so we won't be put through it ever again."

"Please, Tom," Constance tried a personal touch. "For me? Try to get along. Who knows. You might even grow to like him."

"That will be the day."

Constance sighed. Her mother had warned her. Men could be as stubborn as mules when they put their mind to it. "That's why the Good Lord created women," her mother once commented. "Without us there wouldn't be any common sense in the world." Now, like then, the comment made her grin, but she was careful to hide her amusement from her husband. If she was going to mend fences between Tom and Jed Adams, she had her work cut out for her.

7

A better name for Vinegar Flats might have been Dust Flats. Dust covered the buildings; dust caked the hitch rail and the horses tied to the hitch rail. A combination saloon and general store bore a sign that read KITTLE'S LIQUOR AND MERCANTILE EMPORIUM, EVERYTHING UNDER THE SUN AND THEN SOME. There were also a corral, several sheds, an outhouse, and a pump for the well, all as dusty as everything else.

Reining up at the hitch rail, Jed Adams remarked, "That's some sign. The man who owns it must think highly of himself or have a good sense of humor."

"I don't get it, Pa," Pitney said.

"You will when you're older." Jed twisted in the saddle to glance eastward. The prairie schooner was a ways out yet and would take a while to get there. He had seen no sense in continuing to ride with a man who did not want his company, and had brought his sons and their packhorses on ahead.

Bret was gazing back, too. "That

Heather sure is nice, ain't she, Pa?"

"If you're fixin' to court her, you'd better mind your speech. The word is isn't, not ain't. Women like it when a man babbles proper."

"Court her?" Bret blurted. "I ain't about to do any such thing. Or I isn't." But his blush put the fib to his words.

"I don't see how anyone can like girls," Pitney said. "That Sally Waldron didn't do nothin' but tease me. Why, she said she could see my nose hairs when she bent and looked up my nose."

"Females says the strangest things," Jed agreed as he dismounted and looped Hickory's reins around the rail. "Light and rest a spell, gentlemen. I'm thinkin' we'll stay here a day or two before we push on. Our horses can use the rest and we're mighty tuckered out ourselves."

"Ain't that the truth," Bret said. "Or isn't it."

"Remind me to have a talk with you later, son," Jed said. Horses were in the corral and a open-bed wagon was parked nearby. The outhouse was in use; someone inside was whistling merrily.

"Can we get somethin' to eat?" Pitney asked. "My stomach is so empty it's growlin' at me."

Bret stopped gazing at the distant prairie schooner to say, "I was sort of surprised, Pa, when you didn't take Mrs. Waldron up on her offer to feed us breakfast. Why didn't you? It was awful nice of her."

Jed almost answered, *I didn't want to choke on Mr. Waldron's food.* Instead he shrugged and replied, "She's a nice lady. The same can't be said of all her family."

They weren't stupid, his sons. "Mr. Waldron doesn't seem to like us much, does he?" Pitney asked.

"Some folks have too much acid in their system," Jed said, and slid his carbine from the saddle scabbard. "Now how about we quit all this jawin' and go inside and grab us a bite to eat?"

"Now you're talkin'." Pitney was off his horse in a twinkling. "Do you think they'll have hard candy like we used to get back home?"

"Hard candy for breakfast? Your ma would rise up out of her grave and beat me with a stick." Jed had to duck a bit to go through the doorway, then stopped to let his eyes adjust.

On the right was a bar, a long plank laid out on stacked crates. Behind it were shelves lined with bottles. Of the three tables only one was in use, by four dusty men playing cards. To the left was the mercantile half or, more appropriately, two-thirds, since it took up most of the establishment. There was a counter, which, like the bar, consisted of a plank set on crates, and a pickle barrel and a cracker barrel, both duly marked. Clothes and blankets were piled neatly on display, and tools and odds and ends were nicely arranged. There were also canned goods, lined up in long rows.

The neatness made Jed say, "I wonder."

Another moment, and an attractive woman wearing an apron and a brown dress came out of the back. She had a mane of dark brown hair that spilled to her waist. Quite buxom, she had hips wider than most men would call ideal but her waist was quite slim. She came forward, extending her hand as a man would do. "Howdy, strangers. I'm Ruth Kittle but I don't answer to the Ruth much. Most people call me Kit."

Jed shook. Her eyes were emerald green, the same color as Melanie's. "Pleased to make your acquaintance, ma'am," he said, snatching off his hat and glancing sharply at the boys so they would take the hint and take off theirs. "I'm Jed Adams and these are my wild ones, Bret and Pitney. Fine place you and your husband have here."

"Who said anything about a husband?" Kit responded. "I had one but he went and died on me. He was unloading the wagon when a pig spooked the horses and he tried to reach the seat and stop it but he fell and the front wheel broke his neck. Damned stupid way to die, if you ask me."

Jed couldn't say which shocked him more, her language or her attitude. "I'm sorry to hear that, ma'am."

"Why? You didn't know him?"

"I'd have shot the pig," Bret said.

Kit smiled. "A man after my own heart. I took my shotgun and blew its brains out. The rest made good eating." One of the men playing cards called her name and she said, "Excuse me a moment. I need to refill some glasses."

"I like her, Pa," Pitney whispered as she walked off. "She makes me think of ma for some reason."

"I like her, too," Bret said. "She comes right out and says what she thinks."

"I swear," Jed sighed, "you two are becomin' downright woman crazy. Next thing I know, you'll marry those Waldron girls and I'll have Yankees in the family."

Bret blushed again, darker and deeper. Pitney sputtered and declared, "Marry a *girl?* Why, I'd rather marry my horse, if I was ever to marry, which I won't, because I never will, not that there's anything wrong with it, since Ma and you were, but that's how I feel."

"I will remember to quote you six or seven years from now," Jed told him, "if I could figure out what you just said."

"Want me to say it again?" Pitney asked.

"No. It would only confuse me more."

The four men were staring at them. Jed studied the quartet more closely. They had cold, unfriendly faces. Their dusty clothes had seen a lot of use. Three wore wide-brimmed hats, as was the custom in Texas, the fourth wore a bowler tilted back on a crop of curly red hair.

"Well, if it ain't a Reb."

A familiar stab of resentment pierced Jed, and he asked, "Do you have a problem with that, mister?"

"Not me." The man smiled, revealing buck teeth. "I wasn't in the war. But you Rebels had the right idea. Niggers ain't good for nothin' but slaves and lickin' the boots of us whites."

Kit was filling glasses at the bar. "That will be enough, Cooter. You know I don't like that kind of talk."

"Sure, Kit, sure," Cooter said. "But

you'd best hope the Klan never hears how kindly you are toward darkies. They might pay you a visit in the middle of the night."

"Is that why they wear those white hoods and sheets?" Kit replied. "To hide the yellow streaks down their backs?"

Cooter laughed, but his eyes glittered with resentment. "That mouth of yours will get you in trouble one day, woman."

"In case you haven't heard, the only thing that will get a man hung faster than stealing a horse in these parts is harming a woman," Kit said matter-of-factly. "But you go ahead and keep on with your threats."

One of the other players, who had a big belly that stuck out over his belt, cackled and smacked Cooter on the back. "Best wave a white flag, pard. She got the better of you."

"Shut up, Tooley," Cooter snapped.

Jed moved to a display of clothes. Each garment had a tag attached with the size and the price written on it. They were separated as to shirts, pants, and dresses. He stepped to a pile of boys' pants and began inspecting them.

"Anything I can help you with, Mr. Adams?"

Jed had not heard her come up behind

him. "My sprouts can use new britches. Theirs are about worn-out."

Kit gazed at where Bret and Pitney were excitedly admiring revolvers and derringers in a gun case. Then she selected several pairs and said, "I believe these are about the right size. Two that might fit your younger boy but only one for your older boy. I'm expecting more in my shipment next month. They can try them on in the back, if you like. There's a little room just past the curtain."

Jed called the boys over and they reluctantly went to see if the pants would fit, Pitney grumbling in protest.

"I don't know what it is about boys and trying on clothes," Kit said with a smile. "Girls can do it all day and not complain once." Her smiled faded and her green eyes narrowed. "Do you feel the same way Cooter does, Mr. Adams?"

Jed had been trying to avoid looking at her face. Those green eyes brought back too many painful memories. But now he glanced up in bewilderment and said, "I beg your pardon?"

"About blacks, Mr. Adams. Your uniform. The recent difficulties between the North and the South."

Jed resented being asked the question. But

she was a woman, and he had been taught to always respect the fairer sex. "I don't hate blacks, if that's what you're askin'."

"I'm sorry. Have I hurt your feelings?" Kit gave him a searching look. "Then if I'm not overstepping myself, why did you enlist on the Confederate side?"

"It seemed like the right thing to do at the time," Jed said. "And you are oversteppin' yourself."

"Oh. I'm sorry." Kit's cheeks grew pink and she walked past him and over behind the counter. "If I can be of any more assistance, let me know."

Jed was annoyed at himself. He had no call to be so testy with her. But after the night he had just spent, he was prickly about his uniform and what it stood for. When they had arrived at the wash, Constance had invited him and his boys to climb down and partake of some stew. He'd met their daughters, and the man they had picked up out on the plain. The whole while, Tom Waldron kept giving him a look. It was a way Yankees had of staring spitefully at Southerners, as if all Confederates were what came out the hind end of a horse. He would have left if not for Bret and Pitney. They were glad to be among other folks, and it was good to see them having fun.

Shaking his head at his foolishness, Jed walked over to where Kit was arranging tins of tea. "I'm sorry."

"There's nothing to be sorry for," she said stiffly. "You put me in my place and I deserved it."

"No, you didn't." Jed waited for her to turn, then said, "I honestly and truly hope you will forgive me. I've had so many folks look down their noses at me for wearin' gray, my feathers ruffle too easy."

Kit leaned against the shelf and folded her arms across her chest. "Apology accepted. It's nice for a change to meet a man who isn't so full of himself he's forgotten how. Where are you and your boys bound?"

"Nowhere in particular," Jed said. "It's not so much where we're goin' as what we're gettin' away from."

"Ah," Kit said, her green eyes unfathomable. "Well, you're welcome to stick around Vinegar Flats as long as you'd like. You can put your horses up in the corral. I don't charge to board them but I do for the feed."

"This whole place is yours then?"

"You sound surprised. Isn't a woman supposed to try and make good? Can't she run a business?"

"Whoa, there." Jed grinned. "Is it me, or do you keep puttin' words in my head? Women can do whatever they're of a mind to, as far as I'm concerned. Truth to tell, I admire your grit, ma'am."

Kit's cheeks were making a habit of becoming pink. "I guess I'm the one who should apologize now. With you, it's your uniform. With me, it's being female. You wouldn't believe some of the things I have to put up with." She shot a meaningful glance at the poker tables, and one player in particular.

"You would have it a sight easier back east — that's for sure," Jed allowed.

An awkward silence fell between them, broken by the plodding thud of heavy hooves and the creak and rattle of the arriving prairie schooner. Tooley got up and walked to the window. "Well, look here, boys. Some sodbusters are passin' through. What say we have some fun?"

"I heard that," Kit called across the room, "and there will be none of your shenanigans or I'll ban you from the premises."

"I'd like to see you try." This from Cooter, the buck-toothed man in the bowler. "We generally do what we want, when we want."

"Not in my place you don't," Kit said.

Tooley returned to his chair, saying, "I don't know about you, Cooter, but I don't much like havin' my entertainment spoiled. How much longer are we goin' to twiddle our thumbs before we head for Denver?"

Sunlight streamed through the entrance as Tom Waldron and Constance entered, trailed by their daughters. "Clothes!" Constance exclaimed and made straight for the garment section, with Heather and Sally close behind.

"Quite the good-lookin' woman you have there, mister," Cooter said to Tom Waldron. "Your older girl ain't bad, neither."

"I'll thank you not to talk about them that way," Tom curtly replied. "Where I come from, men show respect for women."

"Where I come from," Cooter mimicked him, "men who put on airs are treated to lead poisonin'."

Tension crackled. Cooter and Tooley and one of the other poker players slowly rose, their hands near the butts of their revolvers. Constance paled and started toward Tom.

Jed was debating whether to side with them when a shadow filled the doorway and in walked Vantine.

8

Constance Waldron was terrified. She honestly thought the men at the table were about to draw on her husband. Then in walked Vantine and something happened. Something changed. She could not say what it was other than a subtle wariness came over the buck-toothed man and his friend with the big belly. They forgot all about Tom and intently watched Vantine as he walked to the bar and turned so his left elbow was on the counter and his right hand was low at his side, near his pearl-handled Colt.

"What does a gent have to do to get some whiskey around here?" the man in black asked no one in particular.

Jed Adams did not know what to make of Vantine. When they met the night before, he had the same feeling he did as when he saw a mountain lion or a prowling bear. But the man had acted friendly enough, as far as it went. They hardly spoke ten words to each other since.

Now Ruth Kittle was moving toward the

bar, saying, "All he has to do is speak up. I'm Kit. I own this place."

"I'm right pleased to make your acquaintance, ma'am," Vantine said. "Maybe along with that whiskey, you can explain some of the local customs."

"Customs?" Kit said as she came around the far end.

"Why is it the men hereabouts play cards standin' up?"

Cooter and Tooley seemed to have forgotten all about Tom Waldron. They glanced at each other and slowly sat back down, their hands on the table. Tooley checked his cards and added a few coins to the pot.

Kit was filling a glass. "Here you go, mister. If there's anything else I can get you, give a holler."

"I need a horse," Vantine said. "Mine is feedin' buzzards right now, courtesy of a Comanche." He took a swallow and smacked his lips. "This is fine Monongahela, madam."

"I don't water it down like some do," Kit said. "As for a mount, I'm afraid I don't have any spares at the moment."

"That's all right." Vantine swallowed more whiskey and turned toward the four poker players. "I aim to make do with theirs."

99

The four men stopped playing. Cooter's face creased in a lopsided sneer and he said sarcastically, "You reckon we're goin' to sell you one, just like that?" He snapped his fingers and chuckled.

"No. I reckon you won't have any use for yours." Vantine glanced at Kit. "That reminds me. I don't suppose there's an undertaker handy?"

"Are you serious?" Kit asked uncertainly.

"It's just that I'm not all that fond of diggin' graves," Vantine said, and polished off the rest of his drink in two great gulps. Then he set the glass down and moved a few feet from the bar and hooked his thumbs in his gunbelt. "Now how about we get down to business, boys?"

"I don't know what in hell you're talkin' about," Cooter said. "And what was that business about an undertaker and us not needin' our horses?"

"Dead men don't do much ridin'," Vantine said.

Cooter opened his mouth to respond but Kit beat him to it.

"Hold on there, stranger. I don't allow gunplay. If you have a grievance against these men, I suggest you take it outside."

"I'm sorry, ma'am," Vantine said, "but I've already let the cat out of the bag, and I can't put it back in."

A doubled-barreled shotgun hung on pegs behind the bar. Kit started to reach for it, remarking, "This is my saloon and you'll do as I say."

Vantine's hand moved, and the Colt's nickel-plating gleamed in the sunlight streaming in the window. He didn't point it at her, he just held it and wriggled it back and forth. "I wouldn't, were I you, ma'am. Oblige me and come on around from back there."

Kit's fingers were inches from the scattergun. "And if I don't, you'll blow a hole in me — is that it?"

"I have this to do," Vantine said. "I'm sorry, but I must insist."

A twinge of resentment shot through Jed Adams. He had not known Ruth Kittle long enough to have any feelings for her but he objected to men threatening women on general principle. Still, this was none of his affair. He sidled to where Bret and Pitney were still admiring the revolvers in the case and touched each of them on the shoulder. They turned, and he nodded toward the man in the black and whispered, "Don't move. Don't talk. When the lead starts to fly, hit the floor."

Tom Waldron was speechless. He had

heard about men like Vantine, but he certainly never expected to meet one, and he never in a million years imagined anything like this. He saw Constance start toward him and quickly motioned for her to stay where she was and went over to her instead.

Kit was backing away from the shotgun but she was not happy about it. "Whoever you are, I'll see that word gets out. Texas men don't like it when women are mistreated."

"I'm Lone Star born and bred, myself," Vantine said. "And I can't see how askin' you not to blow me in half with the cannon is mistreatin' you. But you're welcome to slap me after if it will make you feel better."

"I don't think I like you very much," Kit said.

"Most folks don't. That's what comes of hirin' my man stopper out for a price, I reckon."

"Don't sugarcoat it," Kit said. "You're a killer. I knew it the instant you came through that door."

"Fine eyesight you have, ma'am," Vantine said amiably. "But I prefer to think of myself as a pistolero."

Kit reached the end of the bar and stood with her hands gripping the edge, her white knuckles a testament to her anger. "There. Satisfied?"

"Thank you, ma'am." Vantine twirled the Colt into its silver-studded holster. "Now then, where were we?" he said to the four card players.

The whole time, Cooter and Tooley and the other two had been as still as stones. Now Cooter slowly placed his cards down and said, "You were sayin' as how you're aimin' to ride off on one of our horses."

"You'll be on the others," Vantine said. "Bellies down."

Tooley laughed a vicious laugh. "You're plumb loco, mister. What did we ever do to you that you walk in here fired up to make wolf meat of us?"

Vantine hooked his thumbs in his gun belt again and moved closer to the table but not so close that they could jump him. "This isn't about me. It's about you, Lester Tooley, and your friends, there. Hiram Cooter, Arthur Soostan and Ren Krebs."

The four men visibly tensed and Cooter rasped, "How in hell do you know our names?"

"A man in my line of work can't afford to bed down the wrong hombres," Vantine answered. "But this time it was easy. When

I got to Houston, her father already knew all I needed."

"Houston?" Cooter said. "We've never been there."

Vantine sighed, and said more to himself, "They always deny it. Even when there isn't a shadow of a doubt." He paused. "The four of you stayed at a cheap boardin' house on Fourth Street for over a month. You spent most of your time drinkin' and gamblin' and makin' nuisances of yourselves. The marshal had to throw you in jail overnight twice for drunk and disorderly."

Tooley appeared stunned. "How does he know all this?" he said to Cooter. "What in God's name is going on?"

"Shut up, you damned jackass," Cooter snapped.

"You were seen," Vantine said. "A bootblack was settin' up down the street and heard her screams. He hid behind a water trough and saw the four of you run by. He followed you to the stable where you had your horses, and after you rode out, he went back and waited for the marshal to show up."

"You're lyin'," one of the other men said.

"What reason would I have, Krebs?" Vantine retorted. "I didn't track you halfway across Texas for the fun of it. Her father hired me. He wasn't willin' to sit around waitin' for the law to do the job."

Kit took a step past the end of the bar. "Do you mind telling the rest of us what this is all about?"

"Not at all, ma'am," Vantine said. "Three months ago, in Houston, a seventeen-year-old girl by the name of Amy Skimmerhorn got up early to go visit her grandmother. She was a sweet girl, one of those who was friendly to everyone and wouldn't harm a fly. The sun wasn't quite up when she started out."

Tooley and Krebs squirmed in their chairs.

"She was takin' a shortcut down some back streets when she ran into four men who had spent the night drinkin' at a saloon just around the corner. The bartender had tried to shoo them out but one of them pulled a gun on him and told him to keep servin' drinks for as long as they wanted, and closin' time be damned. Shortly before dawn they finally left. As best the marshal could work it out, they ran into Amy Skimmerhorn and dragged her behind a building and raped her. They weren't gentle about it, neither. The sawbones says she had a busted nose and three broken fingers and a few cracked ribs. To cover it up, they slit her throat. Or one of them did. The same bastard carved on her some. He did things I can't talk about in mixed company. Then they left her lyin' in her blood and skedaddled. That's when the bootblack saw them."

"Dear God!" Constance exclaimed. She could tell by the expressions of the four men at the card table that they were guilty of the crime. As guilty as sin, and more than a little afraid.

Jed Adams thought of the horrors the Skimmerhorn girl had gone through, and was tempted to shoot the four himself.

"Her father is Dan Skimmerhorn," Vantine went on, "one of Houston's leadin' citizens. He's made a tidy amount of money in the freight business and spent quite a bit findin' out all he could about these polecats here, even hired the Pinkertons. They were the ones who learned the names. Once he had all the information he needed, Skimmerhorn sent to San Antonio. And here I am."

"Aren't you going to take them back to Houston to stand trial?" Constance asked.

"No, ma'am. These four aren't leavin' this room."

They had it, then. Three of the four

paled, and the fourth, Cooter, began to rise up out of his chair but thought better of the notion and sat back down, declaring, "I tell you it wasn't us! You can't just walk up to someone and kill them. There are laws."

"You're a fine one to lecture me," Vantine said. "Accordin' to the Pinkertons, you and your friends have seven murders to your credit, and probably more no one knows about. Amy Skimmerhorn was your last. It ends here, boys, and nothin' you can say or do will change it. I've been paid to put windows in your skulls. So whenever you want to roll the dice, feel free."

"Just like that?" Cooter said.

"Just like that."

"There's four of us and only one of you." Cooter glanced at Tooley, Krebs, and Soostan and his chin bobbed ever so slightly.

"My Colt has five pills in the wheel," Vantine said, "enough with an extra to spare. But it's considerate of you to fret about my health."

"Go to hell," Cooter said.

"One day," Vantine said. He lowered his arms to his sides and his grin faded. "Dan Skimmerhorn sends his regards. At first he wanted me to fetch you back so he could do to you what you did to his daughter. But that's not practical and he's a practical man. So I'm to tote your bodies back as proof I've earned my fee."

"You expect it to be that easy?" Cooter demanded.

"Easy or hard doesn't make any difference," Vantine said. "Get it in your head that it's you or me and do what you have to do."

Tooley had broken out in a sweat. "This ain't right, mister. What if I agree to be taken back alive?"

"Did you hear me askin'?" Vantine rejoined.

"You can't shoot if we don't go for our hardware," Cooter said smugly, picking up the deck and riffling the cards. "That would put you in trouble with the law."

"Do you think the law will care after what you've done?" Vantine asked and flexed the fingers of his right hand. "Now then. You can die like sheep or you can die pretendin' your men. That's the only choice I'll give you and it's more than you deserve."

For half a minute nothing happened. Then, snarling an oath, the man called Krebs came up out of his chair with his Smith and Wesson sweeping clear. But as fast as he was, the man in black was faster. Vantine's pearl-handled Colt boomed and Krebs was punched backward, flipping over his chair as he fell. For long moments no one else spoke or moved. Then Vantine did a fancy flip with the Colt, returning it to its silver-studded holster.

"Who's next?"

Tooley was gaping at the body on the floor. "Did you see, Cooter? He ain't all bluff and ballast. He's the real article."

"Don't wet yourself," Cooter said. "We still have him outnumbered. On the count of three we take him."

"Let's not be hasty," Tooley said. "Maybe we can reason with him. How about it, mister? Will her old man settle for havin' us hung? Take me back and turn me over to the marshal for trial."

"Not me!" Soostan cried and came out of his chair clawing at his hogleg. He never cleared leather. The pearl-handled Colt flashed and spat lead and smoke and Soostan staggered and pressed a hand to the hole over his heart, and fell.

Once again Vantine holstered his revolver. "And then there were two."

"I want no part of this," Tooley said. He was quaking like an aspen leaf and tears were trickling down his pudgy cheeks.

"Oh, hell," Cooter said and threw himself to the left, taking his chair with him and drawing as he dived. He was counting on the table to shield him for the second or two it would take to bring his revolver to bear.

But Vantine sprang to one side, drawing as he moved, and he fired as Cooter's six-gun rose. Cooter shrieked like a gut-shot cougar and tried to steady his arm, and Vantine fired again, fanning the hammer with his left hand. Then he swiveled toward Lester Tooley.

"I can't draw. I'm too scared."

"I know."

Tooley closed his eyes. "Make it quick, will you?"

"Sure," Vantine said and shot him through the head.

9

Constance Waldron raised her arm to wave, then lowered it again. No one else was waving so why should she? Besides, she was glad to see Vantine leave. She still liked him, and was grateful for his help against the Comanches, but she would never forget what he had done to those four men and never forgive him for exposing her daughters to such language and so much bloodshed.

"He was a strange one," Tom Waldron commented for lack of anything better to say. Strange, in that as sick as he was of war, as sick as he was of fighting and killing, he could not conceive of someone doing it for a living.

"He sure was quick on the trigger, wasn't he?" Bret said to his father.

"The quickest I've ever seen," Jed Adams admitted.

They were standing under the overhang with the Waldrons, watching Vantine lead three horses draped with bodies off to the east. His last words to them were, "You folks did me a favor. If I can ever do the same for you, let me know."

"Did you see those brains all over the floor?" Sally said to Pitney. "I wanted to poke them with a stick."

"You, too?" Pitney said.

"Sally Ann!" Constance declared in dismay. "No more of that talk, if you please. From this moment on, we will never mention it again."

"But, Mother," Sally said, "we saw the whole thing. How can we not talk about it?"

"Never you mind." Constance disliked it when her children argued with her. "It's best to forget these things so you can sleep at night."

Jed Adams remarked, "Some things we can't forget."

Tom was inclined to agree but he was making it a point not to talk to the Reb unless he absolutely had to. "Let's go in and pick dresses for the girls," he suggested to his wife.

Ruth Kittle had a bucket and mop and was cleaning up the mess. Stray wisps of hair had fallen over her face and she brushed them back. "Give me a few minutes and I can help you folks."

"There's no rush," Constance said. She was going to ask if she could lend a hand but all that blood made her queasy. "I don't see how you can do that."

"Live out here long enough and you get used to just about anything," was Kit's response. "Once I had to stitch up a buffalo hunter who was gutted and left for dead by hostiles. There's nothing like pushing a person's intestines back into their body to help you get over being squeamish."

Jed came in with his boys in tow. "We'll be leavin' along about sunset," he announced. He refused to stay longer with Waldron treating him as if he had the plague. "You wouldn't happen to know how far it is to the next water?"

"Nonsense," Kit said.

"Ma'am?"

"Your families are the first to come by in weeks. If you think I'm letting you slip off so soon, you have another think coming. I'd like for you and the Waldrons to be my guests for supper." Kit held up a finger when Jed went to object. "And I won't take no for an answer, Johnny Reb, so you might as well get used to the idea."

Delighted at the invitation, Constance nonetheless said, "We don't want to make nuisances of ourselves."

"I'm the one being the nuisance," Kit said. "I expect to hear all the latest news and what womenfolk are wearing these days and anything else you care to share. I'm so starved for people to talk to, half the time I talk to myself."

"There's no one here but you?" Tom said. He knew she had lost her husband but he would not have thought that anyone, particularly a woman, would live all alone in that godforsaken country.

"There's Three Fingers Bob but he's next to worthless." Kit stooped down and picked up a piece of skull bone and dropped it in the bucket. "Most of the time he's too booze blind to tell his fingers from his toes. He's sleeping off his latest binge somewhere."

"I'm surprised he didn't hear all the shooting and come to help you," Tom Waldron mentioned.

Kit snorted. "That walking whiskey vat could sleep through the Second Coming. He's as next to worthless as it gets."

"Then why do you keep him around?" Constance asked.

"I guess because he has no one and I have no one, and when he's not alkalied, he's better company than a toad."

"You're sure you want us to stay?" Jed asked. Inwardly, he was tickled as could be, although having to spend another night in Tom Waldron's company wasn't to his liking.

"You'll find, Mr. Adams," Kit said without looking up, "that I generally say what I mean and mean what I say. I've got some deer meat left from a buck Three Fingers Bob shot up in the mountains, and plenty of potatoes and canned goods to make the meal more interesting."

"Why do you call him Three Fingers Bob, Mrs. Kittle?" Heather broke her long silence.

"Because that's how many he's got left on his right hand, dearie," Kit said. "The other two he lost to a Kiowa lance. He carries them around in a pouch to show folks."

"I'd like to see them!" Pitney piped up.

"Well, I wouldn't," Constance sniffed. "Why anyone would be so silly is beyond me."

Jed gestured for his son to follow him back outside. "If you'll excuse us, I reckon we'll tend to our horses." With Jed leading the pack animals, they took their mounts over to the corral, with Pitney following along.

"That Mrs. Kittle sure is a fine-lookin' lady, Pa," Bret mentioned. "It's hard to believe she doesn't have a husband."

"I thought you were partial to Heather?" Jed said, and was rewarded with a blush. His older son was setting a new record.

"Mrs. Kittle is a mite too old for me. But if a man your age happened to be in the woman market, he could do worse."

"I had no idea you were an expert on romance." Jed was amused and irritated. Only a few weeks ago his sons had shocked him by mentioning that it would be nice if someday they had another ma. He'd never even thought about remarrying. Melanie had been the love of his life, the one God put on earth for him and him alone. He could never love another woman as much as he had loved her. Or could he?

"Do you hear something?" Pitney asked.

"It sounds like you late at night," Bret remarked, and they chortled.

To Jed it sounded like a goose being strangled. The sounds came from the shed next to the corral. The door was ajar, and when he pushed it open with a toe, he saw tack hanging from pegs and a saddle past its prime in one corner. Under the tack, curled up on his side with an empty whiskey bottle clasped to his skinny chest, was a man in his late fifties or older whose clothes were on the verge of coming apart at the seams. One of the hands wrapped around the bottle only had three fingers.

"It's Three Fingers Bob!" Pitney exclaimed, and pinched his nose. "What's that stink? It's worse than cow manure."

Suddenly the old man's eyes snapped open. Bright blue, they seemed out of place in a face so wrinkled and weathered. "Why all the shoutin'?" he demanded in a voice reminiscent of the growl of a dog. "A man can't sleep for all the racket."

"We're sorry for disturbin' you," Jed said, since his offspring apparently couldn't find their tongues.

"You should be, damn it," the crotchety old-timer snapped, squinting up at them. "It's gettin' so I can't have any peace and quiet around here." He glued his lips to the empty bottle and, after a few fruitless swallows, dropped it in disgust. "Calamity has struck. This hell keeps pilin' on the woes."

"There's no need to cuss," Jed said. He had never been much of a swearer, himself. Maybe because his folks never swore, or because he never felt the need, or because he wasn't much of a talker.

"What are you, a parson?" Three Fingers Bob snapped, and shielded his eyes with his left hand. "I'll be damned! You're one of Robert E. Lee's boys. Howdy, Reb. I'd have worn the gray myself only they said I was too old. Can you imagine?"

"You do seem kind of ancient, sir," Pitney said.

Jed was as surprised as everyone else. "That's not necessarily a nice thing to say, son."

Three Fingers Bob threw back his head and cackled. "No, no, that's all right. I admire a boy who speaks his mind. I do it myself every time I open my mouth." He got his hands under him and slowly sat up. "What the hell time is it, anyway? Why, it's still daylight! And here I thought it was the coffin varnish."

"The what?" Brett asked.

Three Fingers Bob shook himself and tried to crawl out of the shed but lacked the energy and sat back down. "The whiskey, boy, the whiskey. After a bottle or two I sometimes get the powerful shakes and see bright lights where there aren't any. Like when it's snowin' and you're holdin' a lantern and you're lookin' up into the snow."

"I've never done that," Bret said. "We didn't get much snow in South Carolina, and when we did, it hardly ever stuck."

"Is that where you're from? The jewel of the South, boy, the jewel of the South."

Three Fingers Bob held out the hand missing the two fingers. "Give me a yank, will one of you, and help an old critter to his feet?

Bret and Pitney didn't budge so Jed stepped forward and hauled the oldster up. "There you go."

"I'm obliged." Three Fingers Bob staggered a few steps, blinking and smacking his lips, then adjusted his sorry excuse for a hat and grinned broadly, revealing that half his teeth were missing and those still there were a spectacular yellow. "I don't suppose you have a bottle?"

"No," Jed said. "I'm not much of a drinkin' man."

Three Fingers Bob recoiled as if he had been smacked. "Well, now I've heard everything. What the hell kind of a Reb are you, anyhow? Most I've known could swear rings around a tree with one side of their mouth while paintin' their tonsils with liquor with the other. Do you have a puny stomach?"

Jed shrugged. "I married kind of young."

"Say no more," Three Fingers Bob said, holding up his namesake. "That explains everything. Women have been the ruin of more men than smallpox. Why, my five wives were enough to drive me to drink, and look at me now."

Pitney was astounded. "You've been married five times, sir?"

"Sure have. My first left me for a drummer. The second was a marriage of convenience, which I suspect you're too young to savvy, and she left when it was no longer convenient. The third was to a half-breed gal, part white, part Kiowa, a regular panther under the —" He caught himself and said, "By the way, you can call me Three Fingers Bob or you can call me Three Fingers or you can call me Bob or you can call me Hazelton, which is my last name, but you sure as hell can't call me sir. It makes me think I'm back scoutin' for the army."

Not it was Bret who declared, "You were an honest-to-goodness scout? Did you fight many Injuns?"

"A few, boy." Three Fingers Bob used his remaining three fingers on his right hand to scratch himself, low down. "All this jabberin' is dryin' up my throat. I don't reckon any of you gents is willin' to part with the coins I need to slake my thirst?"

"Sorry, no," Jed said.

"We're havin' supper with Miss Kittle," Pitney informed him.

To which Bret lamented, "It's been a coon's age since we had home cookin'. I can't wait."

Three Fingers Bob nodded. "You're in for a treat, young'uns. She can cook up a storm, that gal. It's a cryin' shame she ain't curlin' the toes of some man on a nightly basis. I'd court her myself but I suspect she likes men with teeth and fingers."

"I thought you said marriage ruins a man?" Jed reminded him.

"It sure as hell does." Three Fingers Bob winked. "But if a man's got to sink, he might as well do it in petticoat quicksand."

"That makes no kind of sense," Pitney said.

"It would, boy, if you had peach fuzz on that chin of yours." Three Fingers Bob wiped a sleeve across his mouth. "I sure am dry. Don't know how much more of this I can take." He noticed their horses. "Say. How about if I strip your animals for a dollar. A measly dollar. That's fair."

"We don't have a lot of money to spare," Jed said. "We're lookin' to find us a homestead."

"Do tell? I know a place. Pretty as the mornin' dew. Up in the Guadalupe Mountains, not all that far as the crow flies. Has grass and water and in the winter there's snow to make your young'uns happy."

"Is someone sellin' it?" Jed asked.

"Sell, hell. You just go up there and dig down roots. You can always file a claim if you ever get to Austin or thereabouts." Three Fingers Bob began to tremble and bit his lower lip. "Are you sure I can't part you from a dollar? I work cheap. If not the horses, anything you want, I can do. I'm right handy. It comes from being as old as Methuselah."

Bret and Pitney glanced at Jed in earnest appeal. "I suppose you can unsaddle our horses and strip our pack animals for the price of one drink and one drink only."

"Damnation. Don't you have a drop of sympathy in your soul, Reb? But if that's all you can afford, that's all you can afford, and we've got us a deal." Three Fingers Bob spit into his right hand and held it out. "Shake."

Jed had no desire to have the man's spittle smeared on his palm but he shook, then wiped his palm on his pants.

Three Fingers Bob noticed. "I'd take that as an insult, sonny, if I didn't need the drink so damn much. What's the matter? I've got lice in my hair, not in my mouth." Not waiting for an answer, he turned to the horses. "I'd better get started before I get the shakes so damn bad I can't stand up."

"I really would be grateful if you didn't cuss so much around my boys," Jed said.

Three Fingers Bob grinned and responded, "Tell you what. For a whole damn bottle, I'll never swear around your sprouts again." He crossed himself. "May the Almighty strike me dead if I do."

"You never give up, do you?"

"Hellfire, sonny. How do you think I've lived so long?"

10

Tom Waldron had climbed into the seat of his prairie schooner and was about to flick the reins when the old man with three fingers on his right hand came out of Ruth Kittle's store cradling a whiskey bottle and grinning in delight. The old man stopped and regarded him a moment.

"Who might you be, friend? I don't believe I've made your acquaintance."

Tom had been inside when the old men rushed in and ran to the bar and pounded on it for service. Tom had decided then and there he wanted nothing to do with him. Nonetheless, he had to be polite. He said who he was.

"I'm Three Fingers Bob."

"I know." Tom was anxious to move the prairie schooner. His wife and daughters were in the store with the Confederate and his sons, and he was eager to rejoin them.

"A Yankee, I gather," Three Fingers Bob said. "I'd have worn the blue but they said I was too old. Can you imagine?"

"You're against slavery?" Tom was favorably impressed. "It's the reason I went off to fight. No one should have the right to lord it over another human being."

"I couldn't agree more," Three Fingers Bob said, "which is why I've never owned one of those big plantations with a lot of blacks to wait on me hand and foot. Well, that, and I've never had more than a hundred dollars to my name my whole life long, and those plantations cost more than a hundred dollars."

"Considerably more," Tom said. "Now if you'll excuse me . . ."

"Hold on." Three Fingers Bob came from under the overhang. "I take it you're fixin' to park your rig and put your horses in the corral. How about if I lend you a hand for a dollar? Or do it myself for a bottle?"

Tom was about to say he did not need the help when he realized it would permit him to get back inside with Constance and the girls that much sooner. "Do you have much experience unhitching a team?"

"Hell, sonny, I was a freighter once. Made the Santa Fe run more times than there are stars in the night sky. I can unhitch your animals with my eyes closed." Three Fingers Bob showed his yellow teeth. "Does this mean you're willin' to part with a bottle?"

"You already have one. What do you need with another?"

"What do you need with two ears?"

"Very well," Tom said. "Climb up." When the old man was perched beside him, he shouted, "Get along, there!" and goaded the team into motion. Then he sniffed. "Is that you?"

"Afraid so. I tend to be a bit whiffy when I don't take a bath every six months or so."

"You smell as bad as the hind end of one of these horses," Tom remarked. "Don't sit so close, if you don't mind."

"Sorry. I'd forgotten how sensitive some noses can be." Three Fingers Bob arched an eyebrow. "Say. What are you doing in this neck of nowhere? Have they run out of breathin' space back east?"

"I hope to start my own ranch," Tom said. "With the war over, the demand for cattle will climb, and a man with cows stands to make a good sum."

"Where did you have in mind?"

"It doesn't much matter so long as it's prime cow country," Tom said. He gazed out over the bleak, baked landscape. "I figure if I keep going west I'm bound to strike green eventually."

"I know a place," Three Fingers Bob

said. "It's up in the Guadalupe Mountains. A valley with grass enough for a big herd. The only one of its kind in these parts."

"Why haven't you claimed it for yourself?"

"Hell, what do I want with grass? My nourishment is of a different sort." Bob grinned and caressed the whiskey bottle.

"How remote is it?" Tom was only mildly interested. He doubted Constance would want to settle anywhere near that part of Texas.

"A three-day ride if you start early and ride late." Three Fingers Bob patted the seat. "In this four-wheeled ship of yours, about seven or eight days. I know a pass that will save you a lot of time. And for a bottle of bug juice, I can be persuaded to take you there."

"You sure like your whiskey."

"Booze is like gold. A man can never have enough." Three Fingers Bob nudged Tom's arm. "How about it? What do you say to the proposition?"

"I'd have to talk it over with my wife." Tom never made a decision without consulting her. Well, except for enlisting. And leaving Ohio. And wanting to start a ranch. And raise cows.

"Say no more. I've been married seven

times, myself. It's a lot like being in the army. Yes, ma'am, and no, ma'am, and whatever you say, ma'am." Three Fingers Bob chuckled. "I had me a Mexican wife once who about wore me out with her do this and do that. But Lordy, nights with her were nights to remember."

"I don't care to hear about your love life," Tom said.

Three Fingers Bob snickered. "Sort of the prissy type, ain't you? Seems to me a fella who has brought two girls into the world ought to have more appreciation for the act that brought them into it."

"I'll thank you not to mention my daughters in that vein."

"Land sakes, sonny. You make it sound like a disease. But sure, whatever you say." Three Fingers Bob shifted and peered at their belongings. "What the hell did you do? Bring your whole house?"

"Pretty much," Tom said. "I kept telling Constance we were supposed to travel as light as we could to spare the horses but she couldn't leave the grandfather clock and she couldn't leave the stove and she absolutely refused to leave her china."

"My Maria was fond of crosses. Crosses on the walls, crosses on the doors, crosses everywhere. She was real religious. When I poked her, she would scream Mother of God until my ears hurt."

"I won't tell you again," Tom said.

"About what? Oh. That vein. Sorry. I tend to let my gums flap before my brain knows what they're flappin' about."

"So I've noticed." Tom brought the prairie schooner to a stop alongside the corral with the team facing the emporium. He hopped down and heard Constance laugh and wondered if she was talking to the Rebel.

"I should be done in half an hour or so," Three Fingers Bob said. "I ain't as spry as I used to be, which is why I need my spry juice." He patted the bottle. "And don't you worry. I'll do as good a job as anyone. Ask Kit. I might be roostered most of the time, but when I say I'll do something, by God I do it."

Tom thought of his wife and Jed Adams and grabbed his Sharps. "The teams needs feed and water."

"Hell, any fool can see that. Now scoot. And give some thought to that valley I told you about. If you don't claim it, someone else will."

"Sure, sure." Tom was already heading for the store. He felt like an utter fool when he discovered Constance was chatting with Ruth Kittle, not Jed Adams. His daughters, though, were over by the clothes tables with the Adams boys. He tried to come up with an excuse to forbid Heather and Sally from talking to them, but couldn't.

"Our youngsters have hit it off."

Tom turned so abruptly he nearly tripped over his own feet. "I didn't realize you were standing there."

"Sorry. I didn't mean to startle you," Jed Adams said. He didn't much like this Yankee but he would try to get along with him for the sake of his sons, if no other reason.

"You didn't," Tom said. Then, to cover his embarrassment, he asked, "Are you heading out at first light tomorrow?"

"I'm not rightly sure," Jed said. "I might give my boys a treat and let them sleep in for a change."

Tom was willing to bet that Heather and Sally would love to do the same. They were tired of life on the trail and he couldn't blame them. He was tired of it, too.

Jed gazed at the ceiling. "It's nice havin' a roof over our heads, even if it ain't ours. Makes me hanker more than ever for a place of our own."

"I know how you feel." Tom shared those sentiments. "Sometimes I wonder if I did the right thing dragging my family out here."

"I wouldn't have left South Carolina if my wife hadn't died," Jed said. "I'd had my fill of death in the war, and life goes and takes her from me, too. It wasn't fair. Wasn't fair at all."

"I was sick of all the killing, too," Tom admitted. "The Battle of Shiloh, where our side lost thirteen thousand men out of forty thousand. Chickamauga, where sixteen thousand Federals died in two days."

"There were heavy losses on both sides," Jed said sadly. The flower of Southern manhood had been blown to bits in more than two thousand engagements, and it would take the South decades to recover.

"All those lives, and for what?" Tom shook his head. "It was stupid."

Jed had never heard a Yankee say that before. Most strutted around like peacocks, boasting of how they had single-handedly won the war. Or so it seemed. "I reckon we have more in common than I thought."

Tom did not like being reminded of the war. He glumly gazed out the window and saw Three Fingers Bob over by the prairie schooner. Bob had unhitched one of the horses and was resting from his labors by chugging on the whiskey bottle. On an impulse, Tom turned and asked, "Would you mind if I bought you a drink, Reb?"

"Why not, Yankee?" Jed figured he might as well be sociable.

"No need to bother her," Tom said, indicating Kit, who was conversing gayly with Constance while the two inspected a dress. He went around the bar and asked, "What's your poison?"

"So long as it burns goin' down, it doesn't much matter."

A full bottle of Scotch caught Tom's eye. He snagged a pair of glasses and carried everything to a table and plopped down. "It's been a while," he remarked as he opened the bottle.

"You and me, both," Jed said. "I haven't had anything to celebrate since Hector was a pup."

"Who?"

"Hector. In that book about the Greeks. It's a sayin' in the hills where I'm from. Here's another." Jed solemnly paused. "I've had enough of war to plague a saint."

"I'll drink to that," Tom said, raising his glass. "To the end of war!"

"To the end of war!"

Tom refilled their glasses and immediately toasted, "To the North and the South and the brave men who died on both sides!"

"To the North and the South!" Jed echoed.

"To Ulysses S. Grant and Robert E. Lee!"

"To Grant and Lee!" Jed drained his glass and smacked it down. "My turn," he said, and had to ponder a bit before he came up with one he liked. "To Texas and startin' a new life!"

"To Texas!"

"To my dear, departed wife, the woman I loved more than I've ever loved anythin', taken by consumption when I couldn't be there to comfort her!" Jed raised his glass and then saw that Tom hadn't raised his. "What's the matter, Yank? Won't you drink to the memory of my wife?"

"Of course I will, Reb," Tom said. "But consumption, you say? And you weren't there? I didn't know." He hiked his glass. "To your wife, one of the two best women who ever lived!"

"Two best?" Jed said, then grinned. "Oh, I get it. To our women, then!"

"To our women!"

"To our kids!" Tom reached for the bottle and missed. "Is it me or is everything spinning around?" He tried again and succeeded.

"I'm not spinnin' so much as I am seein' two of everythin'," Jed said. "You've got two noses, Yank, and two chins."

"To two noses and two chins!"

"To noses and chins!"

"I don't know about you," Tom said, "but I can't seem to form a coherent thought. I must be drunk."

"If you can use a word like coherent, you're not drunk enough."

"Good point. To coherent!"

"To coherent!"

And then, as if from on high, a female voice asked, "What in God's name are you two doing?"

Tom blinked up at his wife and stated the obvious, "We're drinking."

"I can see that, Thomas," Constance said. "But why? And isn't it a trifle early to indulge in hard spirits?"

Inwardly, Tom cringed. She never used his given name unless she was perturbed, and the last thing he wanted was to anger her. "Jed and I are becoming better acquainted. Didn't you say you wanted me to be friendlier?" He grinned at his cleverness.

"Friendly, yes. Soused, no."

"It's partly my fault, ma'am," Jed came

134

to the Yankee's defense. "Our toasts multiplied like rabbits."

"I see," Constance said, her tone implying she did not see at all.

Jed became aware that someone was laughing and he twisted in his chair. "Is that you, Mrs. Kittle? What do you find so funny?"

"Men, Mr. Adams," Kit responded. "Men are the most hilarious creatures on God's green earth."

"To men!" Tom said, raising his glass.

"To men!"

"Oh, Thomas," Constance said. "I don't know whether to laugh or beat you with a broom."

"To brooms!" Tom exclaimed.

"To brooms!"

Constance Waldron sighed.

11

The meal was delicious but Jed Adams was in no shape to enjoy it as much as he should have. His head was pounding, for one thing, and for another, his stomach resented every mouthful. But he forced a smile and said to their hostess, "This is some of the best venison I've ever ate, ma'am."

"Thank you, kind sir," Kit said. "When a woman has labored over a hot stove for an hour, she loves to hear her cooking complimented."

Tom Waldron was picking at his meat. He wanted to eat. He truly did. But the thought made his stomach imitate a fish flopping about on dry land.

"None of my wives could whip up a meal half as tasty," Three Fingers Bob commented. "And before I forget, I thank you for the invite. I'm just glad I'm sober enough to remember which is the fork and which is the spoon."

"No one can be that inebriated," Constance said.

"Beggin' your pardon, ma'am," Three Fingers Bob responded, "but there have been a few times when I've worn so many calluses on my elbows, I couldn't remember my own name."

"Well, let's not discuss that now," Constance said, with a meaningful glance at Heather and Sally.

"Again I beg your pardon," Three Fingers Bob said. "It's been so long since I've been in mixed company, I tend to forget my manners, not that I ever had a lot to begin with."

Pitney said, "My brother and me have to have manners. Pa makes us whether we want to or not."

Bob was about to bite into a piece of venison, but he wagged his fork at the youngest Adams. "Listen to him, boy. I wish to thunderation I had heeded my pa when I was your age. But I was a hellion and had to learn things the hard way. So when I was about your brother's age, I told him good riddance and struck off to see the world."

"Did you get to Europe?" Bret asked with keen interest. "I've heard they have a city over there built on water."

"What with one thing and another, I never made it out of Texas," Three Fingers Bob said sadly.

"Tell us about how you lost your fingers," Pitney urged.

Jed glanced up sharply. "Pitney Beauregard Adams, that will be enough out of you. You know better."

"That's all right, Mr. Adams," Three Fingers Bob said. "I don't mind. Although I won't tell the story if Mrs. Waldron or her girls object. It's not exactly what I would call a fittin' supper story."

"We don't mind," Constance said to be polite, although she was hoping he would refrain.

"In that case," Three Fingers Bob grinned. "It was back when I was with the Texas Rangers and —"

"*You* were a Ranger?" Tom interrupted skeptically. Tales of the Rangers had spread even to Ohio. Glorified in newspaper and gazette accounts, they were reputed to be the toughest law officers on the frontier or anywhere else.

"Why are you so shocked?" Three Fingers Bob responded. "I was young once, and a fine, strappin' figure of a man, if I do toot my own bugle." He paused. "Now where was I? Oh, yes. I enlisted in the Rangers in thirty-nine or maybe it was forty. This was right after the Comanches drove all the whites out of Bastrop County. My folks

138

lived there. It's where I was raised. And when they had to join the exodus or lose their scalps, it naturally made me powerful mad. So I went and joined up with Captain Kendall's company. I wasn't sure they'd take me. To qualify, a man had to show them he could ride like the wind, shoot the eye out of a blackbird at twenty paces, track like an Apache, and fight like Hercules and Samson combined."

"You could do all that?" Jed asked with a smirk.

"Hard to believe, ain't it?" Three Fingers Bob said. "Anyway, they took me on and I was in some scrapes that would curdle your blood. Then, one day, three Comanche chiefs showed up out of the blue in San Antonio and said they wanted to parley. They were willin' to stop killin' if we were."

"Did you believe them?" Constance asked, caught up in his story despite herself.

"I did, ma'am, yes. A Comanche may be a lot of things but he ain't a liar. When he says he intends to kill you, he intends to kill you. When he says he wants peace, he wants peace. But it wasn't up to me. I didn't amount to shucks. Colonel Karnes set up the parley, but he told those Comanches that to prove it wasn't a bluff, they had to bring in all the white captives they had." He forked a slice of meat into his mouth and talked while chewing. "A lot of whites, ladies mostly, went missin' back in those days and ended up in some Comanche's lodge."

"It sounds so exciting!" Heather declared.

"So is being ate by a grizzly but I wouldn't recommend it, missy," Three Fingers Bob said. "Anyway, came the day for the next parley, and a bunch of Comanches showed up with just one captive. A poor girl of fifteen they had abused somethin' awful. To punish her, they had burned her nose down to the bone."

Constance squirmed and said, "Perhaps we have heard enough."

"Oh, Mother, please," Heather pleaded. "I won't be up all night tossing and turning. I promise."

"Me neither," Sally said.

"Very well." Constance glanced at Bob. "But I expect you to be tactful and not dwell on all the gory details."

"Don't worry. I've got enough brains to grease a skillet." Three Fingers Bob reached into his mouth and took out a wad of meat and looked at it, then stuck it back in his mouth. "As I was sayin', Matilda

Lockhart — that was the girl with the bone nose — she told the colonel that the Comanches had at least fifteen more captives she'd seen with her own eyes. Well, that riled Karnes, and he sprung a trap he'd arranged in case the Comanches tried any tricks. Next thing you know, there were bodies everywhere: men, women and children, some of them with their innards hangin' out and their throats slit and — "

"Mr. Hazelton!" Constance said sharply.

"Yes, ma'am?"

"Tact, remember."

"Yes, ma'am. Sorry. The funny thing was, we later learned those Comanches had been tellin' the truth. Matilda was the only captive in their band. All those others she saw belonged to other bands. So the people who died that day died for nothin'." Three Fingers Bob chortled.

"You find that humorous?" Constance challenged him.

"Dyin' can be hilarious when you look at it right. And there was a heap sight more, I can tell you. The Comanches went on the worst war path since who flung the chunk. They burned the town of Linnville, stole two thousand horses, and headed home, thinkin' they had showed us who was the meanest dog. But they should have remembered that

141

when you kick a cur, sometimes it gets back up and bites you. Ninety of us rode deep into the heart of Comanche territory and paid them back."

Constance saw that the children were hanging on every word the old man said. In an effort to goad him into getting to the point, she inquired, "All this relates to your hand how exactly?"

"I'm gettin' to that, ma'am. You see, we found a few more captives, and I was part of the party ordered to ride back with them. We'd gone about ten miles when some Comanches jumped us. I had a little girl in front of me in the saddle, and my arm was around her in case she took the notion to bolt. Some of the young ones would. The ones taken when they were babies and didn't know they were white."

Constance thought of how close she had been to being abducted and repressed a shudder.

"So there we were, ridin' along, when arrows and lances came flyin' at us from every which way. I tried to rein out of there, and a lance meant for me caught that little girl in the side and passed clear through her body and out the other side, slicin' off two of the fingers to the hand I was holdin' her with."

After a long silence Ruth Kittle said, "Why haven't you ever told me this before? All you ever said was that a Comanche lance had done it."

Three Fingers Bob shrugged and speared another piece of venison. "I didn't reckon the particulars much mattered."

"How long were you a Ranger?" Tom asked. Like the rest, he had been deeply moved by the account. It showed the old drunk in a whole new light, and he had to remind himself not to assume things about others. He had been doing the same thing with the Johnny Reb.

"Eight years, or thereabouts," Bob said, "until I got tired of the killin'. That's pretty much all a Ranger did back then. Ride and kill, ride and kill." He smiled. "But I got to see pretty near all the state, which came in handy when I scouted for the army later."

"So that's how you know about that valley you mentioned," Jed Adams inserted. He had been wondering if there even was one, and felt guilty for doubting the old man.

"He told you about it, too?" Tom asked in mild alarm.

"What valley? And where?" Constance quizzed them. "How is it no one bothered to inform me?"

Three Fingers Bob helped himself to a hot roll and began to butter it, saying, "It's up in the Guadalupe Mountains, ma'am. About the prettiest place you'll find anywhere. If I had a wife and young'uns I might stake it for my own."

"Are other families there?" Constance had not said anything to Tom but she definitely did not want to settle so far out in the wilds, they were the only people for miles around.

"Not yet," Bob said, "but it's big enough for two or three if they were willin' to divide it up." He looked from Tom to Jed and back again. "You boys could make a go of it, I reckon."

The suggestion so stunned Tom that he didn't reply. He was starting to like Adams a bit, true, but that didn't necessarily mean he wanted the Confederate as his neighbor.

Jed Adams could tell the Yankee wasn't too fond of the notion, and neither was he. He planned to settle somewhere he could be alone with his sons, although they might not cotton to the idea as much as he did.

"Is it the valley you showed me once?" Kit asked.

"Yes, ma'am," Three Fingers Bob said. "I

came across it years ago when I was with an army patrol chasin' a pack of renegades."

Kit looked at Jed Adams. "It's not all that far. There's timber for building and the stream flows year-round. It's well off any trail so you would have it to yourselves. Your only real worry would be the lawless element. This Pecos country has always been wild and woolly, and every longhair with spurs does his best to uphold the tradition. But there's far worse."

"How so?" Jed asked while trying to figure out if she was extending an invitation that had nothing to do with the valley.

"The Comanches, for one thing. They don't often get down this way anymore. The trouble you had was the first time anyone has seen a Comanche in these parts in two years. It's the outlaws you need to consider, those from north and south of the border."

"That would be the border with Mexico?" Tom said.

Kit nodded and absently fluffed her luxurious hair, which she had done up with a red ribbon for the occasion. "Mexican banditos drift north now and then to cause trouble. Vasco Cruz is the worst. He has ten or twelve pistoleros riding with him. They jumped some immigrants last year and murdered every member of the wagon train. By the time the Rangers arrived, Cruz had gone back across the Rio Grande and there wasn't a thing they could do."

"How horrible," Constance commented.

"Texas outlaws aren't any better. You met Hiram Cooter. He's small fry compared to some, like Mort Sayer. The Beast of the Tierra Vieja, they call him, and he's more than earned the name. He gets up this way from time to time. I could mention eight or nine other killers who roam these parts, but you get my point. Thou shalt not kill doesn't hold out here. It's kill or be killed, and if you won't, or can't, then you've no business being west of the Pecos, and might as well head back wherever you came from."

"Are you tryin' to scare us off?" Jed asked with a grin.

Kit shook her head. "No, not at all. I would love to have some decent folks to visit with for a change. But you don't want to make your decision with blinders on. You need to know exactly how it is."

"I thank you," Jed said.

Constance had been listening with growing dread. "How is it, Mrs. Kittle," she wondered, "that none of these terrible people bother you? Aren't you at all afraid, living here by your lonesome?"

Three Fingers Bob stopped chomping to remark, "Why would she be scared when she has me to protect her?"

Neither Kit nor Constance paid any attention to him, and Kit said, "I would be a fool not to be. When my husband was alive I never gave it much thought. Afterward, I gave it a lot of thought, and almost closed up and left. But we'd always dreamed of having a store like this when we were back in New York. We knew that one day more people would come, and we could make a pretty good living."

"But the danger," Constance persisted, "and those killers you mentioned, Cruz and Sayer."

"Cruz has left me alone so far. Maybe he figures one woman isn't worth the bother." Kit folded her arms and leaned them on the table. "Sayer worries me some. He's been by three times. Never says much, but then he doesn't have to. His eyes say it all."

Tom had been weighing the good points and the bad points and the bad points were winning. "What has this Mort Sayer done that he's known as the Beast of wherever it was?"

"What hasn't he done?" Kit retorted. "He's an outcast. An animal. He lives deep in the wilderness and only comes out every blue moon. Word has it he once chopped a man to bits."

Constance had to laugh. "That's preposterous."

"Live out here as long as I have, then say that," Kit responded. She thoughtfully regarded each of them. "The point I'm trying to make is that if you do decide to settle, it won't be a bed of roses. You'll need eyes in the back of your heads and you can never go anywhere unarmed. One mistake, one slip, and you'll wind up dead."

"There's nothing to fear in that regard," Constance said. "After what you've just told us, I wouldn't settle in that valley if it were the only land left on earth."

12

"It's beautiful," Constance Waldron breathed in joyful awe. "Everything you claimed it would be." She had let herself be talked into coming because it was a welcome break from their monotonous westward travel in the prairie schooner.

"I told you," Three Fingers Bob said.

Tom Waldron agreed with his wife. The valley was all the former Ranger and scout had promised, and then some. They had left Vinegar Flats several days ago on horseback. The team horses were not only broken to harness — they doubled as mounts when needed. Tom wasn't happy about leaving the wagon but Ruth Kittle promised to protect their worldly possessions with her life.

The first day had been more of the seemingly endless dry desert plain. The second day they climbed steadily through foothills and into the Guadalupe Mountains. Now here they were.

Jed Adams was also impressed. Born and bred in the Blue Ridge region of South

Carolina, he was a mountain dweller at heart. "I saw signs of deer, bear, elk, and a mountain lion on the way up," he mentioned. "It's not as if a family would starve."

"Or two families," Constance said.

Tom didn't like the sound of that. He wasn't entirely sure this was the spot to start their new life and he intended to talk to her about it later.

The Guadalupe Mountains were a spectacular range of high peaks, steep canyons, and sheer cliffs. The highest of the peaks had the same name as the range and was the highest point in all of Texas. The cliffs and the sides of many of the mountains were exposed rock that made a person think of stone pillars reaching for the sky.

To get to the secret valley, they'd climbed more than two thousand feet in two hours. It was quite a transition from the cactus and yucca of the dry prairie to the fertile green valley with its oak, ash, bigtooth maple, and madrone. And there was grass, acre after acre of rich green grass — an oasis of vegetation created by a year-round stream, which, as they shortly discovered, had a peculiar trait. Parts of it flowed aboveground and parts of it underground. At the upper reaches of the valley, there were stretches where the stream seemed to disappear, while at the lower level, where the grass was thickest, the water flowed blue and pure and deep, forming wide pools in spots where thirsty cattle could slake their thirst.

"I think we should stay overnight and explore," Constance proposed, admiring how the sun shone brightly off the surrounding sandstone cliffs, and how the green and the blue of the valley floor contrasted sharply with the reds and browns above.

"Are you sure?" Tom asked. They had planned to stay a short while and then head back down.

"Of course I'm sure. I love it here. How about you, girls?"

Heather and Sally had spent most of the long ride in the company of Bret and Pitney Adams. They had talked and laughed and talked some more and were becoming fast friends. Heather seldom left Bret's side, a fact her parents and Jed could not help but notice.

"I know a likely spot," Three Fingers Bob said. "I think you'll like it."

The valley floor wasn't level. It climbed gradually another thousand feet to a belt of timber. There, amid the trees, was a deep pool, the water so clear they could see the bottom.

"Look at those big fish!" Pitney declared.

"They're twice the size of the catfish we used to catch back in South Carolina," Bret said. "We should try and catch one for supper and see if they make good eatin'."

They did. That night, with stars dappling the vault of heaven, they sat round a crackling fire and feasted on delicious fish and bread and butter Kit had kindly supplied.

Constance Waldron breathed deep of the crisp mountain air and said, "I love it more every minute."

"So do I," Jed Adams admitted. After the flat plains and mile after mile of dry desert country, the mountains were a welcome change. They weren't the rolling emerald mountains of South Carolina. They weren't lush with vegetation and laced by scores of waterways and rife with more wildlife than a man could shake a stick at. But they would do. They would more than do. A man could make a home here. He could carve his own niche and provide for his loved ones.

Tom sipped his coffee and felt his jaw muscles tighten. The valley had all a

152

person could ask for. He wouldn't deny that. But it wasn't the kind of place where he had imagined they would settle. It was too isolated, to begin with. And his wife and the Reb seemed to have forgotten all about Ruth Kittle's wise words of warning. "What about all the outlaws and hostiles?"

"What about them?" Constance said. "They wouldn't bother us up here, and if they did, it would just be too bad for them."

"Says the woman who has never shot anyone in her life." Tom was bewildered by her drastic change of mind. "Down in Vinegar Flats, you claimed you wouldn't settle here if it was the last land left on earth."

"We all says things we have to take back," Constance said. She encompassed the surrounding mountains with a sweep of her arm. "Besides, the valley is protected on three sides. The only way in is through the mouth to the south."

"One way in is one too many," Tom said, "if we're talking about bandits and renegades."

"Not if we erect a fence and a gate we can bar and lock," Constance said. "We could withstand a siege up here."

"Listen to yourself. What do you know of sieges? The four of us can't hold off a gang of bandits."

"The seven of us could, with a little luck," Jed Adams said. In the war, he had grown accustomed to fighting against impossible odds.

"That's another thing," Tom said. "If all of us settle here, how do we divide up the valley? It isn't as if we can draw a line down the middle."

"Why not?" Jed rejoined. "You take one half and I'll take the other. We'll draw lots or flip a coin to make it fair."

Constance said, "Or better yet, our families can share the valley."

Suddenly Tom lost all interest in the fish he was eating. "The idea is preposterous."

"Why?" Constance asked. "We'll build our house wherever we want, Jed will build his where he wants, and our cattle and his roam the rest of the valley as they wish. Or we can share the cattle and split the proceeds when we sell some." She paused. "The valley is big enough for a large herd, isn't it?"

Jed scratched his chin and calculated. "I make it five miles from north to south and three miles from east to west. That's big enough for all the cows in South Carolina."

"Speaking of cows," Tom thought of another argument, "where are we to acquire these cattle of ours? They don't grow on trees. I have enough money for ten head at the most. It would take years to build them into a herd."

"You're better off than me," Jed lamented. "I barely have enough to buy two cows, and not good breedin' stock, neither."

"Maybe we're getting ahead of ourselves," Constance said. "Maybe a ranch is out of the question and we should be content with homesteads."

Three Fingers Bob was licking the three fingers on his right hand clean. "I know where you can get your hands on all the cows you'll ever need, free for the takin'."

"We're not rustlers," Tom said.

"Hell, you couldn't steal a calf if it was blindfolded and trussed up," Three Fingers Bob agreed. "No, I'm talkin' about wild cows and bulls. More than there are blades of grass in this valley. Millions, some folks says. And you can help yourselves to as many as you'd like."

"Have you been nippin' at that bottle you brought?" Jed asked.

"I know something you boys don't because you're not natural-born Texicans." Three Fingers Bob hunched toward them. "A long time ago, the Spanish settled this part of country. Some of their cattle strayed off and have been runnin' wild ever since, multiplyin' like rabbits. No one can say exactly when it was, although a padre at a mission told me it was Coronado himself who lost the first bunch, and when the next Spanish explorer came through, there were thousands."

"Why haven't we seen any of these wild cows?" Tom Waldron was skeptical. "We covered half the state getting here and never came across a single one."

"Not quite half, and you're in the wrong place," Three Fingers Bob set him straight. "The wild ones are all east and south of the Pecos. Not out on the plains but in the timber and bottomland. In the Nueces River country, they're are thick as fleas on a hound dog. Longhorns, we call them. You could go down there, help yourself to as many as you want, and bring them back."

"You make it sound easy," Jed said, "too easy."

Bob grinned and wriggled his three fingers. "You're a smart one, Reb. When I said the critters are wild, I wasn't talkin' to feel my tongue wag. They've never been roped, never been penned. Most haven't ever set eyes on a human being. Catchin' them will be like catchin' rattlesnakes. Tricky, but it can be done, since others have done it."

"It sounds excitin', Pa!" Bret declared. "I say we should try."

"Not so fast, son," Jed said. "First we have to decide if we really want to settle here." Personally, he was torn. He had to admit the valley was as perfect as could be. But sharing it with a Yankee was asking for trouble.

Tom Waldron said to his wife, "We need to talk this over in private." He went to rise so they could walk off a ways.

"What's wrong with right here?" Constance asked. "The girls have a stake in this, too, and should hear what we have to say."

"Yes, they do, but they're family," Tom agreed. "Others here aren't." To stress his point, he gestured at the Adams clan and Three Fingers Bob.

"Since Jed and his boys might be our neighbors, they have a right to know where we stand," Constance said.

Tom could not believe what he was hearing. "Family matters are best discussed in private. I'm not about to do it in front of strangers."

"Is that all there is to it?" Jed asked.

Normally he would never presume to stick his nose into a spat between a husband and a wife, but since their decision would affect him and his, he reckoned he had the right. "Or could it be you don't want to settle here because you don't like the color of my clothes?"

"Your uniform," Tom corrected him. "And no, I don't care to walk out my door every morning and be reminded of something I'm doing my best to forget."

"I'm tryin' to forget it, too," Jed said. But not because of the North and the battles and the blood. Every time he thought about the war, he thought about Melanie.

"Then it would be stupid of us to pretend we could ever get along," Tom said bluntly.

His wife saw it differently. "I thought it was a waste of everyone's time and energy, too, until we got here. Now I'm not so sure. We could search for months and not find another spot half as nice."

"I'm with Mother on this," Heather said. "I'm tired of riding in the wagon day after day. I'm tired of the dirt and the dust and the heat. I'm tired of rationing water and eating the same food. I'm *tired,* Father, and I won't have it anymore."

"Watch your tongue," Tom scolded her.

Now two of them were against him. He deserved their support, not their condemnation. "It's been rough on all of us but you don't hear your mother or sister or me complaining."

Sally fidgeted and said, "I complain a lot. Just not when you can hear me. I'm as sick of it as sis."

"My own family," Tom said. Setting his plate and fork down, he rose. "Excuse me, I need to be alone for a while." Simmering with anger, he strode off. He had to get out of there before he said something he would regret. The direction he went was unimportant. When the trees abruptly thinned and he found himself on a rise overlooking the lower portion of the valley, he halted. He could hear the stream somewhere to his left. A sliver of moon was rising to the east. The scene was breathtakingly beautiful.

"What am I to do?" Tom asked the night. He could force Constance and the girls to go on but they would hold a grudge for who knew how long. They were good at holding grudges. His wife might even deny him her affections for a while. Years ago she had made him sleep on the settee for over a week after they argued about something he could no longer recall.

The brush crackled, and out came

Constance. She had thrown a blue shawl over her head and shoulders and was as pretty as the day he married her. "You're being childish, Thomas. What will everyone think?"

"Everyone? Or Jed Adams?" Tom responded, knowing his words were a mistake the instant he said them.

"Surely you're not suggesting what I think you're suggesting?" Constance was losing her patience. Men could be so pigheaded and always at the worst moments. "If I thought you were serious, I would slap you."

Tom bit off a sharp reply and said, "Explain something to me. Why the change of heart?"

"I already have explained it." Constance looped her arm through his and gave him a playful shake but he would not look her in the eyes. "It's gorgeous here, Tom, and we would have it all to ourselves."

"Not quite."

"Will you stop? So what if you and he were on opposite sides? He's a decent person and his boys are about the same ages as our girls. Heather and Sally wouldn't only have themselves for company."

"You want to be a grandmother? Is that what this is about?"

"You're being silly. This is about the ranch you've dreamed of, and making that dream come true, about having everything you've ever wanted. But to get it you have to take the first step. You have to seize the moment."

Tom felt as if he were being lectured to. "But what if the moment isn't the right one? What if we make a mistake we'll regret?"

"Those are the chances we take," Constance said. "The important thing is that we —" She stopped and turned her head. "Did you hear something?"

Someone else was coming through the timber. Tom figured it would be one of the girls or maybe both but it was neither. Out of the brush shambled a large hairy shape that snorted and reared onto its hind legs, its claws glinting dully in the moonlight.

"Dear God! It's a bear!" Constance shrieked.

13

Tom Waldron stepped in front of Constance, prepared to sell his life dearly to preserve hers. He had never been this close to a bear before, never even seen one back in Ohio. The few that had not fallen to hunters were wary of humans and there had not been a bear attack recorded in many years. West of the Mississippi River, the situation was different. Bears were still numerous, and in the northern Rockies, grizzlies mauled or killed people each year.

Grabbing at the flap to his holster, Tom felt Constance's fingers dig into his arm. She was as scared as he was. The black bear lumbered toward them, growling and baring its long teeth. "When I tell you to, run! I'll hold it off so you can get to the others!"

The sound of his voice brought the bear to a stop. It lifted its head and sniffed, then grunted and dropped onto all fours.

Tom braced himself. Here it comes, he thought, his hand wrapping around the Starr. It took a heavy-caliber slug to stop a bear and he had foolishly left his Sharps back at the clearing. He started to jerk his revolver when the black bear suddenly wheeled and plowed into the undergrowth.

Constance let out the breath she had not realized she was holding. If there was one thing she dreaded more than hostile Indians, it was being torn to pieces by a wild animal. She had not told her husband but she had nightmares now and then of her and the girls falling prey to wolves or cougars or bears — nightmares so vivid, she always woke with her heart hammering.

"It's gone!" Tom said in amazement. But he drew the Starr anyway and put an arm around his wife. "Let's get back."

Pressing her face to his chest, Constance whispered, "Thank you." That he had been willing to sacrifice himself so she could flee touched her deeply.

"You're welcome," Tom said, although he was not entirely sure why she was so grateful. He had not done anything other than stand there and fumble with his revolver.

"Oh, Tom," Constance said tenderly and kissed him on the neck. "You have your flaws, like any man, but being a coward isn't one of them."

Tom didn't know whether to be annoyed at her low regard for men or flattered by her praise. "Maybe it was an omen." She tended to see omens in everything, and he could use that to his advantage. "A sign that we're not supposed to settle here. That it's too dangerous."

Constance turned her face up to his. "You're right. It is an omen. But not the way you think."

"I don't follow you," Tom said. But then, female logic was often puzzling.

"The bear didn't attack. It ran off and left us alone. That's a sign we're supposed to stay. It's the Lord's way of showing us our fears aren't justified."

Tom hated it when she brought God into things. He couldn't very well contradict the Almighty. "What about the outlaws and banditos? They're not likely to run off at the sight of us, and I may not always be able to protect you." He shook his head. "There are too many risks involved, Connie."

"Oh, darling." Constance kissed him again. "Life itself is a risk. We go from cradle to grave never knowing when our time will come. Didn't you tell me that once, after you came home from the war?"

Another thing Tom hated was when she used his own words against him. Wives did it all the time, then wondered why their husbands never said much. "Even so —" he began.

"Please, Tom. Can't we at least try? For my sake? We'll give it a year, and if we're not happy with how things have gone, we can always pack up and move on. That's reasonable, don't you think?"

"Yes," Tom admitted, but in that year's time a lot could happen, and all of it bad. "I worry, though, that we're making a mistake."

"So we'll learn from it and go on with our lives. It's all anyone can do." Constance rose on her toes to mold her lips to his, then stepped back and smiled. "What do you say? Can I break the news to the others?"

Tom was desperately trying to come up with an argument she could not refute but all he could think of was the feel of her body against his and how long it had been since they had been intimate. "What about Jed Adams?"

"What about him? He's a nice man and his sons are well mannered. They'll make fine neighbors."

"He's a Rebel, Connie. I served on the Union side. In the war that made us enemies, and I can't help feeling bitter. I honestly don't know if I can forget and forgive."

"Thomas J. Waldron, the war is over and

done with and you can't go around disliking everyone who was for the Confederacy. Isn't there enough of that going on? The country is a mess and the only way to end the hatred is to remember we were Americans before we were blue and gray and we're still Americans now."

Tom sighed, recognizing defeat. "I'll try to get along with him but I'm not making any promises. It's the best I can do."

"That's all I ask," Constance said happily, taking his hand. "Come on. Heather and Sally will be delighted."

Jed Adams slowly lowered his Morse carbine. He had been about to shoot the black bear when it turned and ran off. Now he watched the Waldrons depart hand in hand and pondered what they had said.

He had come after them to talk about the valley. To say that maybe it wasn't such a good idea. They were Yankees and he was a Reb and mixing the two was like mixing dogs and cats. They should forget settling there and go their own ways.

But maybe he was being hasty. If they were willing to give it a try, why shouldn't he? If the Yank was willing to put the war in the past, could he do less?

Cradling the carbine, Jed trailed after them. He wasn't one of those who hated Yankees on general principle. He still harbored resentment over their heavy-handed treatment of the South since Lee surrendered, but he couldn't blame Tom Waldron for all the carpetbaggers and other swindlers.

Life had become too complicated, Jed reflected. He missed the old days when the most he had to worry about was keeping food on the table. Everything had been so much simpler. It would be nice to live that simply again, to forget about the outside world and all the troubles the war had brought.

What better place, Jed asked himself, than there in that valley? They could live as they pleased. It would be their own little world. No one would be looking over their shoulders, telling them what they could and couldn't do.

By the time Jed came to the clearing, he had made up his mind. Hunkering by the fire, he refilled his tin cup with hot coffee and took a sip. The Waldrons were being treated to another of Three Fingers Bob's stories, while his sons were keeping the girls entertained. Or maybe it was the other way around.

Pitney strayed over. "Where have you been, Pa? I have somethin' I'd like to get off my chest."

"I'm listenin'."

"Bret and me have been talkin' it over and we want this to be our new home. We'd like to have beds to sleep in again. We want land where we can fish and hunt. And Sally and Heather sure are nice, for girls."

"That's some speech," Jed said.

"It's how we feel, Pa. We'll move on if you want but we'd just as soon not." Pitney fell silent and waited all of five seconds. "Well? What will it be? We'd really like to know."

Jed rose and drew his knife and tapped it against the tin cup to get everyone's attention. "I have something to say," he announced. "My boys and me like it here. It's everythin' Bob said it would be, and then some. If the Waldrons are willin', we'd like to make a go of it."

Tom became aware that all eyes were now on him. He'd figured that he would have more time, that nothing would be decided until they returned to Vinegar Flats. But between his wife and the Rebel, he had been backed into a corner.

"Well, Father?" Heather anxiously prompted.

"It's up to you," Sally said.

Their hopeful expressions were daggers in Tom's belly. "Your mother wants to stay and that's good enough for me." Later, if things went wrong, he could always remind them it had been her idea. "We'll work out where to build our homes in the morning. The rest of the valley will be for both our families to share."

Heather squealed and clapped her hands and Sally giggled and hugged Constance.

Jed Adams extended his hand. "I reckon we should shake on it, Yank."

Reluctantly, Tom shook.

Three Fingers Bob tittered and said, "Now that that's settled, what are you fixin' to call this ranch of yours?"

"Call it?" Tom said.

"A ranch has to have a name and a brand. You need to mark your cattle to discourage rustlers, and so when you take them to market, you'll know which ones are yours."

Pitney beamed and said, "How about if we call it Melanie after Ma?"

Jed had never loved the boy more but he responded, "That wouldn't be fair to the Waldrons. The valley is as much theirs as ours."

They spent the next hour hashing it out.

Everyone took part. Sally wanted to call the ranch the Big Fish after the big fish in the stream. Heather said they should name it Heaven because the valley was heavenly. Constance liked the Waldron and Adams ranch, or, if Jed minded their name first, the Adams and Waldron ranch. Tom thought that was too much of a name and suggested the Waldron-Adams or the Adams-Waldron. Pitney was depressed because they couldn't call it Melanie. Bret was of the opinion they should name the ranch Heather, which raised a few eyebrows. Jed couldn't come up with any he really liked.

They had talked themselves out and were sitting there thinking it was, as Tom put it, a lost cause, when Three Fingers Bob chuckled and slapped his leg.

"You folks sure are a bundle of laughs. How you have lived so long and know so little is a wonderment. The name should be short and something you can use on a brand. Since this here valley is in the Guadalupe Mountains, why not just call it the Bar G and make the brand a G with a bar under it?"

"The Bar G?" Jed tried it on for size. "It does have a ring to it."

"Of course you would say that," Tom

said. "The G could stand for gray as well as anything else. Why not the Bar B for blue? Or the Bar T for Texas?"

Constance nudged him with her elbow. "You're nitpicking. Cut it out. We'll take a vote and I vote yes."

It was unanimous, although Tom had to be nudged again before he would raise his hand to show he would go along.

Shortly thereafter, they turned in for the night. Jed lay on his back with his fingers laced under his head and stared at the sparkling stars without seeing them. He had another reason for settling there, a reason he had not mentioned, a reason he could not mention. Or maybe it was more of a hope than a reason. A hope he felt great guilt over.

Jed had always felt that when a man and a woman vowed to love, honor, and cherish each other, they should love, honor, and cherish to the grave. When he had lost Melanie, he naturally figured he would spend the rest of his days alone. She was his one true love. There would never be another.

But time healed all wounds, or so folks were fond of saying, and if time didn't truly heal, it did mend a wound enough that a man could think the unthinkable.

That a man could look at the long, lonely nights he had left on this earth and maybe not want to spend them alone. That a man could start to let himself think there was life after love, and maybe, just maybe, another love.

It was much too soon to say. But Jed was interested, and he had not felt the feeblest spark of interest in a female since Melanie's passing. It could be that Kit wanted nothing to do with him, or to just be friends, in which case he was feeling all that guilt for nothing.

Jed glanced at Constance, peacefully sleeping with her head on her husband's shoulder. A strange constriction formed in his throat and he had to tear his gaze from her before he choked.

His last thought before he drifted off was that life was strange, stranger than anything anyone could imagine, and it didn't do to have set notions of how it should work out. The best anyone could hope to do was let the flow carry him along and hope the current didn't become too strong.

At daybreak they rode down out of the valley that would soon be their home. Three Fingers Bob was in the lead and did not look around when Jed brought Hickory up next to Bob's mount.

172

"I have a proposition for you."

"Uh-oh," Three Fingers Bob said. "Every time I hear that, I want to plug my ears with corks. It usually means work or trouble and I'm allergic to both."

"How would you like to come to work for us?" Jed asked and held up a hand to cut a protest off. "Hear me out. You know this country. You know the land and the people. You know cows or enough about the wild cattle we're goin' after that we stand a chance of bringin' some back. We'd be forever in your debt."

"I'll think it over. But I won't work on the ranch and that's final."

"Suit yourself. But we'd let you work when you wanted and not work if you would rather not. What we need more is your advice. My pa always said that, if a man has to learn, he should learn it from the best."

Three Fingers Bob laughed. "You mean I'm good for somethin' other than growin' a cowlick?"

The descent was easier than the climb. By late in the evening of the second day, Vinegar Flats was in sight. They were a quarter of a mile out when Three Fingers Bob rose in the stirrups and suddenly drew rein. "God in heaven, no!"

Jed and Tom rode up next to him, and Tom asked, "What's the matter? You look sick."

"Do you see that big roan at the hitch rail?"

"You can tell what kind of horse it is from way out here?" Tom marveled. "You must have the eyes of an eagle."

"What about the roan?" Jed asked.

"There's only one hombre I know of with a horse like that." Three Fingers Bob paused. "That there animal belongs to none other than Mort Sayer, the Beast of the Tierra Vieja."

14

One of the hardest things Jed Adams had ever done was casually ride up to the hitch rail in front of the emporium and casually dismount and casually stroll inside. Right away he saw Mort Sayer.

The Beast of the Tierra Vieja had to be seven feet tall, or close to it. His shoulders were twice as wide as the chair he filled to overflowing. None of his bulk was fat. It was all solid muscle, from his broad chest to his tree-trunk thighs. His face was bearded and brutish and caked with the dust of many miles of travel. He wore a floppy hat and a shirt and pants in grave need of washing. On the table in front of him was a Spencer rifle. A Remington and a Bowie adorned his hips. "Who the hell are you?" he greeted Jed suspiciously.

Jed smiled and said, "Someone in need of a drink." He walked to the bar, every nerve jangling.

Ruth Kittle had been doing something behind the counter. She straightened up and looked at him and instantly looked away, but not before he saw the bruise on her right cheek and her swollen left eyebrow. "What can I get for you, Mr. Adams?"

"Whiskey will do," Jed said, bubbling with fury. "How much do I owe you?"

"It's on the house," Kit said, "since it's the last drink I'm ever serving."

Jed tried to keep his voice level while asking, "You're closin' up? I thought you liked this place."

"I do," Kit said, "but Mr. Sayer has come all the way from the Tierra Vieja to ask me to be his bride and I can't rightly refuse."

A shadow fell across them and Mort Sayer plunked the Spencer down on the counter and leaned on his elbow. "A man gets mighty lonely livin' by himself, and she's a fine figure of a woman. She'll be fun to ride at night, wouldn't you agree?"

His voice made Jed think of thunder booming in the distance. "A gentleman doesn't talk about ladies like that in public." He never saw the blow that smashed into his ribs and felled him to his knees. But he did see the ham-sized hand that gripped the front of his shirt and shook him so hard, his teeth cracked together.

"Are you sayin' I ain't a gentleman, Reb?

Because if you are, I'll have to set you straight the hard way."

"Mort, please," Kit interceded. "He didn't mean anything. You can't go beating on my customers."

"I can do any damn thing I please," Sayer growled. "And I'm not stupid. I should snap his puny neck for insultin' me like that."

"I didn't," Jed willed his vocal cords to work. A hand of solid iron gripped the back of his head and twisted it so he was nose to bulbous nose with Mort Sayner. Fetid breath nearly made him gag.

"I've killed men for less." Sayer's brown eyes were oddly dilated and the right one would not stay still. It moved from side to side and up and down, glancing everywhere except at Jed.

"Is this what our life will be like?" Kit asked. "It's bad enough you're dragging me off. Must I watch you commit murder as well?"

"What's his life to me?" Mort Sayer said. "As for you, I've thought about it and thought about it, and it's high time I had me a woman. A white woman, not a breed or a redskin or a greaser. And you're the only one in these parts."

Jed girded himself. Sayer had momentarily forgotten about him, and he must use that to his advantage.

"But we don't know each other," Kit objected. "You've only ever been here a few times."

"That's enough," Sayer said. "The first time I set eyes on you, I knew I wanted you. So now I'm takin' you and that's that."

"Like hell it is." Jed uncoiled, putting all he had into a blow to the chin that would have crumpled most men in their tracks.

Mort Sayer was rocked, but only slightly. Rubbing his jaw, he grinned and said, "Well now, the puny Reb wants to play." His hand closed on Jed's throat and he shifted and shoved.

To Jed, it was akin to being propelled from a cannon. He crashed into a chair and his legs became entangled and down he went. He was beginning to think riding in alone hadn't been all that smart, but he couldn't very well put the children and Constance in jeopardy, and Tom had to stay to safeguard them. As for Three Fingers Bob, his last comment as Jed rode off was "The last time the Beast was here, he knocked one of my teeth out and I ain't got that many to spare."

Now Mort Sayer advanced with a

mocking smirk and his huge fists bunched. "What's Kit to you, Rebel? Why did you stick your gray nose in here?"

"She's a friend," Jed said, pushing the chair off him. His carbine was on the bar and he didn't own a pistol. He had his knife but Sayer's Bowie was bigger. *Everything* about the Beast was bigger.

"A friend or more?" Sayer asked harshly. "It could be you've been triflin' with her when my back was turned."

Kit was hurrying around the bar. "Leave him alone, Mortimer! You have no right to beat on him!"

The Beast halted and bowed his shaggy head as if in thought. He waited until she was passing him to go to Jed, then whipped around, backhanding her across the face. The blow sent her sprawling.

"No!" Jed was off the floor and charging, his arms raised to ward off punches. He was so intent on Sayer's huge fists that he failed to notice an equally huge boot until it slammed into his chest and lifted him clean off his feet. He came down on top of a table and the legs splintered like kindling. Scrambling erect, resisting ripples of agonizing pain, he set himself. "Come on, you woman-beatin' bastard."

Mort Sayer's brutish features became

more so. "Most folks have the sense not to rile me, Reb. I've killed forty-one men, over thirty of them with my bare hands. Say your prayers."

"I'm surprised the Rangers haven't put an end to you," Jed said.

The Beast lurched to a stop mere feet away. "Those peckerwoods? The last pair they sent after me, I cut up into pieces and left for the coyotes to eat."

Jed glanced at Kit and an icy chill seized his soul. "Would you do somethin' like that to her?"

Those broad shoulders shrugged. "Who knows? Maybe after I tire of her other charms. Most of the females I take don't last more than a few months."

"You're not takin' her," Jed vowed.

"Oh?" Laughter rumbled from the Beast's chest and he crouched with his arms spread wide. "Here's where I crack your bones."

"Just try," Jed said. Hardly was the challenge out of his mouth than a two-legged battering ram plowed into him and steel bands encircled his waist and he was raised into the air and held there.

Mort Sayer was a talkative brute. "Folks wonder why I'm the way I am, but it's easy to understand. I like to kill, and have ever since I was old enough to strangle a goose."

Jed's spine flared with torment that nearly blacked him out. His insides were being squeezed to mush, and there wasn't anything he could do. Or was there? He slugged Sayer on the jaw but it was like striking a boulder. He pushed against Sayer's chest but he might as well have tried to move a mountain. He kicked Sayer in the legs with no effect except to make Sayer laugh.

"When the blood comes gushin' out your nose, you're done for."

Jed's head felt fit to burst. He only had seconds left and then it would be all over. Frantic to break free, he gouged his thumbnails into the Beast's eyes.

Howling like a stricken wolf, Mort Sayer jerked his head back and twisted it from side to side. When that failed to dislodge Jed's thumbs, he roared like a maddened bull and hurled Jed to the floor. Jed's right shoulder bore the brunt, and he would have sworn he heard a crack. But he could move his arm, and he levered away and up and gained his feet, swaying unsteadily.

The Beast had his palms pressed to his craggy face. Lowering his huge hands, he glowered, blood trickling from both eyes.

"No one does that to me and lives!" His arms outstretched, he rushed in to apply another bear hug.

Jed had other ideas. Skipping backward, he discovered they were on the dry goods side of the store when he bumped into a shelf of plates and cups. At the last instant he darted aside and Sayer smashed into it and sent pots and pans crashing down. Jed circled, seeking to get back to the bar and his carbine. Or the Spencer, if he could reach that.

But for all his bestial fury, Mort Sayer guessed what Jed was up to and side-stepped to cut him off. "No guns, Reb. This is just you and me, man to man, and when it's over it will just be me."

"You're not fightin' a woman now," Jed taunted. He saw Kit stir and roll on her side, and to keep the Beast too occupied to notice, he suddenly sprang forward and kicked at Sayer's knee. A broken kneecap would bring down even the biggest of men. But Sayer was as fast as he was big and he nimbly avoided the kick, and sneered.

"Is that the best you can do? No wonder you Confederates lost the war."

A childish barb, yet Jed grew warm with anger and took the bait by leaping and swinging. Both fists connected but it was like punching a tree. He hurt his hands more than he hurt Sayer. Then Sayer's fist landed, and if Jed's ribs weren't broken, it was a miracle. He staggered and doubled over, his lungs laboring for breath. His leg hit something and he glanced down to find it was an upended chair. As quick as thought, he bent and seized it by the legs and swung it with all the strength he could marshal.

The Beast of the Tierra Vieja brought up his massive arms to cushion the blow. The chair splintered and slivered but seemed to have no effect. Growling, Sayer pounced, and Jed darted to the right out of reach. Jed's back was now to the front window, and he realized that, if he wasn't careful, Sayer would back him into the corner where he would be at the man's mercy. He started to glide left but Sayer blocked his way.

"No, you don't. This time I've got you."

The man sure did love to flap his gums, Jed thought, and an idea was born. Suddenly stopping, he asked, "Why don't you do the rest of the world a favor and turn yourself over to the Rangers so you can be hung?"

Mort Sayer paused, his weight balanced on the balls of his feet, his hands hooked into claws. "That's the stupidest thing I've ever heard."

"Your folks must be real proud of their son," Jed stalled. "The shame will put them into early graves."

"Shows how much you know," Sayer scoffed. "They've been six feet under since I was fourteen. That's when I took an ax to my pa and then went into the kitchen and strangled my ma."

"You murdered your own parents?" Jed was genuinely shocked. "What kind of abomination are you?"

"I've already told you. The kind who loves to kill. I get these urges and I can't help myself." Sayer's giant frame relaxed slightly. "After that goose, I couldn't kill enough. I strangled the rest of the geese and broke the necks of the chickens and drove a pitchfork through the cow. Not at all once. Every few days I would kill one and hide the body, but I couldn't hide the cow, and by then my folks knew it was me. So my pa told me they were kickin' me out. Me, their own flesh and blood! That's when I took the ax to him and split his skull as easy as can be." Mort Sayer laughed.

"That's funny?" Jed said.

"I'd always figured people would be

harder to kill. But they're not. People are easier than geese and chickens and cows. Most are too scared to fight back, or when they do, they don't know how to go about it. They're not born killers, like me."

"I'll kill you if I can," Jed promised, which proved a mistake.

"That's a big if, Reb," Sayer responded and came in swift and low in an attempt to tackle him.

Jed's only recourse was to spring back out of reach, which put him right where the Beast wanted him — in the corner. He feinted right and went left but Sayer only had to take a step to block him. He dodged right but again Sayer was too fast for him. With a sinking feeling, he braced for the final rush.

"I told you," Sayer crowed. "Now I get to play with you like I did those animals." He flicked a right hand and laughed when Jed recoiled. "Ready to meet your Maker and —" He stopped. He had noticed Kit, who was on her feet and limping toward the bar. He was on her before she could take another step, his fingers locked in her long hair. "Tryin' to help your lover, is that it, bitch?"

Jed went to her aid. He was afraid the Beast would snap her neck but Sayer saw him coming and flung her at him. He could have sidestepped but he caught her and absorbed the force of their fall with his own body. Flat on his back, with Kit on top, he looked up into the blood-rimmed eyes of the rabid killer.

"And now it ends," Mort Sayer said.

"You've got that right, you miserable gob of spit!" a new voice intruded. "I owe you for a tooth."

Three Fingers Bob was in the doorway, a revolver held low in his right hand, a whiskey bottle in the other. He swayed slightly and his hand was not as steady as it should be, but not even Sayer would rush an ex-Ranger with a cocked pistol.

"Get out of here before you annoy me, old man, and maybe, just maybe, I'll let you live."

"Who appointed you God?" Three Fingers Bob asked and squeezed the trigger.

Jed had seldom seen so beautiful a sight as that of the slug coring Sayer high in the right side. Scarlet mist sprayed, and Sayer grabbed his shoulder and bellowed and took a step toward Bob. Again the revolver boomed, and this time it was Sayer's left thigh that exploded in drops of blood.

Suddenly whirling, Sayer vaulted over Jed and Kit. He tucked his head low and smashed into the window, disappearing in a shower of glass shards. Jed heard shouts and then the blast of a heavy-caliber gun. Tom's Sharps, he reckoned. Hooves pounded, and the Sharps thundered again.

Jed hurt all over but he was in no hurry to get up. Kit's hands were clinging to his shoulders and her face was nestled against his neck. Tears dampened his skin.

"Damn me all to hell," Three Fingers Bob was saying. "I couldn't hit the broad side of a barn if I was inside it." He swayed over to them and chugged some whiskey. "We got tired of waitin' and came for a look-see. Half a bottle of red-eye, and I'm as brave as any man." He leaned down. "How bad are you two hurt?"

"I'm fine," Jed said, putting an arm around Kit. "Just as fine as can be."

15

Jed Adams spent two weeks in bed in a room at the rear of the emporium. As near as they could tell without the services of a sawbones, he had two cracked ribs. His right shoulder and his lower back were so badly bruised, he could barely stand or move his right arm. Kit tended to him and brought his meals and they spent many idle hours talking. Bret and Pitney shared another room and were happier than Jed had seen them since they left South Carolina.

Tom Waldron, in the meantime, was kept busy. He bought tools and some other items they would need and with Constance along took the prairie schooner to the valley. He parked it where she wanted their house built, on the same rise where they had encountered the bear, and unhitched the team.

Three Fingers Bob came along to help unload in return for another whiskey bottle. As they were sliding the mattress out, Tom mentioned, "That was a brave thing you did the other day, going in alone.

I should have gone with you."

"Someone had to stay with your wife and the girls," Three Fingers Bob said. "And don't make me out to be braver than I'm not. It took half a bottle to give me the courage."

"You were a Texas Ranger once," Tom reminded him, "and no one has ever accused them of a lack of bravery."

"Once I was. But once ain't now. I'm not half the man I used to be."

"Is it because of that girl you were holding when that lance went through her?" Tom inquired.

"You ask too damn many questions, Yank," Three Fingers Bob said gruffly. "Let's just say I got sick of all the bloodlettin' and let it go at that. The thing for you to remember is that you can't count on me in a tight spot."

"You underestimate yourself," Tom said. "As far as I'm concerned, you've proven your mettle."

Three Fingers Bob scowled. "Why is it some folks always think they know how other folks think even when the other folks don't think like they think they do?" He firmed his hold on the mattress. "Don't forget what I told you about not relyin' on me or you might come to regret it."

"Well, anyway, I imagine we've seen the last of Mort Sayer. I think I hit him with one of my shots, which was hard to do with him hanging from the side of that roan. How he could ride like that, I'll never know."

"It's an old Comanche trick," Three Fingers Bob said. "And no, we ain't seen the last of him. Sayer will hate us something fierce for the lead we put in him, and when he's good and ready, he'll come back to put some into us."

"By then we'll be settled in," Tom said. "Let him come. We can handle him."

"If you don't mind my sayin' so," Bob said guardedly, "the only thing worse than a fool is a fool with confidence. For the sake of your wife and those pretty girls of yours, don't rest easy until Sayer is dead."

Once the prairie schooner was unloaded, Tom climbed up and removed the canvas, which he then used to cover the more valuable of their possessions. "I don't like leaving all this stuff here," he commented when he finished and stepped back.

"It should be safe," Three Fingers Bob said. "I haven't seen any sign of Injuns, and I doubt there's an outlaw alive who knows about this place."

"What about rain?" Constance asked,

with a glance skyward.

"At this time of year? In Texas?" Three Fingers Bob cackled.

On the return ride to Vinegar Flats, Tom rode beside his wife. "It's still not too late to change your mind. We can pack everything back up and keep on west until we find a place you like more."

"I'm happy here," Constance said. The more she saw of the valley, the more she loved it. The sea of grass, the red and brown of the timber, the high cliffs bright with sunlight, the gurgling of the stream in the quiet of the night, filled her with a sense of belonging. "We've made up our minds and we will stick by it, come what may."

Tom tried one last argument. "What if Bob is right and Mort Sayer pays us another visit? Do you want him getting his hands on Heather or Sally?"

"Honestly, Thomas," Constance said peevishly. "Of course I don't. But burying our heads in the sand like one of those ostriches isn't how to deal with life. We take the bad with the good. We have a home now, and we'll defend it with our lives, if we need to. End of discussion."

Tom was glad to see Jed Adams up and about when they arrived at the emporium.

The Rebel was in a chair near the busted window with his carbine across his lap. "How soon before you're in shape to go after cattle?"

"We can leave in the mornin' if you want," Jed said.

From behind the bar, where Kit was arranging bottles, came, "Don't listen to him, Tom. He needs another couple of days. A week would be better but you men can be so impatient."

Tom sensed a change had taken place but he did not comment on it. The Reb's personal life was none of his business. "I've drawn a map of the valley with an X where we're building our house." He slid the paper from a pocket and unfolded it. "Connie said I should be sure you have no objections."

"None at all," Jed said after studying it. "I plan to build my cabin here." He touched a spot on the map that corresponded to the north end of the valley just below the timber line.

"We'll be about a mile from one another." In times of trouble, that was a lot of ground to cover. "Maybe we should be closer. Why not build your cabin in the clearing where we spent our first night?"

"We'd be breathin' down each other's

necks," Jed said. "I wouldn't want to crowd you."

"Constance wouldn't mind," Tom said. Neither would he, but he would not own up to it.

"I'll talk it over with my sons," Jed said. He had taken to asking their opinions on everything so they would feel they had a part in the planning of their new home.

Tom turned to the window and the hot air that blew in off the prairie. "It's too bad about the glass," he said to make conversation.

"Kit says it will be a couple of months before she can get in a new pane. Until then she sticks a sheet up at night to keep out the dust."

"What about the things Bob says we'll need for the brush country? The boots and the spurs and the" — Tom paused — "what were they again? The chaps?"

"The Spanish called them *chaparejos,* or so Kit tells me," Jed said. "She has a couple of angoras that have been gatherin' spiderwebs and she'll let us have them for danged near free. She also has spurs and boots." He extended his legs to show off the pair of each he had picked.

"How do you walk in those high-heeled monstrosities?" Tom asked.

"It takes some gettin' use to," Jed said, "but once you do, you don't want to wear any other footwear."

"That will be the day." Tom bent to study how the spurs were attached. "Those prongs could tear a horse up."

"They're called rowels," Jed enlightened him, "and Bob says we should file the points so they're blunt, not sharp."

"You don't say?" Tom reached out and flicked one with a finger and it spun round and round. "If he says we need these, then we need them. But I'll be damned if I'm wearing a high-crowned hat like his. I'm perfectly content with the one I have."

"You, too?" Jed said. He would wear his Confederate cap until the day he died. There were certain allowances he was willing to make but his uniform wasn't one of them.

"There's something else I've been meaning to talk to you about," Tom said, uncomfortable broaching the subject.

"Heather and Bret," Jed guessed, and when the Yankee nodded, he said, "They've been makin' cow eyes since they met. Bret goes on forever about how pretty and smart your girl is."

"Ah. Well, I have it on her authority that your older boy is the handsomest male who ever lived." Tom frowned. "I think they're getting too serious. We should do something about it."

"About two young'uns in love?" Jed grinned. "Why, we might as well try to stop a river in flood or the sun from settin'. Bret is old enough to make a miration of your girl if he wants, and if they marry up, so much the better."

Tom was momentarily speechless. They were talking about his daughter. He reminded himself that Southerners tended to think differently than people north of the Mason-Dixon line.

"That would make us in-laws," Jed said. "We could let them pick a plot in the valley so they don't go and move off like so many their age do."

"We're getting ahead of ourselves," Tom said. "My Heather isn't old enough to marry yet."

"No? She's pushin' seventeen, I hear. That's how old Melanie was when I married her."

"In the North we tend to wait a little longer." Tom had heard that Jed's kind married their girls off at thirteen and fourteen.

"I see." Jed sat back. "I'll respect your wishes but don't blame if they get tired of waitin' and get carried away."

"Surely you're not suggesting, Reb, that my daughter would do anything improper?" Tom challenged him.

"Human nature is what it is, Yank," Jed said. "When they're that young, they think with their hearts, not their heads. Don't you recollect how it was when you fell in love?"

"Certainly. I courted Connie with her father's permission and never touched her the first year."

"Really?" Jed was flooded with memories of Melanie and him giving free rein to their passion every chance they got.

"Why do you sound surprised?" Tom asked. "There are right ways and wrong ways of courting, and I won't have my daughter treated like a fallen dove."

"Bret would never do that," Jed said hotly.

"See that he doesn't." Tom would stand for a lot of things in the interest of getting along but that wasn't one of them.

Jed never had liked people telling him what to do. He was set to give the Yankee a piece of his mind when Kit appeared at his elbow.

"I couldn't help overhearing. I've seen the two of them together, and Bret is always the perfect gentleman. Your daughter's virtue is safe, Mr. Waldron."

"Let's drop it, shall we?" Tom said. Few subjects were more distasteful to him, especially with regards to his daughters.

"I'd take Bret with us when we go," Jed mentioned, "but we need Bob more. I'll tell the boy to be on his best behavior, or else."

"Don't worry," Kit said. "Constance and I will keep an eye on them. Things won't get out of hand."

"I'm grateful," Tom said, almost sorry he had brought it up.

Two days later Three Fingers Bob led them southeast across the prairie. Tom brought up the rear, leading a pair of packhorses and two extra horses they would use for saddle mounts. He twisted to wave to his family and saw Heather standing next to Bret. "Did you remember to have that talk with your oldest son?"

"I sure did," Jed said. "He promised not to make any babies until we get back."

Three Fingers Bob chortled but Tom did not find it at all amusing.

The distance was three hundred miles and more to the Nueces River. Once they left the baked plain behind, they entered fertile lowland that rose no higher than three hundred feet above sea level, according to Three Fingers Bob. Brush and timber became common. Game was abundant. Hardly a night went by that they didn't dine on fresh meat. Twice they had wild turkey.

With each passing day, Tom fretted less about his family. Constance and Kit were capable women, and as much as he resented Bret's interest in Heather, the boy could shoot and ride and was only a shade on the younger side of manhood. They would do all right without him.

The days became weeks and eventually there came an evening when Three Fingers Bob announced they had come far enough.

Tom and Jed could not hide their excitement. Their dream of owning a ranch depended on their success, and they sat around the campfire debating how many cattle they needed.

"You're both wrong," Three Fingers Bob said after Jed mentioned that they should have at least a hundred head and Tom thought it should be two hundred. "Anything less than three hundred is a waste of our time."

"We can handle that many?" Jed asked. "I thought you said these are wild cattle?"

"The difference between wild cattle and

tame cattle is the mossy horns will gore you if you give them the chance and we won't give them the chance." Bob sipped some coffee. He had not touched a bottle since leaving Vinegar Flats and was as sober as they had ever seen him. "The old bulls are the worst. Some are downright snake mean. They'll come at you to kill and you'd damn well better shoot them dead or we'll be buryin' what's left of you."

"You make it sound like the war," Tom joked.

"It is. It's us against them. Make no mistake. They're tougher than we are. They can endure the hottest hot and the coldest cold. They can run like antelopes and go through the heaviest tangles like it wasn't there. Thorns are nothin' to them but without those chaps you wouldn't have any legs left after the first day."

Tom said, "They're just cows."

"Anything but. They're big-eared, coarse-haired demons with hooves, and don't you ever let down your guard. They're muscle and hide and horns — God, those horns — and they can rip you open so quick, you'll have your guts in your hands before you know what's what. They'll turn on you in the blink of an eye, always when you least expect. Do exactly as I say and maybe, just maybe, we'll make it through alive."

"The important thing is they're free," Jed said.

Tom Waldron stared into the inky timber beyond the circle of firelight and wondered what on earth he had gotten himself into.

16

First they needed to find a likely spot to hold the cattle they caught. As Three Fingers Bob explained, it had to have grass for grazing and plenty of water and it would help if the lay of the land was such that the cattle wouldn't stray off before they were ready to head for the Guadalupe Mountains.

The site Bob chose was a broad hollow ringed on three sides by hills and bordered on the fourth by a creek. "We'll start in the mornin'," he said as they were stripping their mounts. "I just wish we had more horses."

"Isn't two for each of us enough?" Tom Waldron asked.

"Not hardly. Five or six each is better. Ropin' longhorns will be harder on our horses than it'll be on us, and it will be hell on us, which reminds me." Three Fingers Bob took one of the new ropes each of them had. "Let's limber these up some."

Tom held his in both hands and asked what he thought was an obvious question: "How do you work this thing, exactly?"

Three Fingers Bob was making a loop in the end of his and looked up in amazement. "Please don't tell me you've never thrown a rope."

"I've never thrown a rope," Tom said. "Why would I? In Ohio there wasn't any need. Our cows come when we call them."

Jed Adams was trying to fashion a loop like Bob's. "We didn't have much call to rope animals in South Carolina, either."

"Good God," Bob declared. "It's worse than I reckoned."

There was a day's delay while they were given lessons in the basics of rope handling. Tom was impressed by the things Three Fingers Bob could do. The oldtimer was a virtuoso at roping anything from any position — standing, sitting, running, riding. Jed wanted to learn tricks like stepping into a whirling loop and then swinging it up and over the body but Bob said that had to wait.

"First you learn to toddle, and then you learn to walk. We'll stick to the simple stuff until you can rope somethin' without fallin' off your horse."

The first throw he taught them was the overhand toss. To Tom it looked simple until he learned the rope had to be thrown in a certain way so that the moment he let go, the back of his hand was to the left, with his thumb down.

Bob took a rock and drove a waist-high stake into the ground for them to practice on. After watching a few tentative throws, he frowned and said, "If you can't rope somethin' that's standin' still, how in hell do you expect to rope a movin' cow? Here. We'd best try bigger loops."

Soon Jed was snaring the stake every time but Tom would miss as often as not, leading Three Fingers Bob to remark in exasperation, "Forget the blamed rope. I'll give you a club and you can beat the cows senseless."

They practiced until it was too dark to see; then Jed kindled a fire and put a pot of coffee on to boil while Tom gathered enough firewood to last the night and Three Fingers Bob sat on his blanket with his back to his saddle muttering to himself.

"Let me do any ropin' that needs doing," the former Ranger said when the coffee was done. "You two just swing yours and yell a lot and maybe the cows will take the hint."

"We're not that bad," Tom said defensively.

"You're worse. Hell, I've seen vaqueros who can do things with a rope that would make you think the rope was alive. The Mexicans are a sight better at it than we are but we're catchin' up."

That night Tom could barely sleep, he was so excited. His dream was finally coming true. Soon he would have his own ranch or, rather, half a ranch and half the cattle. He didn't like the arrangement as much as Constance did. He would much rather have the entire ranch. But for the sake of marital harmony he would go along with her wishes, for now.

It seemed to Tom as if he had only been asleep a few minutes when a hand roughly shook his shoulder.

"Unless you want a pot of cold water on your face, I'd get up," Three Fingers Bob said. "We have a lot to do and time's a-wastin'."

The sun wasn't up yet. A cup of coffee served for breakfast. Then they were in the saddle and riding at a walk in single file through brush so thick, Tom would have been lost on his own. He soon realized why Bob had insisted they buy the angora chaps. The trails they were following — cattle trails, he suspected — were so narrow that limbs and thorns tore at his legs and thighs.

Jed couldn't understand why they were

sticking to the brush. Everyone knew cows liked open country. They came to the edge of a wide plain. He started out on it and Three Fingers Bob hissed like a riled snake.

"Where in tarnation do you think you're going? Get back here and hide or you'll spoil our surprise."

"But how will we get any cattle?" Jed protested.

"They'll come right to us soon enough."

Jed reined back and leaned on his saddle horn and scanned the plain for signs of life that weren't there. Gradually the sky to the east brightened. He was about convinced the old man didn't know what he was doing when specks appeared far off. Soon the specks grew in size and took on the shape of cattle.

Jed was expecting cows similar to those back in South Carolina, only wilder. But these weren't cows. They were monsters. As best he could judge, most weighed upward of a thousand pounds. High at the shoulders and lean at the flanks, they had wicked-looking horns that curved forward like those on buffalo, only these were longer. Their skulls were also long and thick. In their mannerisms they were more like deer than cows. They constantly sniffed the air and looked about, alert for peril.

Bob had mentioned that most of the wild cattle were black but browns and grays and pale red and yellow were much in evidence. Some were a mix of red and white or other colors. Not one had an ounce of fat on its powerful frame. They were living examples of raw power, and watching them approach was enough to almost give Jed second thoughts. Almost, but not quite.

The longhorns did not look like normal cows; they did not act like normal cows. Nor did they graze like normal cows. All other cows grazed during the day and rested at night. Longhorns grazed at night, and when day broke, they headed for thick timber, where they would lie up until the next evening. That was why Three Fingers Bob had them wait at the treeline. There was no need to go after the cattle; the cattle would come to them.

Bob was whispering instructions. "As soon as they see us, they'll stampede for the brush. Rope one and tie it down like I showed. Then move on to another. We won't have a lot of time. If we get four each, we'll be lucky."

Tom did not see how he could get even

one. A man with a rope on a skittish horse against behemoths that could disembowel either of them was not a situation to his liking. More than ever, he wished he had not given in to Constance. He should have insisted they move on. There were bound to be other locales as nice as the valley, bound to be cattle that weren't as fierce as grizzlies.

"Wait until I say," Three Fingers Bob whispered.

Tom's mouth was dry and his palms were sweaty. He shifted his grip on his rope, then froze. One of the steer was staring right at his hiding place. He thought for a moment he would go undetected but his horse chose that moment to stamp a hoof and flick its ears.

A snort from the steer, and bedlam was unleashed. Instantly, the lead cattle galvanized into thunderous motion, and within seconds, hundreds of longhorns were hurtling toward the timber in a long line of horn and sinew.

Tom thought he had been scared during the war. He thought he had been scared the night Connie was taken by that Comanche. But the fear that spiked through him now was worse by far, a rippling wave of fright spawned deep in his being, fright that made his flesh crawl with goose bumps. He came within a whisker of reining around and getting out of there.

Then Three Fingers Bob bawled, "Now, boys! Now!" and applied his spurs to his horse.

Jed immediately did the same, unleashing a Rebel yell. He had his rope ready to throw, holding it as Bob had taught them.

Of their own accord, Tom's legs moved and his spurs did what spurs were designed to do. The next moment he was galloping toward a living wall of horn and sinew that was bearing down on him like a herd of buffalo gone amok.

Disaster seemed inevitable. Three Fingers Bob was out ahead, expertly whirling his rope. Tom could not bear to watch the old man be killed but he couldn't turn away. He braced for the crunching, crushing impact of tons of hurtling cattle with the ex-Ranger and the ex-Ranger's mount, but a miracle took place. At the last instant the cattle veered to either side to avoid him. Bob's rope darted out, and just like that, a mossy horn was roped and down.

Then Tom had his own life to think of. The cattle were almost on top of him, their horns bristling like the spear tips in a

Greek phalanx. He picked an onrushing brindle and swung the rope and threw, and missed. He drew rein as the cattle went flying past, their horns so close to his legs and to his horse that he tensed with the expectation of imminent disaster. But the longhorns thundered by and he was left sitting there on his horse with his rope on the ground.

"I could use some help here, Yank!" Jed Adams hollered. He had snared a big black bull by the horns. The bull was digging in its hooves and tossing and turning in a ferocious attempt to break free. The rope was as taut as piano wire, but try as he might, Jed couldn't bring the bull down. It was a stalemate. He did not dare unwrap the rope from his saddle horn to try to gain a little extra leverage because the bull would tear it out of his hands and be off like a shot. "Bring him down if you can!"

Tom coiled his rope and closed in, the loop low to the ground. He was not much good at the overhand toss but maybe an underhand throw would work as well. All he needed to do was get the noose up under the bull's forelegs and they would have the brute where they wanted it.

"Hurry!" Jed yelled. None of their horses except Bob's were cattle trained, and Hickory wasn't happy about being so close to the longhorn. Hickory's eyes were wide and his nostrils were flaring, and Jed wouldn't put it past the horse to rear and plunge and try to bolt. "I don't know how long I can hold this critter!"

Tom saw that roping the bull's front legs wouldn't work; they were planted like stakes into the ground. So he rode in alongside it and swung the loop neatly over its head and horns, then jabbed his spurs and sent his horse toward Jed's. He was moving fast, and when he came to the end of the rope, his mount's momentum, combined with the constant pressure Jed's rope supplied, did what needed doing. The bull crashed to earth.

Jed spurred his sorrel so he could get in close and tie the bull off but Three Fingers Bob beat him there and accomplished in seconds what would have taken Jed a minute or more.

The drum of hooves receded into the timber. Tom glanced around and was delighted to see two other wild cows tied down, a testament to Bob's skill. "We did it!" he exclaimed. "We got three!"

"*We?*" Three Fingers Bob said in more than mild disgust. "Where do you get that *we* from, greener? If it hadn't been for me, you wouldn't have one." He shook his head as he coiled his rope. "I don't know about this. It's dangerous enough without havin' to nursemaid two lunkheads who don't know a hooley-ann from a Mother Hubbard loop."

"I caught hold of one," Jed said. Considering it was his first try, he was proud he had done even that.

"Sure. And if that critter had charged you instead of fought the rope, you might be lyin' in your own innards about now."

"You're just sayin' that to scare us," Jed said.

"You're damn right I want you scared. Fear can do more than brains to keep a man alive. But you're missin' my point. At the rate we're going, it will take a month of Sundays to get enough cattle for your herd."

Jed swung down to undo his rope from the bull's horns. "So what else do we have to do? Or is it you have an important engagement somewhere we don't know about yet?"

A smile spread across Bob's seamed features. "You're a regular know-it-all. But after we get these cattle to camp, you two are spendin' the rest of the day practicin' how to rope. You'll throw loops until your arms are so heavy you can't lift them, and you'll thank me for it later."

Tom was sure the three wild cattle would fight savagely to free themselves once they were allowed to get up, but to his utter astonishment they let themselves be led along as tamely as dogs on a leash although the bull snorted a lot and tugged at the rope now and then.

Three Fingers Bob had insisted on buying a lot of extra rope at Kit's. Now Tom and Jed learned why. The Texan rigged a rope corral and placed the three cattle inside. "There we go."

"You can't be serious," Tom said, giving the rope a shake. "This wouldn't hold a pair of sheep."

"Keep that up," Three Fingers Bob said.

"Keep what up?"

"Shakin' the rope. A rope brought them down and they were led into the corral by a rope and now they're penned by a rope. They're learnin' to respect rope and do what we want them to do. God help us if they ever lose that respect and figure out how puny we are."

"It's silly," Tom said. "They could break out without half trying."

"You know that and I know that but they don't," Three Fingers Bob said. "Always remember they're stronger than us and meaner than us but they're also dumber than tree stumps. That's our edge. The only edge we have."

Jed could not take his eyes off the three magnificent specimens, the start of their very own herd. He imagined the valley in the Guadalupe Mountains, the Bar G, overflowing with cattle just like them. "Give us a week and we'll be ropin' eight of these a day."

"Even at that rate it would take us forever to gather herd," Bob said. "I know how to do it faster but there's a problem."

"What sort of problem?" Tom inquired. He was all for speeding things along if he could be with Constance and the girls that much sooner. He never cared to be apart from them. During the war it was his hardest burden to bear.

"It could get us killed."

17

Constance Waldron did not like to impose on people, particularly people she did not know, and she did not know Ruth Kittle that well. When Kit offered to put her daughters and her up in rooms at the rear of the emporium, Constance politely declined. They could make do up in the valley, she said, and would live in a tent until the men returned. But Kit would not hear of it.

"Stay alone up there with just your girls? Didn't the Comanches and Mort Sayer teach you anything?"

Constance had been offended by the suggestion she could not take care of her own, but before she could defend herself, Tom, who had overheard, surprised her by saying, "I think Kit has the right idea. With Bob gone, there won't be any men around. You two should stick together so you can look out for one another."

Just then Bret Adams cleared his throat. "My pa is leavin' me here to watch over them, Mr. Waldron. I won't let them come to harm."

"That's nice," Tom said.

There were times, Constance had reflected, when she wished her husband had more tact. The boy was only offering to help and Tom made it sound as if Bret was barely out of diapers. "The girls and I will be fine at the valley. I have your revolver and I can shoot." Shortly before they left Ohio, Tom had taken her out into the fields and taught her how to load and fire the Starr. He set six bottles up for her at ten paces and she shattered three of them in twelve tries.

"Please, Connie," Tom said. "I don't often ask for much but I'm asking now. It would take a great worry off my shoulders."

It was true. He rarely asked a favor. So Constance felt compelled to agree. But now, with the men gone over a month, she yearned more and more for the green valley that would soon be their new home.

Kit was dusting shelves in the dry goods section when Constance came down the narrow hallway from the back. "Have you seen that youngest of yours?" Kit asked. "She promised to give me a hand cleaning and she's nowhere around."

"Sally is probably off with the others," Constance said. Her girls and the Adams boys had been spending a lot of time together, a circumstance with which she was not entirely happy in light of Heather's continued interest in Bret.

"Can I ask you a question?" Kit said. "Be honest. Do you like me?"

"I beg your pardon?"

Kit turned from the shelves. "Ever since the men left, you've clammed up. You're not as friendly as you used to be. I have the impression you don't care for me much and I'd like to know what I did to cause it. I was hoping we would be friends for a long time to come."

"It's not you," Constance said. "It's this whole situation. I don't feel comfortable, and I guess it shows."

"I've done all I can to make you feel at ease."

"I know, I know. Don't feel bad. It's not you. It's me. I won't be happy until I have a roof of my own over my head again."

"I understand," Kit said. "I felt the same way when my husband, Ken, built this place. It was wonderful to have a home again. But it can also lull you into thinking things are wonderful when they're not."

"How do you mean?" Constance asked.

"A roof over my head made me feel safe, made me feel sheltered. I didn't think anything would ever go wrong, so I never actually considered what would happen if Ken died. I never expected to be running the emporium alone."

"You can't blame yourself. Accidents happen."

"Oh, I'm not saying I could have prevented Ken having his neck broken. We're none of us God. But I would have been a lot better prepared to handle his death if I had not been feeling so safe and content."

Constance did not see herself having the same problem. She would never feel entirely safe ever again. As it was, she was worried sick about Tom and spent many a sleepless hour late at night tossing and turning in her bed and praying he made it back safe and well.

Kit had resumed dusting. "I suppose the smart thing to do was to close the emporium and go back east. But Ken was proud of our store. He was always looking ahead to the future and he was sure one day soon people would flock into west Texas and we would be at the crossroads of the migration. His exact words."

Constance hated to admit it, but her Tom rarely thought that far ahead. He tended to act more on impulse, as his abrupt decision to pull up stakes and head for the frontier showed.

"Closing up or selling out would be the same as saying Ken's dream was worthless," Kit was saying. "I had to stay. As much for the memories as to prove him right. Not that there isn't a day I don't re—" Kit stopped and cocked her head toward the sheet that hung over the window. "What was that?"

"I didn't hear anything," Constance said. If not for the wind and the occasional whinny of a horse or the cluck of a chicken, a person might think the outside world no longer existed.

"I did." Kit went behind the bar and took down the double-barreled shotgun. From under the counter she brought out a box of shells and fed one into each of the twin barrels.

"Is that necessary?" Constance asked.

"Remember what I said about not letting a roof lull you into thinking you'll live forever?"

Constance followed Kit outside. The horses in the corral were resting in the midday heat. The only other sign of life was a lizard skittering about.

"I don't see the children anywhere. Do you?"

"Sally? Heather?" Constance called, and when there was no reply, she stepped from under the overhang into the blazing sun. "They have to be around somewhere."

Kit moved to the right. "I'll check around back."

"Give a yell if they're there." Shielding her eyes with her left hand, Constance turned from west to east and back again, scouring the parched plain. Shimmering heat waves created illusory lakes of water. "Sally? Heather?" she repeated, only louder. "Where are you?"

A giggle brought Constance up short. Suspecting it came from the shed by the corral, she marched over and yanked on the handle. No one was inside. Another giggle drew her to the shed near the pump. A spare pump handle and other parts were stored inside. Furtive whispering and snickering persuaded her to move quietly. She gripped the door, and pulled.

The four were there, Sally to the left with her hands over her mouth, Pitney to the right with his mouth agape. In the center stood Heather and Bret, the latter with his back to the door. Constance could not quite see what they were doing but their heads were bent at suggestive angles. At the flood of sunlight, both jumped and spun, and Heather bleated, "Mother!"

"What are you up to in here?" Constance demanded. "Didn't you hear me yelling?"

"We came in to get out of the sun," Heather said.

A bald-faced lie, if Constance ever heard one. It was stifling in the shed. "Do you think I was born yesterday?" Bret was red in the face and would not meet her gaze. She turned to Sally. "Let's hear your excuse, young lady, and make it a good one."

"I don't have one," her younger girl said. "I just do what Heather wants me to."

"How about you, young man?" Constance asked Pitney. "What are you doing in here?"

"Mainly sweatin', ma'am."

"Come out of there, the four of you," Constance directed, and after they complied, she closed the door and put her hands on her hips. "I wasn't born yesterday. And I don't enjoy being fibbed to. Into the store with you, and we'll have us a little talk."

"Oh, Mother," Heather said petulantly, "you're embarrassing me. There's nothing to this, nothing at all."

"Of course not," Constance said. "Young ladies your age spend hours in sheds with young men Bret's age. Into the store," she repeated. "I can do with a glass of water

220

and I'm sure all you can, too." She almost laughed as the children trudged along with their heads hung low like prisoners on their way to the gallows — except for Pitney, who appeared to be quite pleased that Bret was in hot water. "You really should have answered me when I called, Heather."

"We didn't hear you."

"Then either your ears are in need of cleaning or those shed walls are thicker than I thought."

"You think you know everything," Heather sulked.

"That will be quite enough, young lady. And you, Bret Adams. Your father said you were to heed me while he was gone, did he not?"

"Yes, ma'am," Bret said so softly she barely heard him.

"What do you think he will say when he hears of this escapade of yours?" Constance fed his shame.

"I reckon Pa will be upset with me," Bret said. "But Heather is tellin' the truth, Mrs. Waldron. Nothin' much happened."

"It's the much part that concerns me more than the nothing," Constance said. "I can't be watching you two every hour of every day. I expect you both to be on your best behavior and it disappoints me no end when you let me down."

"Yes, ma'am," Bret said.

"I haven't done anything," Pitney piped up, "so there's no need to tell my pa on me, is there?"

"You're as pure as the driven snow — is that how it goes, young master Adams?" Constance asked.

"I've never seen much snow, driven or otherwise" was the younger boy's response, "but I wish I may be shot if I ever do with Sally what Bret was doin' with Heather."

"Pitney!" Bret declared angrily.

"Let him speak," Constance said. "He's the only one among you who has no reason to stretch the truth."

"Please, Mother," Heather said, "don't make a mountain out of a molehill. I'm begging you."

By then they were at the store. "In you go," Constance said. It was a relief to be out of the burning sun. She went behind the bar, where Kit kept a pitcher filled with water, and set five glasses out and filled them. "Here you go."

Pitney came over first and gulped his as if he had just crossed the Mojave Desert. "Thank you, Mrs. Waldron. Our ma would do kind things like this, too."

"I bet your mother was a fine woman," Constance said sincerely.

"Yes, ma'am," Pitney proudly declared. "Ma was the finest ever. Every day she hugged us and told us how much she loved us. On Sundays she always baked cookies." Pitney coughed and bowed his head. "I miss her somethin' terrible."

Constance thought of Jed and Kit. Their mutual interest in each other was as plain as plain could be even though they acted as if nothing out of the ordinary were taking place. "Maybe one day you'll have a new mother."

"Maybe," Pitney said, "but it won't be the same."

Sipping some water, Constance fixed her gaze on her oldest. "Now then, what am I to do with you, Heather Elizabeth Waldron?"

"I haven't done anything."

"And you, Bret Adams? Do you maintain you haven't done anything, too? Or has your father taught you better?"

"We were only —" Bret began, but could not finish. After a bit he managed, "I didn't mean any harm, ma'am."

Heather was tapping her foot. "We have nothing to be sorry about. You don't need to apologize to her."

"Then why were you hiding in the shed?" Constance asked.

"Because I knew you would act like this," Heather said. "I knew you would make more out of it than there was."

"Would you like to spend the rest of the day in your room?" Constance threatened her. "And we'll see if your father agrees I made too much of it when he gets back." She was trying not to lose her temper but her older girl always had a way of aggravating her.

The mention of Tom had its desired effect. Of the two of them, Tom was much more strict. He was fond of saying it was his duty to protect his daughters' virtue, and no father ever protected it more earnestly. Any breech of what Tom deemed proper behavior was swiftly and severely punished.

"Must we bring Father into this?" Heather worriedly asked. "Why bother him with trifles?"

"Maybe he'll think it's of more consequence," Constance said. "The same with your father, Bret."

Tears of anger filled Heather's young eyes. "There are days, Mother —" she said, and stopped herself.

"Yes?"

"Forget it." Heather spun and moved toward the hallway to the rooms at the back, her entire body shaking as if she were about to throw a fit.

"What's the matter with sissy?" Sally asked. "Is she sick?"

"It's nothing a good tongue-lashing won't cure," Constance predicted, and she was just the one to give it to her once Kit returned and could watch the others. The thought made her wonder where Kit had gotten to, and it dawned on her that she had not let Kit know she had found the children. "I'll be right back," she said, coming around the counter. She noticed Heather had stopped, and that her oldest was as rigid as a board. "Heather? What is it?"

"Dear God in heaven!" Heather blurted and backed away from the hallway. "Mother, look!"

Out of the back came Kit. But she wasn't alone. The Beast of the Tierra Vieja towered above her, a huge hand gripping her throat. He stopped and laughed and shook Kit as if she were a rag doll, then grinned. "Did you miss me? I was shot full of holes the last time I was here and I figure to give as good as I got. Who wants to be first?"

18

They settled into a routine.

Each morning they were up an hour before sunrise and in position near one of several plains before dawn broke. They waited on anxious edge for the longhorns to drift toward the timber, and when the wild cattle were close enough, they burst from cover and roped and tied down as many as they could before the cattle dispersed into the thick brush. Hardly a day went by that they didn't add eight or more cows to their rapidly swelling herd.

In the afternoon one of them would stay at camp while the other two ventured into the timber in search of more. It was dangerous business, flushing longhorns in the brush. Often they did not see the cattle until they were right on top of them, and the critters were as apt to charge as to run.

One morning Tom and Three Fingers Bob were out scouring the undergrowth. Tom had fallen behind and was yawning and trying to remember when he last had a good night's sleep when a snort and a crash startled him into sitting straight in the saddle just as a brindle bull hurtled out of the tangle and slammed broadside into his horse. It did not use its horns, thankfully, but the impact was enough to stagger the horse and send Tom tumbling. He jarred his left shoulder and winced as he sat up. Then he suddenly imitated stone.

A mountain of muscle was regarding him with baleful intent. Fetid breath fanned Tom's face. He was nose to nose, eye to eye, with the bull. He sat stock-still and tried not to blink or do anything that would incite the behemoth to finish what it had started.

Tom's horse had moved off a dozen yards and was well out of reach. His rope was nearby but it might as well have been on Mars. He could not look to Bob for help; the ex-Ranger was out of sight.

The bull pawned the ground and swung its head from side to side, and Tom thought his end had come. He considered rolling to one side and scrambling into the brush but it would be futile. The longhorn would be on him before he got to his feet. One of its horns dipped and he closed his eyes and braced for the inevitable.

There was another snort, then the dull thud of hooves, and Tom cracked his eyelids to see the bull shamble leisurely off into the vegetation, the intrusion on its domain forgotten. Exhaling, Tom wasted no time in collecting his rope and climbing back into the saddle.

"What the hell is keepin' you?" Three Fingers Bob had returned and impatiently beckoned. "We have us a heap of mossy horns to rope and I'm not gettin' any younger."

Tom did not tell him about the encounter. Bob would only criticize him for being so careless, and he had every right to be mad. It *had* been careless. Tom was fortunate to be alive.

Another mishap occurred a few days later, but that time to Jed.

They were up at the usual time and in position near a plain at the usual time. As always, the longhorns drifted toward cover at first light, grazing as they came. A yellow bull caught Jed's eye. He reckoned it would make a fine addition to their herd, and when Three Fingers Bob whooped and galloped from cover, Jed voiced his Rebel yell and made for the yellow bull.

Usually a bull would turn to either side but this one stood its ground and lowered its horns. Jed threw his rope in a perfect toss and the noose settled around the bull's head and thick neck, but when he tried to bring it down, the bull wouldn't fall. Instead it suddenly charged. It was Jed who had to frantically turn Hickory aside, and then the bull was past him and bounding for the timber.

Jed went after it. Bob had warned him about allowing too much slack in the rope. He must keep the rope taut to keep the cattle under control. But before he could, the bull came to a tree and in a twinkling had angled left to avoid it. Jed tried to follow suit but he was to the right of the tree. Another second, and the bull had wrapped itself around the trunk and was about to impale Hickory.

Jed reined aside, or tried to. The rope hindered him. So long as it was looped around his saddle horn he wasn't going anywhere. But if he unwound it, the bull would take off, with the rope still attached.

A horn missed Hickory's leg by the width of Jed's hand. Jed cut toward the tree and at the last possible instant hauled on the reins and flew by the bull. He looked back just as the rope caught the bull across the legs and the animal went down hard.

Later the same bull proved intractable. As they were herding the nine longhorns they had roped that morning toward camp, the yellow bull repeatedly broke toward the brush. Jed had to cut it off and herd it back.

Along about the tenth time, Three Fingers Bob looked at him pointedly from across the other side of the bunched cattle and said, "He's one of yours, so you get to decide. Shoot him or let him go."

Some bulls simply wouldn't cooperate. Their spirits were too fiery, their natures too independent. They fought the rope, they fought being tied down, and they would fight every foot of the way along the trail. They caused more trouble than they were worth, as Bob put it one evening, and the only thing to do was kill them or send them back into the wild.

Tom Waldron didn't much care one way or the other. He would as soon shoot them and be done with it. But Jed was not fond of committing needless slaughter. He admired the longhorns too much, admired their courage and how they never gave up. They reminded him of a tattered army of men in gray who fought until the very last, an army he had been proud to be part of.

Once again the yellow bull broke toward the brush, and this time Jed did not try to stop it. "We still have eight left. Not bad for a mornin's work."

"We're doing a lot better than I expected," Three Fingers Bob said, "what with having to work with you two lunkheads."

"Thanks for the confidence," Jed said dryly.

"You're doing fine, son, you and the Yank. You both can handle a rope almost as good as a Texan. It won't be long before we have the full three hundred and can start the drive to the Bar G."

Jed was eager to get back, as much to see his sons as to see Ruth Kittle. He thought of her often and, at night, would lie under his blankets thinking thoughts he kept to himself.

"We've been lucky so far," Bob said, "but no one's luck holds forever."

His comment was prophetic. Ten minutes after they arrived at camp, and the new cattle had been added to those already there, Tom Waldron came up and exclaimed, "One of our cattle is missing!"

Three Fingers Bob chortled. "I told you before. We're bound to have one jump the rope and hightail it into the woods now and then."

"No, you don't understand," Tom responded. "This one was stolen."

"You're sure?" Jed asked.

"I've found footprints. I'm no tracker,

but I think someone helped himself when we weren't looking. The only thing is —" Tom hesitated.

"What?" Jed prompted.

"You'll think I'm crazy, but they were barefoot."

"Show us the spot," Three Fingers Bob said.

It was directly across from their camp at the base of the low hills. The old scout dismounted and walked about reading the sign. "You're right, Tom. It's just one man and he wasn't wearin' shoe leather. But that's not unusual. We haven't come across any yet, but there are homesteads scattered from here to the Gulf. Poor folks, mostly, who scrape by as best they can. Likely as not it's one of them. He roped one of our cattle in the middle of the night and snuck out."

"If they're that poor he's welcome to the meat," Jed said. His whole life he had to struggle to eke out a living for his family; he would not begrudge someone in the same plight one longhorn.

"No, he's not," Three Fingers Bob disagreed. "I'm going after him to fix his hash."

"Why bother?" This from Tom. "One measly cow is one measly cow. I agree with my partner."

Jed looked at Tom. It was the first time the Yankee had referred to him that way. "Thanks, pard," he said with a smile.

"Kids," Three Fingers Bob said. "I'm workin' cattle with kids." He indicated their herd. "It's only one now but if we let him get away with it he'll be back for more. Worse, he'll spread the word we're a weak-sister outfit and we'll have cow thieves swarmin' out of the backwoods to help themselves."

"You're exaggerating a tad," Tom said.

"Not even a smidgen. You don't know this country like I do. You don't know the people. They're curly wolves with no hankerin' for brotherly love and all those other highfalutin ideas. They live in the backwoods because they like it that way, and they do as they damn well please."

"Which makes them a lot like men," Jed said.

"There you go again. Puttin' your thoughts in other people's heads. Do you think because you like to eat eggs that everyone who likes eggs must be the same as you?"

"That made no kind of sense," Jed replied.

"It must be the sun," Tom said, "but I believe I understand his point."

Three Fingers Bob forked leather. "This might take a while. If I'm not back by midnight, I probably ain't comin' back. Carry on as I've taught you, and in another two to three weeks, you'll have your herd."

Jed was quick to propose, "One of us should go with you."

"I'm old enough to wash behind my own ears, thank you very much." Bob rode off up the nearest hill.

"Hold on," Jed said and glanced at Tom, who nodded. "I'm elected, I reckon." He quickly caught up. "I want one thing clear. We're not out to swap lead."

"What would you have me do?" Three Fingers Bob responded. "Ask him pretty please not to swipe any more of our critters? Maybe he'll bust his gut laughin' and solve our problem."

"I mean it," Jed insisted. "We don't provoke anyone if we can help it."

"Maybe in South Carolina stealin' a cow don't amount to much," Three Fingers Bob said, "but in Texas it's as provokin' as stealin' a horse, and we generally treat horse thieves to a strangulation jig."

"I don't want any mention of hangin' when we get there," Jed said. "In fact, let me do all the talkin'."

"Suit yourself." Bob was disgusted. "Just don't blame me if he doesn't kiss your backside out of gratitude."

The tracks were plain enough. The cow

thief had led the longhorn more than a hundred yards to a waiting horse, then ridden southeast into dense timber. Three Fingers Bob was in a sulk and did not speak once the whole ride, only breaking his silence when tendrils of smoke rose in the distance.

"That will be their homestead. Do we sneak up on it, quiet-like, or do we ride up to their door with signs on our chests sayin', `Shoot me. I'm an idiot'?"

Jed was annoyed enough to propose they ride right up to the door but he had not survived the war by being careless. "We'll go in slow and look things over before we show ourselves."

"There's hope for you yet, Reb."

"Comin' from you, Ranger, I'll take that as a compliment."

Three Fingers Bob gave a start. "No one has called me that in more years than you've lived. Until you and your Yankee friend came along, I'd as soon have forgotten I ever wore a badge."

"It's somethin' to be proud of," Jed said.

"Are you proud of all the blue bellies you killed in the war? Because that's all a Ranger is: a killer with a badge. Oh, we enforce the law, but we do it at gunpoint, and our motto was always shoot first and ask questions later. It couldn't be helped. You don't last long if you're slow on the trigger."

"It won't always be that way. One day Texas will be as civilized as the states east of the Mississippi River."

"Good God. I hope not. Civilization is just a fancy word for wearin' a leash, and I never have taken to being another man's dog."

A sentiment Jed shared, although he applied it to the carpetbaggers lording it over the South. The situation was no different in Texas, what with the Radicals running things. But there weren't carpetbaggers nor Radicals in the Guadalupe Mountains.

Three Fingers Bob slowed and shucked his rifle from its saddle scabbard. "Keep your eyes skinned, Reb."

"Maybe we should ride in with out hands empty so they know we're friendly," Jed suggested.

"Do whatever you want. It's your body they'll riddle with bullets."

Jed unlimbered his Morse carbine and verified he had a cartridge in the chamber. Moving quietly, they wound along a foot-path toward the smoke. Suddenly he had the feeling unseen eyes were on them. Twisting, he checked behind them and on both sides but saw nothing to account for it.

"I don't like this," Three Fingers Bob said. "It's too damn quiet."

Only then did Jed realize the woods were as still as a cemetery. No birds were chirping, no squirrels were chattering. Not so much as an insect stirred. That could only mean one thing.

Three Fingers Bob pointed.

Off through the trees stood a cabin or some semblance of one. Whoever built it had left chinks between many of the rough-hewn logs and was content with a roof that sagged in the middle. Strips of burlap hung in the only window, and the door, which was partly open, was attached by rawhide hinges. The small clearing in which the cabin sat was littered with the bleached skulls and skeletons of longhorns.

"What are all those bones doin' there?" Jed asked.

"It's called laziness."

"There's one with some flesh and hide still on. Look at all those flies! And the stench!"

"Forget the damn carcass," Three Fingers Bob whispered. "I smell a trap."

Jed was still convinced they could settle things peacefully. Then a faint sound drew his gaze to a tree beside the trail, to a low limb on which squatted a figure that did not look entirely human, a figure that howled and sprang.

19

Constance Waldron was rooted in shock but only for a few moments. As the Beast of the Tierra Vieja limped out of the hallway with his iron fingers encircling Ruth Kittle's throat, Constance dashed around the corner and ran toward the gun case on the other side of the store.

"Stop right where you are!" Mort Sayer roared. "Or so help me, I'll crush her neck and take you instead!" To demonstrate, he squeezed, and Kit involuntarily cried out in pain.

Constance slowed, debating whether to try for the guns anyway. She had her daughters to think of.

Just then Bret Adams snatched up his rifle and started to snap it to his shoulder to shoot.

"I mean it, boy!" Sayer thundered. "Even if you put a slug in me, I'll kill her! Is that what you want?"

Bret and the rest of the young ones glanced at Constance for guidance. She, in turn, glanced at Kit, who was struggling weakly, her breath choked off, on the verge of collapse. She also saw the Remington in the Beast's other hand, held down low. "All right!" she said, halting. "We'll do as you want! Just don't hurt her!"

Bret wavered and placed his rifle on the bar. "I can't believe you came back," he said to Sayer.

"Did you really think I wouldn't, boy? I didn't get what I came for." Sayer had relaxed his hold but now he shook Kit, hard. "Step to the middle of the room, all of you, and keep your hands where I can see them."

Constance did as he instructed, standing so she was between him and the children. Sally was rightfully terrified, and Heather was trying not to betray how scared she was. The Adams boys were grim and glaring.

"Where's your menfolk?" Sayer demanded, advancing. "And that old fart Kit lets hang around the place?"

"They're gone," Constance admitted. "Off gathering cattle for our new ranch."

"So you're alone?" Sayer grinned and bent over Kit. "Well, now, I came at just the right time, didn't I, darlin'?" He laughed and pushed her so violently, she fell to her knees at Constance's feet. "Stay there with your friends while I ponder some." Sayer limped to the bar.

"Must you treat her so?" Constance asked as she helped Kit up. Finger marks on Kit's throat were proof of how hard he had choked her.

"I've been right nice so far, lady." The Beast holstered his revolver and helped himself to a bottle. "Don't rile me or that will change." Taking several deep swallows, he sighed and wiped his mouth with the back of a sleeve.

"There are limits to what people will tolerate, Mr. Sayer," Constance said. "Harm us or the children and every man in the state will be after you."

"Most don't have the backbone," Sayer said "But you're right. The Rangers would send half a company or more, and there are bound to be others. Not that they worry me any. I can shake most anyone this side of an Apache." He tilted the bottle and, when he was done, commented sourly, "Still, it's the only reason I don't kill you and the lambs where you stand."

"I'm no lamb," Bret said.

"I'd be quiet, were I you, boy," Sayer said. "You're older than the rest and you ain't no female, so killin' you won't stir up no hornet's nest."

Pitney clenched his small fists. "Leave my brother be, mister, or our pa will give you what for!"

"Rebel gnat," Sayer said and came over to a table and pulled out a chair and sat. "You know, now that I think about it, I could kill all of you anyway and make it look like Comanches were to blame. How do you like that idea?"

Kit was rubbing her throat but had stopped gasping for breath, and said unevenly, "Quit it, Mort. I'm the one you came for. Take me and be done with this. Scarin' kids is beneath even you."

"You think you know me but you don't. I'll teach you, though. Before I'm through, you'll be a whole new woman." Sayer laughed viciously.

"Why me out of all the women in Texas?" Kit asked. "Why not a woman who wants to be with you?"

"I told you before, there aren't that many females west of the Pecos. And you're not only one of the prettiest fillies I've ever laid eyes on — you don't have a husband or a father or brothers who will come after me. I can do with you as I please." Sayer patted his lap. "Come over here and sit."

"No," Kit said.

The Beast pulled his revolver and placed it on the table with a loud thunk. "I'll count to five, and if you're not on my knee, I'll shoot the older boy."

"You're real good at threatening women and children, aren't you?" Kit said, but she went and sat on his leg with her arms folded across her bosom and her chin thrust defiantly.

"You've got spunk," Sayer said, "but I'll beat that out of you soon enough, along with your other bad habits."

"What would they be?" Kit inquired.

"The same as all women have. Sassin' a man. Not doing what they're told, when they're told. Not rememberin' who is the master and who is the rib." The Beast patted her shoulder as someone might pat a pet dog. "I've broken mustangs. I can break you."

Constance was staring at the Remington. If she could get her hands on it, they would have the upper hand. Taking a slow step, she said, "Is that all women are to you? What about love and caring and tenderness?"

"What about them? They're excuses weak men make when their women wear the britches."

"I must say, you have an unusual view on things." Constance took another step.

She tried to catch Kit's eye but Kit was staring fixedly at a wall. "In case you haven't heard, a little sweet talk goes a long way. You won't win a woman's heart by abusing her."

"It's not her heart I'm interested in," Sayer said with a leer and a wink at Kit.

Emboldened by his easygoing manner, Constance slowly approached them. "Are you hungry? Would you like for me to make you a meal?" She had to keep him talking, keep him distracted, until she reached the table.

"I could eat a horse," Sayer said, "which reminds me." He pointed at Bret. "Go saddle one of those nags in the corral and bring it to the hitch rail. Kit and me are leavin' soon."

"What's your hurry?" Constance asked. "Don't you want that meal?"

"You might be lyin' about your men. They could be back any minute. Or someone else could happen along. I aim to be long gone when they do." Sayer rested his hand on the Remington. "And you can forget about puttin' windows in my noggin with my own gun."

"Don't take her, Mr. Sayer," Constance tried a different appeal. "When the men do return, they'll come after you. Mr.

Hazelton is a former Texas Ranger, and he's a fine tracker."

"Who the hell is Hazelton?"

"Everyone calls him Three Fingers Bob."

"That old goat was a Ranger?" Sayer laughed and shook his head. "Who would have thought it? He's about as worthless as teats on a stallion."

Kit let fly with a verbal barb, "He shot *you*, didn't he? Too bad his aim was off or you wouldn't be pawing me."

"I haven't begun to paw," Sayer snapped, then touched his shoulder and his thigh. "That bastard put two slugs into me. I owe him." To Constance he said, "Maybe you're right. Maybe I shouldn't be so hasty. Maybe I should stick around until Bob gets back and give him what he gave me."

"Our men nearly killed you once," Constance said. "Why stay and give them the chance to finish what they started?"

"Because I was figurin' on killin' them anyway sooner or later. I can't have folks sayin' I ran away with my tail tucked between my legs. I have my pride." The Beast suddenly rose, dumping Kit unceremoniously on the floor, and trained his Remington on Bret Adams. "I told you to do something, boy, and you'll damn well do it."

"I'm not leavin' these ladies alone with you," Bret said.

Heather gasped and clutched his arm. "Do as he says or he'll shoot you. We'll be all right. If he tries anything, we'll yell."

"Go," Constance urged, afraid Sayer would shoot and maybe hit her daughter. They must not do anything to set him off.

"It ain't right," Bret said, but he went.

Mort Sayer did not lower the revolver until the door had closed; then he jammed it into its holster and glowered at Kit as she picked herself up from the floor. "You're more trouble than you might be worth. If you have an extra dress you want to take or a few geegaws, fetch them. No tricks, or that cute little girl won't be so cute when I get through with her."

Constance turned and held her arms out and Sally rushed into them. "The only way you'll harm a hair on her head is over my dead body."

"Jabber, jabber, jabber," Sayer said. "I'm sick of it. The rest of you sit at the other table until the boy gets back, and not a peep out of you."

Unsure whether he was leaving or staying, Constance ushered the girls and

Pitney to the table farthest from Sayer's and claimed a chair facing him.

Kit was smoothing her dress and had not moved. It angered Sayer, and swearing a vicious streak, he grabbed her arm and practically threw her toward the rear hall. "When I say jump, you jump!" His mouth twitched and he swung the Remington from her to them and back again.

"Careful on that trigger," Kit said. "I'm going. I'm going."

Constance sought to calm him by asking, "Where are you from, Mr. Sayer? I would like to hear about your past."

"Would you?"

"It would help me understand you better."

"And you'd like that? You'd like to understand why I am how I am? I reckon I can help you." Smiling, the Beast walked over to her, and still smiling, he backhanded her across the face.

Constance thought her neck had snapped. The room swam and blood filled her mouth. She heard Sally and Heather cry out. Sagging, she gripped the arms of the chair to keep from sliding off.

"When I say not a peep, I damn well mean not a peep," Mort Sayer fumed. "The next one of you who opens their mouth loses teeth."

Hoping the kids would heed him, Constance closed her eyes. Her temples were throbbing. Until this moment she had entertained the thought that they could talk their way out of this fix, but there was no reasoning with someone whose conduct was ruled by a bestial nature. She must stop acting as if she were back in Ohio among polite society and do what common sense dictated.

"Mother, are you all right?" Heather whispered.

Constance lifted her head. Sayer was at the front door, checking on Bret, his back to them. Sally had tears streaming down her cheeks. Pitney was gripping his chair, his knuckles white. She pressed a sleeve to her mouth and the sleeve came away red. "He didn't hurt me much," she lied. Her lower lip was swelling and her jaw hurt when she moved it.

"We can't let him take Kit."

"I know," Constance said, shifting toward the bar. Bret's rifle lay where he had left it, and the boy always kept it loaded. She coiled her legs under her. "When I move, I want the three of you to duck under the table."

"I want to help," Heather said. "I'll yell and run the other way to distract him."

"And be shot in the back?" Constance shook her head and winced at the added pain the movement caused. "It's under the table and nothing else. I'll deal with Mr. Sayer."

"Are you sure you can?" Heather whispered. "You've never shot anyone before, and Father says some people don't have it in them."

"Now is not the time to quibble." Although now that Constance thought about it, her daughter had a point. She wanted to do it but was wanting enough? *Thou shalt not kill* had been drilled into her since she was old enough to attend church, and breaking one of the Ten Commandments was a sin. "Your father shot enemy soldiers in the war. I can do no less to protect my family." Brave talk, but she was conflicted by sudden doubt.

"I can do it," Heather whispered. "Let me try for the rifle."

"Quit arguing," Constance said. Here their lives were in peril and her oldest was giving her a hard time. Teenagers had to be the most exasperating creatures on God's green earth, next to men.

"Hurry it up, boy!" Mort Sayer hollered. "I could saddle that horse twice as fast with my eyes closed."

Bret answered, but Constance could not quite make out what he said. She had delayed long enough. Pushing up out of the chair, she flew toward the bar and their salvation. Sally called out but she did not glance around. There was no turning back.

A loud crash filled the emporium, and Heather yelled. Constance was within arm's reach of the counter when a heavy blow between her shoulder blades buckled her legs out from under her. She crashed against the bar. Her temple struck hard and then she was on her hands and knees and the room was spinning again, worse than before. "No," she bleated, a heartbeat before another blow to the ribs lifted her half off the floor. She collapsed like a punctured waterskin. She heard Sally scream, she heard another crash and a gunshot, and a cannon went off somewhere. Desperate to save her children, she struggled onto her elbows but her arms would not support her weight and her consciousness was fading fast. Gritting her teeth, she flailed wildly about for something to hold on to, so weak she couldn't raise her arm.

Again Sally screamed, and Constance held off the darkness and made it to her knees but it took every ounce of strength

and will she had left. She swayed, her eyelids fluttering, the world a jumble of colors
and confusion. Her hand brushed the bar
and she braced her arm and began to rise,
or thought she did, because the next instant her cheek smacked the floor and the
world was snuffed from existence as a
flame was snuffed from a candle.

20

The apparition in the tree slammed into Jed Adams and Jed was unhorsed. They tumbled to the ground, with bony fingers seeking Jed's throat while another hand seized his carbine and sought to wrest it from him. Jed landed on his side and kicked out. His boot caught his attacker in the gut and the man was knocked back. Scrambling onto his knees, Jed leveled his carbine.

His attacker froze. It was a tall, spindly man in his forties or so, with a face like a locust's and whiskers down to his waist. He was wearing torn pants. He was not armed.

"One twitch and you're buzzard bait," Three Fingers Bob said, his own rifle trained on the man's chest.

Jed added, "This is no way to treat visitors."

"You don't fool me!" the man declared in a shrill voice. He was burned dark by the sun and as filthy as a dirty rag. "You're here to make worm food of me for the cow."

"We have the right," Three Fingers Bob said. "Rustlin' is rustlin' whether it's one or one hundred."

"All those critters you have and you begrudge a starvin' family a few meals?" the man asked.

"A few, hell. There's enough meat to feed three or four people for a month."

"I've got eight young'uns," the man said, "plus me and the missus. In one week we'll be suckin' the marrow from its bones."

Jed could see Bob was disposed to give the man a hard time, so he said, "Show us this family of yours and you can have the longhorn and be welcome to it."

"Your friend won't shoot me? He looks plumb mean."

"He won't shoot you," Jed assured him, rising. He held out his hand and introduced himself.

"Tobias Secarth," the man said, shaking. "By your accent I take you to be a fellow son of the South. I'm Georgia born, myself. Came to Texas about ten years ago thinkin' it was a land of milk and honey but mostly it's a land of savages and scorpions."

Three Fingers Bob made a sound reminiscent of the bray of a mule. "I've yet to see it fail. Those who can't make a go of it blame the land or the weather or the cycle of the moon but they never put the blame where it belongs, on their own shoulders."

"Do you have a family, mister?" Tobias asked, and when Bob shook his head, he said, "Then you have no business insultin' me. I do the best I can but work is mighty scarce in these parts."

"Then move to where jobs need fillin'," Three Fingers Bob said, "San Antonio or Houston or Dallas."

"Live in a city?" Tobias made the thought sound tantamount to insanity. "I'd rather be boiled in oil. I like the freedom to do as I please without bein' beholden to any man."

"You like starvin'," Bob said.

Jed was climbing onto his horse. "Enough," he said. "Let's visit with these folks. If it's as he claims, I'm givin' him the cow."

The footpath brought them to the clearing in which the small cabin sat. Up close it was even more of an affront. Jed was about to comment on the shoddy workmanship when Tobias Secarth tugged on his long whiskers and proudly said, "I built this myself. Took me six months of sweat but it's ours free and clear." He raised his voice. "Martha, you can come out, and bring the chicks. Every last one."

On the south side of the cabin, tied to a stake, was the missing longhorn, dozing in the sun, unaware its fate was in the balance.

The door creaked wide-open and out waddled a woman as broad as she was tall. Stringy black hair and chubby cheeks caked with grime did not add luster to her appearance. Her homespun dress was little more than a sack, and like her husband, she had bare feet. After her trailed eight children ranging in ages from about three to fifteen, each as filthy and shabbily attired as their parents. They had a wariness about them that reminded Jed of wild animals.

"The fruit of my loins," Tobias said, smiling. "I'd have had more but the wife can't seem to breed my seed like she used to."

"Oh, sure, blame the woman," Mrs. Secarth said, "when it could be you're shootin' blanks."

Three Fingers Bob chuckled. "That's tellin' him, ma'am."

"You stay out of this," Tobias Secarth said. "I'm as spry as I've ever been, I'll have you know."

Jed slid the Morse carbine into his saddle scabbard. "I've seen enough. You folks are welcome to the critter, and if you need one or two later on, come see me. No need to go skulkin' about in the middle of the night."

"We're obliged, friend," Tobias said, "and we'd be honored if you and the ornery one would stay for vittles."

"Who are you callin' ornery?" Three Fingers Bob demanded.

Martha walked up to Jed and placed her hand on his boot. "Please, mister. I ain't much of a cook but we'd like to thank you for your kindness."

"It wouldn't be hospitable to say no," Tobias urged.

Much to Bob's annoyance, Jed accepted. They tied their horses and were ushered inside like conquering heroes, the kids buzzing about them and asking all sorts of questions about the outside world.

"You'll have to excuse my brood," Tobias said at one point. "We don't have many visitors, and they're starved for news."

Jed talked until his lips were fit to fall off. For every answer, the children had two questions. He was glad to use twilight as an excuse to light a shuck, and after thanking the Secarths, he headed for camp, whistling as he rode.

"Quite taken with yourself," Three Fingers Bob said. "Although I suppose they should have renamed one of their kids after you."

"You're just upset because you were wrong," Jed refused to take the bait. "They were as nice as nice could be."

"One of these days you'll learn that trust isn't all it's touted to be. A man can smile and stab you in the back at the same time."

"The world accordin' to Hazelton," Jed said. "Your a cynical old cuss, and I pray to God I don't end my days the same. A person can go through life lookin' for the worst in people or he can go through life lookin' for the best."

"I was as silly as you when I was your age, but life taught me that going through it with blinders on is a surefire invite for heartache."

Jed refused to be drawn into a debate. He felt good and he would not let the old Ranger spoil his mood.

Twilight had fallen and stars sprinkled the firmament. A breeze out of the northwest brought some relief from the heat. Off in the timber a coyote howled. Later an owl hooted at them from high in a tree.

"We should have brought some of that beef for Tom," Jed mentioned as they climbed the hill that separated them from the herd.

"Especially as it was our beef."

On the crest of a hill, Jed reined up to gaze down on the fruits of their toil and was struck numb. "What the hell?"

Three Fingers Bob galloped down the slope, bawling, "Waldron! Waldron! Where are you?"

The cattle were gone. Every last head. Jed rode to the bottom and reined right and then left, seeking some sign to explain their disappearance. "They must have stampeded," he guessed aloud.

"Over here!" Three Fingers Bob called.

The ex-Ranger had dismounted and was bent over a prone figure. Jed swung down and ran to them, dreading the worst, as Bob carefully rolled Tom Waldron over. A wicked gash on his forehead was caked with dry blood. Another above his left ear was still bleeding. His left cheek was badly swollen and his chin bore a nasty dark bruise.

"Someone beat the hell out of him," Three Fingers Bob said. He slid a hand under Tom's head and gently probed. "Just as I figured. He's got a bump the size of a goose egg. Whoever it was, they jumped him from behind, then beat him after he was down."

"Rustlers?"

"Who else?" Three Fingers Bob rose. "Stay with him while I get a fire going. We'll tend his wounds as best we can and head out after them at first light."

Jed hunkered, in near shock from the unexpectedness of the theft. Other than Tobias Secarth's family, they had not seen another living soul in weeks. Yet someone must have been lurking nearby, spying on them, and waiting for the right opportunity to strike. Several someones, since it would take more than one person to rustle a herd the size of theirs.

Tom groaned and his eyelids fluttered. His lips moved weakly as if he were trying to speak.

"Rest easy, pard," Jed said. "It's me and old Bob."

But Tom did not rest easy. "Took me by surprise," he said hoarsely. "Never saw them until they were all over me."

"How many?" Jed needed to find out.

"Five or six." Tom licked his lips, and winced. "They left me for dead and drove off our cattle."

"It'll take more than a few whacks to dent that thick Yankee noggin of yours," Jed said with a grin. "Now be still."

"Don't let them get away. Don't let them steal our future out from under us."

"I won't, I promise." Jed placed his hand on the Northerner's shoulder. "But will you *please* shut up? You're in a bad way and you need to rest."

"Sure, Jed, sure. Whatever you say."

A new emotion filled Jed's breast and he took Waldron's hand and squeezed it. "I'll get whoever did this."

In no time Three Fingers Bob had a fire going. Together, they gingerly lifted Tom and placed him on his back beside it. Everything they owned was gone. All their gear, all their utensils, all their supplies.

Jed had a canteen on his saddle, and he went to the creek and refilled it, then cut strips from his own shirt to clean Tom's wounds and apply as bandages.

"You do that real well," Three Fingers Bob commented.

"I had a lot of experience in the war," Jed said. He didn't delve into the gory details of the many battles and the many wounded.

"I think he'll live," Bob said. "But it won't be for lack of tryin' on their part." He added a broken limb to the fire. "You should stay here. I'll go after the bastards by my lonesome."

"There are too many," Jed said.

"Tom can't fend for himself in the shape

he's in. Someone has to look after him, and you're his partner. Besides, the rustlers can't get that far with that many cattle. I'll catch up before noon, I reckon, and be back with the herd by supper."

"You can't handle all those longhorns yourself," Jed argued. "Not any better than I could anyway. I'm the one who has to go."

"Why you?"

"You said it yourself. I'm Tom's partner. They're my cattle as much as his, and this coon fights his own fights."

"You'll have to kill them," Three Fingers Bob said. "You know that, don't you? In Texas rustlin' is a hangin' offense. They won't let themselves be taken alive. It will be you or them."

"I can't just ride up to them and start shootin'. I'll give them a chance to give up first."

"Then you're not going. You can't go into a gunfight with your hands tied behind your back. Me, I'll gladly blow out their wicks, and good riddance to scum the world is better off without."

"You sure are a bloodthirsty cuss."

"A man does what he has to," Three Fingers Bob said. "Those who can't, those who have more scruples than brains, don't last long. Or don't you want to see those boys of yours again?"

"I can do it," Jed asserted.

"Can you? It's not like the war, where there were rules of engagement and the like. It's kill or be killed. That's the first lesson every Ranger learns. Wantin' to uphold the law is fine. Wantin' to help people is all well and good. But when you strip away the noble ideas, all that's left is you and the other feller and if the other feller shoots you first, then that's too bad, but it's what you deserve for being so damn dumb."

"I could never be a Ranger."

"Don't insult yourself. It's not a great leap from killin' for your country to killin' to keep the peace. The difference is that there are no rules out here. You're either quick or you're dead."

Jed had never looked at it that way. Later, while Bob stood watch he turned in, and tried to get some sleep. But he could not stop thinking about what Bob had said. He was tired and stiff when the first golden rays lit the eastern horizon, and as soon as it was light enough to see, he went over to examine Tom Waldron. The Yankee was sound asleep and breathing evenly. Jed didn't hear Three Fingers Bob come up behind him.

"It's not too late to change your mind, Reb."

"No." Jed saddled Hickory and checked his carbine and forked leather. "If I don't make it back, explain to my boys how it was and how I had it to do."

"I'll do what I can for them," Three Fingers Bob pledged. "But I'd be a poor substitute for their own pa."

Jed looked down at Tom, still sleeping peacefully. "Life sure is strange. Here I am out to avenge a Yankee bein' hurt."

"The important thing is to go on livin'. Show no mercy. They don't deserve any. Shoot as many as you can from ambush and pick off the rest one by one. Don't be fussy about it, neither. A bullet in the back works just as well as a bullet in the front, and they can't shoot you when their backs are to you."

"God, you're coldhearted," Jed said. He smiled thinly and touched the brim of his Confederate cap and lightly tapped his spurs to Hickory. With the rising sun warm on his face, he rode out to do what he had promised himself he would never do again. He rode out to wage war.

21

Constance was aware of sounds. Of rustling and a cough and the scrape of a chair on the floor. Pain was the next sensation, in her ribs and high up on her back and in her temple. She heard someone moan and realized the sound came from her lips; she opened her eyes.

Bright sunlight spilled through a window. Constance squinted and slowly turned her head. She was in a bed, covered by a quilt. She recognized the room. It was Kit's bedroom, and Kit was in a chair, reading. A pan of water and a folded towel were on the bed table. "How long have I been out?"

Kit nearly dropped the book, she came out of the chair so fast. She sat on the edge of the bed and smiled. "Fourteen hours, give or take. Nothing seems to be broken but you won't be doing somersaults for a while."

Constance laughed, a mistake that cost her sharp stabs of agony in her side. Then everything came back to her in a rush and she sobered. "My girls? Were they hurt?"

"They're fine. Heather and I have been taking turns watching over you. She just left ten minutes ago to catch up on her sleep. That's a fine daughter you have there." Kit paused. "Sally has been worried sick and won't hardly touch her food. She dotes on you, you know, but that's normal for a girl her age."

"And the Adams boys?"

"Nary a scratch on either. Sayer took a shot at Bret as Bret came charging through the front door but he missed. They offered to bury the body. I had them take it a quarter of a mile away. No sense in planting the bastard in my own yard, as it were."

"Sayer is dead?"

"He forgot about my shotgun. I had dropped it when he jumped me out back. When he sent me to pack, I went and got it. He was so busy kicking your ribs in that he didn't see me until I was close enough to blow him in half, just about. I gave him both barrels in the chest."

"You killed him," Constance marveled. She had never slain another human being and honestly didn't know if she could.

"It was him or the rest of you," Kit said. "He couldn't leave witnesses."

"I never thought of that."

"He lived about ten minutes more. Asked me to promise I would never tell anyone about how he died. It was too embarrassing, he said, being shot by a woman." Kit's contempt was plain. "Sayer didn't know how to take no for an answer, and he got what he deserved."

"You did what you had to."

"Which is why my conscience is clear. I gave him his chance. Hell, several chances. But he was as arrogant as he was stupid. Some people are like that. They think the sun rises and sets just for them."

"I'm sorry," Constance commiserated.

"For what? I wouldn't have been the first woman he dragged off into the mountains. There are rumors of others. Apparently, whenever he was bored with one, he would pick another. He thought his size gave him the right to do as he pleased. But buckshot will beat size any day of the week."

"Will you let the law know?"

"What difference would it make? Sure, I shot him in self-defense, but a judge might decide it was murder, and who needs that?" Kit set the book on the bed stand and rose. "Would you like something to eat or drink? Then if you're up to it, Heather and Sally will want to welcome you back to the world of the living."

"Soup would be nice," Constance said.

She was halfway done the bowl when her daughters rushed in and Sally threw herself on the bed and into Constance's arm with happy abandon. Heather was more restrained. They embraced, and Heather sat in the chair with her hands folded on her knee.

"We were so afraid," Sally said, tears in her eyes. "If we lost you, I don't know what we would do."

"Your father would take care of you." Constance was watching her oldest for some sign of what Heather was thinking. "He'll be proud of how you handled yourselves, of how brave you were."

"Bret was brave, too," Heather said. "He was nearly shot trying to save us. If not for Kit, he might be dead."

"So I've heard."

"He rushed in without any thought for his own safety. He saw you on the floor and he went to help you and that terrible man shot at him."

"I'll have to thank him," Constance said, but her daughter had more to say.

"I've never seen anyone so brave, Mother. He would have given his life for me — and for you. Yet you treat him as if

266

he is less than we are and don't want me to have anything to do with him."

"I get the point," Constance stressed. Thankfully, Heather dropped the subject, but it gave Constance a lot to think about all that day and most of the next. Kit would not let her get out of bed until suppertime, and then only because she stubbornly insisted.

At mealtime they usually sat in the kitchen at a long table. When Constance shuffled in, her entire body sore and her ribs aching with every breath she took, Bret Adams jumped to hold her chair for her.

"Here you go, ma'am."

Kit was at the stove, not even trying to hide her smile. "Would you like some brandy with your meal? It helps the digestion."

"My digestion is fine, thank you," Constance said, not finding it nearly as humorous. But she sat down and thanked Bret and did not fail to notice that he sat next to Heather instead of across from her as was the customary arrangement. Sally and Pitney were on the other side, Pitney looking about as pleased about the change as he would have been about a visit to the dentist.

Constance made it through the meal and

dessert and was out in front of the emporium in a rocking chair enjoying the evening breeze with Kit when her older
daughter and Jed's older son came out and
stood to one side waiting for her to acknowledge them. She saw no point in dragging it out. "What can we do for you?"

"We would like to have a talk with you,
Mother," Heather said formally.

Kit smiled and stood and excused herself, bending to whisper into Constance's
ear as she went by, "Remember, you were
their age once."

Constance did not make it easy for
them. She stared off across the baked
prairie, pretending to be deep in thought,
until Bret Adams cleared his throat.

"Mrs. Waldron? May we have a word
with you, please? If you're up to it, I mean.
I'm willin' to wait but Heather wants to do
it now."

"My daughter has an impatient streak,"
Constance said. "You'll see it when you're
not blinded by the light."

"What light, ma'am?"

Constance felt a twinge of remorse.
"Nothing. Ignore me. I'm never at my best
when I feel as if I've been run over by a
wagon. What can I do for you?"

"I think you know, Mother," Heather

said in her polite but aggravating manner. "But we will spell it out for you if you like."

Bret glanced at her. "Be nice, will you?" To Constance he said, "I would like your permission to court her."

"Why ask me? It's her father you should talk to. And I would imagine your father might want a say, too."

Heather answered for him. "They're not here and you are. They might not be back for weeks yet. We want your permission so there won't be any hard feelings."

"In other words," Constance translated, "you want my permission so you don't need to hide in sheds and skulk around behind my back hoping I won't notice." She sighed and leaned her head back. "I wasn't born yesterday, Heather."

"I never said you were. But I'm sixteen now and that's old enough, and Bret is seventeen, and we're in love."

There it was, Constance thought. She could have said that sixteen was still a child and seventeen was not a man and that neither of them had any idea what love was, but Kit was right. She had been sixteen once herself.

"My intentions are honorable, Mrs. Waldron," Bret said. "I would never do anything to shame her or hurt her."

"I'm tired of the skulking, as you call it," Heather stated. "You taught us better than to do things behind your back."

Constance stared into the distance. She suddenly felt older than she had felt five minutes ago. She had always known this day would come but she had assumed it would be a while yet. She should have known.

"Will you *please* say something, Mother?" Heather asked.

Bret nudged Heather's arm. "I told you we should wait. Let's leave her be, Hetty. She needs her rest."

Constance looked at them and saw herself and Tom in her father's parlor, Tom with his hat in hand and she as nervous as a cat in a room full of rocking chairs. "Hetty?" she said.

Bret blushed. "It's my special name for her, ma'am. One only the two of us use. Sort of short for Heather."

"I call him Bretty," Heather said and clasped his fingers.

"Well," Constance said. It summed up her feelings quite nicely. But rather than say what she was really thinking and possibly hurt their feelings, she remarked, "I daresay I know two men who will be shocked out of their boots when they return."

"Not my pa," Bret said. "He had a notion how I felt about her before he left and never said I couldn't."

"My father will take it well, too," Heather predicted. "Just before he left, he told me that I'm not his little girl anymore but a grown woman."

Constance suppressed a grim. The young never realized how young they were until they reached middle age, when they could look back on their silliness from a higher rung on the ladder of maturity.

"What about you, Mother?" Heather said. "You haven't told us how you feel. Do we have your approval or not?"

Choosing her words carefully, Constance replied, "My father raised horses. When a colt was born, it was kept in a stall with its mother. Then he would put them in the corral, where the colt could prance around as colts like to do. Later still, he would put them in the pasture and the colt would run with the other horses. Eventually the colt would grow to where it could fend for itself."

"What's your point?" Heather asked. "I'm no colt."

"My point is that there comes a time in everyone's life when they step out on their own. You want to open the gate and run free, and I can't blame you for being true to the call of human nature."

Heather pursed her lips, then smiled sweetly at Bret. "Would you mind if I talked to my mother alone?"

"Not at all. I'll be inside. Give a holler if you want me."

The moment the doors closed, Heather was in front of the rocking chair with her hands on her hips. "All right, Mother. What was all that business with horses really about? And how do you honestly and truly feel about Bret and me?"

"Do you love him?"

"Yes. Sure. Of course," Heather declared. Then she said with slightly less conviction, "I think I do. Why?"

"Courtship is not to be taken lightly. He wants your hand in marriage. He wants to spend the rest of his life with you, for better or for worse."

"Yes. So?"

"Are you ready to make that big of a commitment?" Constance asked. "To devote your heart and soul to him for as long as you shall live?"

"I won't know that until we've spent more time together," Heather said. "But isn't that what courting is all about? To get to know the other person? To find out if

272

they're as special as you think they are?"

"Just so your marriage isn't engraved in stone," Constance said.

"What do you take me for?" Heather leaned down. "You've always taught me to stand up for myself and do what I think is right. Well, I think this is right. But you also taught me not to let life box me in. Remember those stories you would tell about Grandmother? How she never really liked Grandfather but married him because it was expected of her and she spent her entire life miserable?"

Constance nodded.

"I don't want to be like her. I don't want to spend my days in a prison I can't escape. I'll court Bret, but if it doesn't work out, it doesn't work out." Heather smiled. "Someone I look up to has showed me how to do things right and I try to follow in her footsteps."

Constance felt her eyes misting and coughed and looked away. "Perhaps I've misjudged you. Or perhaps it's just that no mother ever really wants her little girl to grow up and face all the hardships and heartaches she's faced."

"Life isn't always easy. Isn't that what you've told me a million times?"

"I didn't think you heard me," Constance

said, and suddenly Heather was hugging her and she was choked with emotion.

After a while Heather remarked, "Bret really is sweet, and so considerate. He always treats me like a lady."

"A man who will do that is a man who respects you, and a man who will respect you is a man who won't ever beat you or curse you or generally make your life miserable. I've known too many women who regret saying, 'I do.' Don't be one of them."

"I told Bret he has to court me for two years before he can propose," Heather revealed. "That should give me enough time to really get to know him, don't you think?"

"More than enough," Constance said and tenderly took hold of both of her daughter's hands. "I'm sorry for doubting you. For thinking you were being rash and headstrong. You're smarter than I was at your age."

"Mother?"

"Yes, dear?"

"If it works out, I'll have your blessing, won't I? You'll be there for our wedding?"

"Need you ask? Just promise me one thing."

"Anything. Name it."

"When your father returns, let me talk to him first. That way, Bret will live longer."

They both laughed.

22

The trail was ridiculously easy to follow. The cattle had carved a path forty feet wide, enabling Jed Adams to move a lot faster than those he was following. He rode grimly, an avenging angel on horseback, although he had never thought of himself as a particularly vengeful man. But this morning he burned with bloodlust. The vicious beating Tom had suffered and the rustling of the cattle they had spent so many weeks toiling so hard to acquire screamed out for justice.

Jed must always keep in mind that he was outnumbered. But he had his Morse carbine and the Smith and Wesson revolver Kit had given him the night before they left Vinegar Flats. An odd name, he thought, for the place to be called, and it occurred to him that he had never asked her why. When he got back, if he got back, he would.

Jed wouldn't delude himself. The men he was after knew the country better than he did, and they would be on the lookout for pursuit. He must exercise extreme care.

If they had pushed the cattle all night, and the signs indicated they did, then they had an eight- or nine-hour lead. But the cattle would slow them down. The herd wasn't trail broke, as Bob called it. The longhorns had taken to being bunched but they were not fond of being driven, and their independent natures would spur the wildest of them to make breaks for cover now and again. If the rustlers didn't want to lose any, they would be forced to round up the strays, causing repeated if brief delays. Or so Jed hoped.

It was shortly after ten in the morning, by Jed's battered old pocket watch, when he happened to gaze ahead into the timber to the left of the broad trail and caught a brief gleam, the telltale glint of the sun off metal midway up a tree. Old instincts took over, instincts he had not relied on since the war.

He wasn't in rifle range yet but he soon would be. His head bent as if he were intent on the tracks, he watched the tree from under his hat brim, seeking the bushwhacker who had to be there. Sure enough, a silhouette presented itself. A man was perched in a fork, rifle ready, waiting.

Suddenly spurring Hickory, Jed galloped left toward the woods. He was ten yards from cover when the rifle banged, a waste of lead since the shot kicked up dirt well short of Jed and his mount. It told him something. No self-respecting soldier would fire when the target was out of range. Whoever he was up against had no military training and knew next to nothing of tactics. He, on the other hand, had learned from some of the best cavalry commanders the South had, and the South had a lot of good ones, men of dash and daring and brilliance in combat.

The instant Jed was under cover he reined sharply toward the tree the man had chosen. He wove Hickory through the brush with a skill that had impressed Three Fingers Bob, and it took a lot to impress the former Ranger.

Jed left the carbine in its saddle scabbard. The undergrowth was thick, and he would be on the man before he had a clear shot. For that, the revolver would suffice. He thumbed back the hammer and held it so the barrel pointed straight up, as he had been taught, controlling Hickory with light pressure from his legs, also as he had been taught, his gaze fixed on the tree and not anything else, as he had been taught.

The would-be killer fired again but the intervening branches deflected the bullet or stopped it because Jed never heard it hit anywhere near him. He rode faster, never in a straight line for more than few yards, reining right and left and back again. And then the rifle cracked and a slug buzzed past his ear and he was close enough now to see the man in the fork frantically trying to reload an old muzzle loader.

Jed fired and thumbed back the hammer and fired again. The figure stiffened and clutched at its chest and toppled, plummeting head-first to the hard earth. Jed reined to a stop near the body, the Smith and Wesson extended, but another shot wasn't needed. A glance assured him there were no others nearby, and he swung lithely from the saddle.

The man lay facedown. With the toe of a boot, Jed rolled him over and frowned.

The tattered clothes, the grimy features, the bare feet, pegged him as a local, the same breed as Tobias Secarth. A troubling notion popped into Jed's head. He left the man and the man's rifle lying where they had fallen and climbed back on Hickory, the saddle creaking under his weight. "I hope to God I'm wrong," he said aloud and spurred his mount on.

Jed returned to the trail. Now he was very wary. If they had tried an ambush once, they might try it twice. Or maybe their confidence in the man in the tree was such that they would think they could take it easy. Predicting was hard, since they were amateurs.

By noon the freshly churned earth and equally fresh droppings warned Jed he was close. He slowed, the carbine in his hand. Tendrils of rising dust made him slow even more. The sounds came next, of cattle on the move and of men coaxing them on with occasional shouts and whoops.

Then the trailing edge of the herd was in sight, with a lone figure on foot in their wake, flapping his arms now and then and hollering. Another ragged man in rags, barefoot and armed with a rifle.

Five or six, Tom had said, but there might be more. Jed did not see the others yet but no doubt some were flanking the herd and there were bound to be one or two riding point.

A cold fury seized him. Jed had worked long and hard to gather up those long-horns. Those cattle were the key to his future, to his new life as a rancher, to the welfare of his family and of his partner's. The men who had stolen them, who had left one of their own to kill him from hiding, did not deserve mercy.

Three Fingers Bob had been right, as he almost always was. Maybe it came from being a Ranger. There were no more capable men anywhere.

But now Jed forgot about Bob and he forgot about Tom and he forgot about everything except what he had to do. He was close enough to see the swishing tails of the longhorns and the puffs of dust that rose from under their hooves. The man bringing up the rear had not yet noticed him yet. His mistake.

Jed bent forward and charged. At a gallop he bore down on the rustler, wedging the carbine's stock to his shoulder. There was a trick to firing at the gallop. He had to hold the upper half of his body as still as he could and his arm as rigid as iron and, at the moment he fired, center the sights on the target.

The man heard him. The man turned. Surprise slowed his reflexes and he was slow to bring up his rifle.

Jed's carbine cracked.

The rustler staggered but got off a wild shot that missed; then he turned to run. He had only taken a few steps when Hickory slammed into him. The man sailed a half dozen feet and crashed to earth.

Jed rode up to him. The man was still alive but the hole in his chest hinted it would not be for long. Dark blood flowed, from the hole and from the corners of his mouth. His lips moved feebly. "You weren't — You weren't —" That was all. The rustler died with a puzzled expression on his dirty face, his last breath ending in a convulsion.

Jed did not linger. He fed a cartridge into the carbine and reined toward the right side of the herd. The shot had not spooked the cattle, as he had feared it might, but that was Bob's doing.

Weeks ago, on a sunny afternoon, Three Fingers Bob had gone over to the cattle they had collected at that point and began banging two pans together. When Jed asked what in the world he was doing, the old man explained that the longhorns had to become accustomed to being around humans, to the loud noises people made, so they were less apt to spook. From then on, once a day or so, the old Ranger would bang pans together until the more skittish of the longhorns got used to it.

Jed had thought Hazelton was loco, as Texans liked to say, but now Bob's efforts paid off. The other rustlers were bound to have heard the shot and would be ready for him. He swept around the right flank, Hickory going full-out, alert for the flanker who had to be there. Another instant and Jed saw him, on one of their stolen horses, another filthy scarecrow of a man in rags. This one had Tom's Sharps, and he was quick to snap it to his shoulder and fire. But he did so one-handed and the recoil snapped his arm. Predictably, he missed. Jed didn't. His answering shot smashed the man back but the rustler did not go down. Wheeling the stolen horse, he fled.

Not once during the war had Jed ever shot a man in the back. Others did. Some members of his company took special delight in shooting down fleeing Yankees. But not him. War was hell and war was brutal but war without honor wasn't war at all — it was slaughter for the sake of the slaughter. He refused to stoop that low. A man had to have some honor, even when up to his waist in the blood of his enemies.

But this wasn't war and the rustlers weren't enemy soldiers. They were thieves and murderers. They did not deserve to be treated honorably because they had no honor.

Jed shot the man in the back. He aimed

squarely between the shoulder blades and the rustler flung out his arms and toppled. He was dead when Jed reached him, and Jed did not stop. He would come back for the Sharps and the horse.

The cattle were slowing.

Jed rose in the stirrups and saw two more riders out in front. They spotted him and yelled to each other words he could not quite catch over the pounding of Hickory's hooves. Then they reined toward the flank, coming after him.

Jed swerved Hickory into the vegetation. He sought a convenient patch of shadow and stopped. There was a trick to fighting in timber, too. He had been taught to always use the shadows to best advantage and stay as motionless as the trees around him until the moment came to move.

The rustlers came on fast. They thought he was fleeing and it made them reckless.

Jed shot the first one in the head. The second one fired in his direction but did not know exactly where he was and the shot went wide. Jed fixed his sights on the man's face, but the shock of recognition froze his trigger finger. He aimed at a shoulder instead, and down the rider went.

The rustler was on his belly, crabbing toward the rifle he had dropped, when

Hickory trotted out of the brush. "I wouldn't, if I were you," Jed said.

Tobias Secarth looked up into the carbine's muzzle. His teeth were clenched and blood was seeping from his wound.

"Why?" Jed asked. "After we let you keep that cow? Why would you take part in this?"

Bitter laughter spilled from Secarth's throat. "Take part, hell! I planned it, you damned Reb!"

"You what?"

"I stole that cow to draw one or two of you off, and it worked. When you and the old man showed up, I kept you at my place long enough for my friends to steal your herd. It worked like a charm."

"You invited us to supper so you could stab us in the back?" Jed was stunned not at the treachery, but that he had been so gullible.

Tobias Secarth grinned. "I should thank you for makin' it so easy. You're a lot more trustin' than that old Ranger."

Jed still did not quite understand. "With all the wild cattle around for the takin', why steal ours?"

"To sell, why else? I can get twenty dollars a cow in Houston, twice that for bulls." Tobias grimaced and swore. "You

284

weren't supposed to catch up. I left Willy to take care of whoever came after us."

"How many others have you done this to?" Jed wondered.

"More than a few," Tobias admitted. "But this is the most we've ever taken. Sellin' all these critters will keep my family in money for years to come."

"But that won't be enough, will it? You'll steal more if you live, you and your friends."

Tobias forgot himself and shrugged, then groaned and swore some more. "Don't act so high and mighty. You're no better than me. Not wearin' that uniform, you're not."

"Meanin'?" Jed was debating what to do. He knew what Three Fingers Bob would do but he wasn't Bob.

"Meanin' you fought for the South. Meanin' you killed to keep the blacks as slaves. Meanin' I'm no more of a sinner than you are."

"I don't murder. I don't steal," Jed said.

"You never shot any Yankees? That's pretty much the same as murder, ain't it? You never went hungry and had to forage for food? That's the same as stealin', ain't it?" Tobias shook his head. "No, you're no different than me, except you did it all nice and legal because there was a war on."

Jed resented the comparison. "It's not what we do. It's why we do it that counts. I did what I did to protect the South, not out of greed." He noticed Secarth's dark eyes flick beyond him and back again, and a sly grin curled Secarth's mouth.

It struck Jed that once again he was being played for a fool. That Tobias was trying to keep him talking so he wouldn't catch on that another rustler was skulking toward him with the intent of shooting him in the back. He started to whirl just as a gun went off, but there was no searing pain. The rustler who had been about to shoot him was crumpling with part of his forehead blown away.

Out of the trees rode Three Fingers Bob, his smoking revolver in his hand. He drew rein next to Tobias and said, "I figured you had a hand in this."

"What are you doin' here?" Jed found his voice. "You're supposed to be takin' care of Tom."

"He was worried sick about you," Bob said. "He nagged and nagged until I had to come to spare my ears. It's a good thing, too. Another second and you would be pushin' up wildflowers."

"I still don't think you should have left Tom alone."

"Take it up with him," the ex-Ranger said. "As it is, the two of us can bring the herd back that much faster." He wagged his revolver at Tobias Secarth. "What do you want done with this bastard?"

"He has a family, remember?"

"When will you learn, Reb? Those high-falutin notions of yours will get you killed one day. As for this piece of trash," Three Fingers Bob said, and shot Tobias through the head. Brains and blood splattered the legs of their horses.

Jed did not criticize the old Ranger. It had to be done, whether he admitted it to himself or not.

"Now then," Three Fingers Bob said, "do you want to ride point or drag?"

23

A lot of things Tom Waldron had not thought were possible had become so.

First, who would ever imagine he would become partners with a Johnny Reb. Second, that their crazy scheme to gather up wild cattle from the Nueces River country and bring them to the Guadalupe Mountains would work. Third, that they could start building their homes before winter set in. And fourth, that he would be happier than he had ever been in his entire life. But he had, and it did, and the Adams cabin and his own log ranch house were well under way, and he woke up every morning with a newfound sense of purpose and more energy than he knew what to do with.

His outer wounds from the beating healed but not the inner ones. Every time he relived the incident in his mind, relived being jumped from behind and savagely struck again and again, he would feel fury such as he had never known and vow nothing like that would ever happen to him again.

They had been back a week when they heard about Mort Sayer. Why the women waited so long to tell them, Tom could not begin to guess. It was one of those unfathomable female things, with which the children went along.

Now it was late November, and Tom was gazing out over the valley on a brisk early morning and reflecting that two of those "children" weren't really children anymore. Heather and Bret had become inseparable, or as inseparable as Constance would allow. They were forever holding hands and whispering to each other and doing all the things young couples in love always did.

Initially, Tom was not so sure he approved. Bret was a fine young man — there was no disputing that — but Tom had always imagined his older daughter marrying someone more substantial. Still, he did not say anything. Constance was of the opinion the romance should run its course, and that if they came out against it, Heather would want to be with Bret that much more.

"She'll fight us tooth and nail," his wife predicted. "At her age, anything we want, she'll want the opposite."

But she can do better, Tom almost said.

"The wise thing to do is to do nothing," Constance stressed. "If it is true love, nothing we do will keep them apart."

Tom had never been a big believer in the notion that a man and a woman were destined to be together. That a person had one true love and one true love only. To him, two people met and grew to like each other and the like grew into love. It could just as well happen with someone else. Circumstance, more than heavenly design, accounted for the union of a man and a woman. Years ago he had brought up the subject with Constance and she had been so appalled at his outlook that he never brought it up again.

Two riders appeared lower down. Bret and Heather were making a circuit of the valley. They had volunteered to check the cattle each day, but they weren't fooling anyone.

And they weren't the only ones smitten by one another. Jed was spending almost as much time at Vinegar Flats as he was at the Bar G. Twice now Kit had stayed overnight at the Adams cabin in an extra bedroom Jed claimed he built just in case someone came to visit.

Constance was tickled by all the love in the air. She was hoping for a spring wedding and was annoyed that Jed had not proposed yet.

"What's gotten into you?" Tom asked after she brought it up one night. "Why have him rush things just so you can have an excuse to buy new dresses for you and the girls? Marriage isn't something to be taken lightly."

His comment had not gone over well.

Now, gazing at the clusters of cattle scattered the length of the valley, Tom turned his attention to more practical matters. They had yet to brand their stock. Three Fingers Bob insisted it must be done, and they had asked Bob if he would do the honors and Bob said he would, but ever since they got back, the old Ranger spent every waking moment with his mouth glued to a bottle.

"He's a strange one," Jed remarked the last time they talked about it. "He never touched a drop the whole time he was helpin' us gather a herd, but now he won't sober up if we got down on our knees and begged."

"It's as if he's making up for lost time," Tom had said. Which was a shame. He'd grown to really like the old-timer. To like and respect him. "He must have more inner demons than we suspect."

291

"We'll give him another week," Jed proposed. "If he hasn't given up the liquor by then, we'll step in."

The week was about up, and Tom had to wonder just how Jed planned to go about weaning Bob off the tarantula juice, as Bob was fond of calling it.

A dress rustled behind him, and a warm hand clasped his. "Isn't it beautiful?" Constance said, inhaling the chill air deep into her lungs. She loved the valley, loved how the aspens on the surrounding mountains had changed colors as summer gave way to autumn, loved watching eagles soar high in the sky. "I never want to move again as long as I live."

"Shouldn't we give it a while before we make a decision like that?" Tom asked. "We haven't even sold our first cow yet."

"Everything will work out," Constance said confidently. "I'm sure of it." She raised his hand to her lips and kissed it. "Admit it. You love it here."

Tom was trying to remember the last time she had kissed him when they weren't behind a closed door.

"Our new home," Constance said with a bob of her chin. "All we could ever hope for. I must admit I had reservations. I was worried sick we made a mistake. But you were right to want to come west."

Tom switched to trying to remember the last time she had said he was right about something. It had been a while.

"Christmas is only a month off," Constance mentioned. "What do you say to inviting Jed and his boys and Kit and Bob over to exchange gifts and drink hot cider?"

"The last I looked, we're short on apple trees."

"Kit has some cider we can buy. And maybe some pretzels and Saratoga chips. And peanut brittle and taffy for Sally and Pitney. Gingersnaps, too."

"I must be a millionaire and not know it."

"Cut it out. You'll have as much fun as everyone else." Constance couldn't wait. Back in Ohio they rarely went to social functions except for a few church socials. Tom was not one for mingling with others. "I'll bake a few pies and tea cakes."

"Whatever you want, dear," Tom said dutifully. When she got like this, it was best to go along with whatever she wanted. "Let's go in. I could use a cup of coffee."

Constance started to turn but stopped. "I wonder what that's about?"

Bret and Heather were across the valley,

riding hard for the Adams cabin.

"Maybe she forgot her shawl," Tom said.

They went inside. The house would eventually have eight rooms but for now only the main room was near complete and two others had walls and beds but that was about it. It was hard work, chopping and sawing and trimming and planing, but the reward was worth the sweat. Kit had ordered nails and Tom had about used up his first batch. He must ask her to get more.

In a corner of the kitchen sat the stove they had lugged west. Beside it sat a box of wood. Tom kindled the fire still warm from breakfast while Constance filled the coffeepot with water from a bucket and put the pot on to boil.

"I hope our window glass arrives by January," Constance said, gazing into the main room at the large window. "Kit says not to get our hopes up, though. That it could take up to six months."

An old blanket, which Tom had folded in half and tacked to the wall, kept the chill out, but it would not suffice once the weather turned really cold. Either they must install a glass pane or he would have to board the window over until spring.

"It would be wonderful to sit here in the comfort of our home and look out over our valley," Constance said. There were so many things she was looking forward to, so much that had to be done.

Tom sat at the table. He rarely took time off like this to talk. Pushing out another chair, he motioned, and his wife came over and sat next to him and giggled like a girl of ten.

"I'm so excited all the time. Does that make any kind of sense?"

"I feel the same way," Tom said. The slow pace at which the work was proceeding didn't suit him. He liked to get a job over with quickly. But it took time to build a house and time to do all things they planned for the valley. For the Bar G.

"Kit was telling me three wagons stopped at her store last week," Constance mentioned, "bound for Santa Fe or somewhere near there. She advised them it was too late in the year for traveling that far but they wouldn't listen."

"Some people just have to learn things the hard way," Tom said, then brought up what was uppermost on his mind. "Answer me true. How do you feel about this whole business with Bret Adams?"

"I beg your pardon?" Constance stalled. She had been quite surprised when he did not say much after Heather broke the news to him. Heather took it for granted he had no objections to the courtship, but Constance knew him better.

"Do you still think we should put a stop to it?"

Constance spoke her mind. "It's a little late to be asking that now, isn't it? The time to say something was the day she told you, right after you returned from the Nueces River country."

"I wanted time to think about it," Tom explained, "to come to terms with my feelings."

"And now you're saying you don't approve?"

Tom fidgeted in his chair. "Look, I like Jed. I never thought I would say that about a Reb, but we went through a lot gathering up the herd, and I know I can trust him. And Bret is a fine enough boy."

"But?" Constance said when he paused.

"But I can't help thinking Heather could do better." Tom held up a hand when Constance went to speak. "Hear me out. Please. Yes, Bret is well mannered and cares for her. But what will he amount to later in life? Can he give her a fine house and all the other things she deserves? We don't want her to spend all her days poor, do we?"

"Thomas Waldron," Constance said, "I never thought I would see the day when you would be so petty."

"I shouldn't worry about our daughter's future?"

"Don't put words in my mouth. You know perfectly well what I mean. So what if they don't have a cent to their name? Did we, when we were their age? They're no different than any other young couple. It's not what they have *now* — it's what they will build for themselves as the years go by."

"You do realize they probably won't stay here? That as soon as they are married, he'll drag her off somewhere? Jed thinks we can bribe them with land but I'm not so sure."

"Honestly. You would think we were supposed to keep leashes on them, the way you talk. They have to court for two years to earn our approval, remember? By then they'll be old enough to do whatever they please, go wherever they want."

"It's not their ages," Tom said, "it's the thought of never seeing her again."

Constance blinked and pursed her lips and in a little bit said, "I'll miss her, too, if it comes to that. But there comes a time when every hatchling flies the nest. Some don't fly that far. Others do. Whether they do or they don't do is entirely up to Heather and Bret. We have to abide by their decision, whatever it is."

"Sometimes you can be so damned reasonable, it's annoying," Tom commented.

"Look at us? Are we living where my parents wanted us to live? Or your parents? They would much rather we were in Ohio than in the hinterlands of Texas."

"That's different," Tom said. "We had already lived there a good many years before we decided to move."

"You decided," Constance amended. "I was perfectly content on the farm. But I came along, didn't I? I'm doing my best to help your dream of owning a ranch come true."

"I never said you weren't."

"And do you know why I am?" Constance asked. "No, don't answer. It should be obvious. I took you for better or for worse. In my mind, Texas was worse, but I love you and try to respect your wishes, so I bit my lip and didn't say anything, and here we are. And yes, I admit I love it here. I admit you weren't as crazy as I thought." She smiled to lesson the sting.

"By crazy you mean selfish? Well, I guess I was, uprooting us like that. But I don't see what our situation has to do with

Heather and her gallant Southern beau."

"Don't you? My point was that there is no predicting what a married couple will do or how things will turn out. All we can do is give them our blessing and pray they live a long and happy life together."

Tom hated being at fate's whim. At moments like this, he had the vague and uneasy feeling that no one ever truly had a say in how their life unfolded.

Soon the coffee was done, and Constance filled their cups and they sat sipping and talking about the thousand and one things that needed to be done. The unfinished kitchen was warm and cozy and they savored the moments they were sharing. Then hooves drummed outside and someone was hammering on their front door, and Tom hurried to open it.

"Saddle up, pard," Jed Adams said. Behind him on their horses were Heather and Bret and even Pitney. "We've had some visitors we didn't know about."

"Visitors?" Tom said quizzically, and fear spiked through him at the memory of how close he had come to losing Constance to Comanches. "Indians, you think?"

"Apparently not, but we'd best go have a look-see." Jed turned to climb back on Hickory.

Constance stepped past Tom. "Heather, I want you to stay. It's not safe with strangers about until we know who those strangers are."

"Ah, Mother," her oldest groused. "Bret and I were the ones who found the tracks. I'll be all right."

Tom was on the verge of informing her that, until she was married, she would continue to do as they wanted, when Jed made a remark that nipped her protest in the bud.

"Do as your ma says. And, Pitney, you climb down, too. I want you here where you'll be safe. I have a bad feelin' about this, and if I'm right, we're in for trouble."

24

Four riders had entered the valley from the south and ridden far enough up the west side to view both homesteads from a bordering slope. Jed discovered where they had lain for hours, their horses concealed among some boulders. "They were spyin' on us," he deduced.

"Indians?" Tom said, still worried about Comanches.

"No, the horses are shod." Jed roved the area, intently scouring the ground. "Look at this," he said and picked up the stub of a long, thin cigar. He sniffed it and broke it in half and rubbed the pieces between his fingers. Then he hunkered and ran a hand over several hoofprints. "They rode out of here sometime late yesterday. Slipped down to the stream first to water their horses."

"Which is where Heather and me found their tracks, Pa," Bret said. "We came to tell you right away."

Jed threw down the pieces of cigar, and frowned. "They went out of the valley the way they came in. Scouts, most likely, sent ahead to find out what they could about us."

"Scouts for whom?" Tom said, perplexed. "What do you know that I don't?"

"There's been word Vasco Cruz has drifted north of the border," Jed informed him. "The Mexican army was nippin' at his heels and he needed to get out of Mexico for a while."

"Where did you hear this?"

"From Kit. She heard it from a parson who heard it from a couple of Texas Rangers who are huntin' for Cruz south of here."

"And you didn't say a word to me?" Tom was stunned. "You didn't think it important? Cruz is the scourge of northern Mexico. They say he's murdered dozens. The Mexican government is offering five thousand pesos for his head on a platter."

"How was I to know Cruz would come this way?" Jed justified his lapse. "Or find our valley?" He abruptly bent down. "What's this? I've seen it before." He held up a small silver crucifix on a broken silver chain. "That parson who went through Vinegar Flats wore one just like it."

"Lots of people wear crucifixes," Tom reminded him.

"But not with the initial H.B. engraved on the back. The name of that parson was Harry Baker. He was comin' east, headed for Houston. I guess he never made it. I bet he was the one who told Cruz about us."

"How do you reach that conclusion?"

"I talked to him down at the emporium. I told him all about the Bar G and our plan to have a big ranch one day."

Tom glanced at the tracks. "We're still only guessing. There might be a perfectly simple explanation for all this."

"It's a damn good guess," Jed said. "Vasco Cruz got his hands on the parson and learned about us so he sent some of his men to see if the parson told the truth."

Tom hoped not. To a bloodthirsty bandit like Cruz, two gringo families with women and possessions and a large herd of cattle in a remote valley would be too tempting to pass up.

Young Bret could see it, too. "Didn't Kit tell us Cruz has a dozen or so guns ridin' with him, Pa? What will we do if the whole gang shows up?"

"We could invite them in for tea," Jed said, "but I doubt they're all that sociable. Cruz would just as soon kill us and steal all we own."

"And take our herd and sell it," Tom said. "Putting an end to the Bar G before it has really begun." He gazed down the valley. "We have to do something. We can't just sit here waiting for the ax to fall."

"What do you suggest?" Jed asked. "Send for the Texas Rangers? To hear Three Fingers Bob tell it, they're aren't enough of them to go around, and they would need proof it really is Cruz before they would come. Even then, all they can do is wait around for him to strike, and they can't wait forever."

"Army troops, then."

"From where? Fort Quitman was abandoned during the war. Fort Stockton was burned down and is being rebuilt. Fort Bliss has troops but they never send patrols this far into the Guadalupe Mountains."

"They have to protect us," Tom insisted.

"We're not the only settlers in these parts," Jed said. "Why should they give us special attention?" He shook his head. "There ain't much the army could do, anyway, unless Cruz was stupid enough to stay in one spot long enough for them to attack him."

"You make it sound as if it's all up to us." Tom refused to accept that. After all the hardship, after all the effort they had gone to, he was not going to stand idly by while a bandit brought their dream crashing down around them.

"We can ask Bob what he thinks we should do," Jed proposed. "If we can sober him up enough, that is." He climbed on Hickory and reined toward the valley floor. "One of us has to stay, though."

Tom agreed. "Bob likes you more than he does me, so you should be the one to talk to him. While you're gone, I recommend having your boys move in with us. Our place is bigger, and we should stick together until Cruz makes his intentions clear."

"I'll go if you want me to," Jed said, but he wasn't being entirely truthful. He would go anyway, for Kit's sake. She couldn't stay at the emporium with Vasco Cruz prowling about.

"I'll go tell Constance. Be careful. Cruz's men could be anywhere." Tom trotted off in the direction of his ranch house.

Jed hurried toward his cabin with Bret close behind. He could not stop thinking about Kit, and how Vasco Cruz might be at Vinegar Flats right that moment, doing the sort of thing bandits sometimes did to women. Belatedly, he became aware that his older boy was saying his name, and he shifted in the saddle and slowed. "What is it?"

"The bandits could already be here. Do you want me to look around for sign of them? I know the valley better than anyone."

That was true, Jed reflected. Bret had explored it from end to end and hunted every foot. "We can't risk them jumpin' you." When Bret opened his mouth to object, Jed quickly said, "Think of the women. Tom can't protect them by himself. I'm countin' on you to lend him a hand while I'm gone. No matter what, you're to keep Constance and Heather and the kids safe."

"I'll do my best," Bret vowed. "But maybe we're getting worried over nothin'. Maybe Cruz won't bother us."

"Don't get your hopes up, son. He's snake mean, this bandito. For twenty years or more he's been raidin' on both sides of the border. About three years go, accordin' to Kit, Cruz came on a wagon train out of Missouri. Six wagons, with men, women, and children. They had just sat down to supper when he and his men took them by surprise. Then Cruz had his fun."

"Tell me more," Bret said when Jed stopped.

"I don't know as I should."

"Why not, Pa? I'm pretty near a grown man. You've said so yourself. You don't need to spare me like you do Pitney."

"I reckon not," Jed admitted. "Very well. Cruz lined up some of the men and used them for target practice. He shot off their ears and their fingers and put a few other holes in them before he got around to blowin' out their brains. They were the lucky ones. The other men were tied to wagon wheels, upside down, and fires lit under them and their brains baked, Apache fashion."

"Sweet Jesus," Bret said.

"Then Cruz turned to the women. He took one into a wagon and let his men have their way with the rest, and after it was over, he slit each of their throats."

"And the children?"

"He had a boy about your age tied to four horses and torn limb from limb. A boy of fourteen was held down by several of Cruz's men and Cruz poured flour down the boy's throat, chokin' him to death."

"Didn't he spare any of them?"

"A seven-year-old boy," Jed said. "Cruz had one of his men leave the boy near a settlement so the boy could tell what had happened. Then he headed south of the border takin' all the girls along. They go for top dollar down there. Or top peso, you might say."

Bret was aghast. "Cruz sold them?"

"That's Kit's guess. He's done it before. Vasco Cruz is bad medicine, through and through, and if he's heard about the Bar G, he might figure we're easy pickin's and come to help himself."

"Can we fight that many bandits by ourselves, Pa?"

"It's either that or we tuck tail and run," Jed said. "And Cruz will still take our cattle and burn down our cabin and Tom's house."

"We can always get more cattle," Bret said. "And we can always rebuild if we have to."

"Then what? Wait around for Cruz to pay us another visit and go through it all over again?" Jed shook his head. "Either we make a stand now or we give up and go elsewhere."

"Why not take Heather and the rest east of the Pecos until Cruz drifts back into Mexico?"

"Because west of the Pecos is where we've chosen to live, and I'll be damned if I'll be run off. This is my home — *our* home — and we should defend it with our lives if we have to." Jed did not say that there was more to it, that he had grown extremely fond of Kit and could no more leave her than he could abandon Bret or Pitney.

The rest of the ride was conducted in silence. Jed scoured the surrounding mountains even though Cruz was too clever to show himself before he was ready. At the cabin he collected all their ammunition and filled a sack with jerked venison and most of the canned goods he had bought from Kit and other articles his boys and the Waldrons might need. Then he brought their spare horses around from the log corral he had built and strapped on the packs while Bret helped Pitney saddle up.

Bret was uncommonly quiet, leading Jed to ask as they were about to head across the valley, "Is something on your mind, son?"

"I've been thinkin' about what you said about Vasco Cruz. About what he did to the people in that wagon train. About what he might do to Heather if he gets his hands on her."

"Let's not forget Constance and Sally and your brother."

"I'm not," Bret said. "It's just that Heather is sort of special, if you know what

I mean, and the notion of Cruz doin' things to her or sellin' her — it scares me, Pa. Scares me more than I've ever been scared my whole life. I won't let anything happen to her. Ever."

Jed placed a hand on his older son's shoulder. "I felt the same way about your ma. It's natural not to want to see someone you love hurt. But it happens. I lost your mother."

"That was different. She came down sick. There wasn't anything you or the doctor or anyone else could do."

Pain knifed through Jed. Not physical pain, although it was as real as a punch to the gut or an uppercut to the jaw. Pain all the worse because it was pain of the heart. "That doesn't make losin' her any more bearable."

"I know," Bret said. "But that wasn't my point." He had more to say but for some reason he changed his mind and climbed on his buttermilk.

During the ride to the Waldrons', Jed made a few comments to draw his older boy into conversation but Bret always responded with a yes or a no or a nod. The boy was deep in thought about something. Jed figured he would talk about it when he was ready, and let it go.

Tom Waldron was outside waiting. He had his Sharps rifle and had put on his Union infantryman's overcoat.

Jed was a bit taken aback. He had almost stopped thinking of the Ohioan as a Yankee. Tom never wore his old uniform. Jed wore his, but only because his cavalry outfit was the only clothing he owned, which was only part of the reason. He also kept wearing it so he wouldn't forget who he was or what he had fought for and what was being done to the South by the greedy victors.

Constance heard them ride up and came outside. She didn't bandy words. "Do you really believe we're in danger, Jedidiah?"

"Yes, ma'am." Jed wouldn't lie to her. She had always treated him decently and with the utmost honesty, and he could do no less.

"Then we should all go with you," Constance said. "Give me fifteen minutes and we'll be ready."

"With all due respect, ma'am, you and the kids are safer here than we would be on the trail. Cruz might ambush us along the way. Even if we reached the emporium, it sits right out in the open plain and would be impossible to defend." The thought made Jed inwardly wince. Kit wouldn't stand a prayer. Three Fingers Bob was also there but the old Ranger was useless when he was in a drunken stupor.

"Yes," Constance said, glancing at the ranch house. "Yes, I can see that. With enough water we can hole up in there indefinitely."

Tom felt he had to contribute, so he said, "I made firing slits in the walls, like Bob recommended, in case we were ever attacked."

Eager to get going, Jed handed Tom the lead rope to the packhorses, then squatted in front of Pitney. "I have to go after Ruth Kittle. Mind your manners and do as Mr. and Mrs. Waldron tell you."

"I will, Pa," his younger son said. "You'll be careful, won't you?"

"Always," Jed said and gave him a lingering hug. Then he nodded at Bret and at Tom and touched his cap brim to Constance and mounted. He was mildly startled when Heather came up and placed a hand on his leg.

"You be careful, too, Mr. Adams."

Jed hated leaving them but it had to be done. He was tempted to ride his horse into the ground but he had the good sense not to. He pushed until midnight each night, so he shaved a half day off the journey. When Vinegar Flats materialized on the horizon, he grinned in relief. He was still grinning when he reined up at the hitch rail and wearily slid down and tied the reins. There was no sign of Three Fingers Bob, who of late had taken up residence in the shed near the corral.

Removing his Confederate cap, Jed swatted dust from his sleeves and went into the store, calling out, "Kit! It's me! I'm come to collect you!"

The response wasn't quite what he expected.

A rifle barrel was shoved at his face and a thickly accented voice said, "*Por favor.* You will so good as not to move, senor, or you will be very dead."

25

Tom Waldron watched the Confederate gray uniform dwindle in the distance. He was uneasy at being left alone to protect their families. Oh, he had Bret's help, but despite the fact the boy had proven he was more than a fair marksman, Tom was not all that confident Bret could hold his own in a fight to the death with a pack of bandits. It was one thing to want to. It was another to stand firm and fire coolly when lead was whistling past and blood was being spilled and people around you were dying.

Tom had found that out in the war. His first skirmish, he was so scared he soiled himself, then been deeply ashamed until he learned he wasn't the only one in his company who thought being shot at was a frightening experience. To his credit, he didn't break and run as some had done. Most returned later, drifting sheepishly into camp singly and in twos and threes, their heads bowed, their shame worn on their sleeves. None were punished. At the next battle, the ones who had fled were the ones who fought most bravely. He never quite understood why that should be. Their commander said it was because they had "gotten the fear out of their system."

As for Tom, he fought because he had to. Because it was required. Because if he didn't, if he stood there dumbly gaping at the onrushing line of shrieking Johnny Rebs, he would not live to see the next dawn.

He never grew to like war, as some did. He couldn't glory in the combat, in the din and the fury and the bloodletting. The best he could do was accept the fact he was a soldier and perform his duties the best he knew how.

When he was discharged, Tom felt over-whelming relief. He had vowed to himself *never again*. Never again would he put himself in a position where he must kill or be killed. Never again would he take up arms against another human being. Never again would he go through that living hell.

Then came the incident with the Co-manches, and Tom was reminded that the world was not a safe place and that, while he might have forsaken violence, others had not. Others were perfectly willing to take advantage of his desire not to harm them and harm him and those he cared for.

All Tom wanted was to be left alone to live life as he wanted without interference and without having someone out to slit his throat. But he wasn't being realistic. In the real world, people killed other people, and all their fine, noble sentiments be damned.

So there he was, once again put on the spot, once again being called on to spill blood he did not really want to spill. Tom swallowed hard and resigned himself to face what was coming.

"Anythin' you want us to do, sir?" Bret Adams asked.

Tom turned. The boy looked eager to help, to please. His brother and Sally looked scared. Heather was hard to read. His wife's brow was knit in thought, but then she was always thinking about something or other. "We need to collect as much water as we can, and chop extra firewood and store it inside. We'll also need to stock up on salted meat."

Constance stirred and said to the younger ones, "None of you are to leave the house without telling Tom or myself where you're going. And no one is to go anywhere alone. Always take someone else along. And always be armed."

"Do I get to have a gun, too?" Sally asked.

Constance looked at Tom. They had never let their younger girl so much as touch one. Heather had fired a rifle a few times, but that was all. "Do you want one?"

"Pitney has his squirrel gun," Sally said.

"We'll see," Constance hedged.

Tom wished they had more firearms. A lot more. There was his Sharps and his Starr revolver and the two rifles belonging to the Adams boys and a revolver Jed had left with them, and that was it. Not exactly an arsenal, he thought ruefully, and hoped Jed had the presence of mind to bring all the extra guns he could carry when he returned with Kit.

The next several hours were busy ones. Constance and the girls made repeated trips to the stream to fill every spare container they had with water. Bret and Pitney chopped wood and stacked it inside against the west wall until it was half as high as the ceiling.

Tom stood guard or, rather, prowled around the house and the stream and the woods, alert for sign of the bandits.

By noon they had enough water and wood, and after a short meal, Tom sent

Bret off to hunt. "We need as much meat as we can lay up. I'd go with you but one of us must be with the women at all times. Pitney wants to go, and I'll leave it up to you whether you take him."

Without any hesitation Bret said, "Keep him here. He's a fair hunter and a fair shot but he's young yet."

Tom did not mention that he had the same view of Bret. "Remember, son, they won't give you a chance if they can help it."

"I know." Bret started to turn and grinned. "That's the first time you've called me that, Mr. Waldron. Son, I mean."

The word had just sort of rolled off Tom's tongue and was not intended in any personal way. He smiled, though, then took up position where he could see the house and most of the valley and the adjoining slopes.

The wait grated on his nerves. Tom had never been the most patient person in the world. Constance liked to tease him that when the Good Lord passed out patience, he was off in the outhouse. But he was profoundly glad that the afternoon went by uneventfully. By evening he dared to entertain the thought that perhaps, just perhaps, the tracks had not been made by Vasco

Cruz's men and Vasco Cruz was nowhere around and they were taking all their elaborate precautions for nothing.

Toward afternoon Bret returned with a buck strung over the packhorse he had taken along.

"Any sign of them?" Tom asked.

"None at all. Pa says that's how it will be until they're ready to jump us. He says they're real sneaky."

Tom had to wonder how a Reb who had never been west of the Mississippi River was so knowledgeable about Mexican banditos, but that was neither here nor there. He helped lower the buck and then helped hang it from a low branch on a tree near the house.

"I'll do the carvin', if you don't mind," Bret offered.

"Be my guest." Tom never enjoyed cutting animals up. All the blood and gore and hair made an awful mess. His first time had been when he was six and his father took him to the barn to slaughter a calf. A calf he liked, a calf he had fed by hand, a calf he had petted every day. Seeing it bled and rendered had been a severe shock. Until then he had not given much thought to where the meat he ate came from. Afterward, he could never take a bite of meat of any kind without remembering that he was eating something that had once been alive and vital.

Bret had been well taught. He butchered the buck as expertly as anyone could, leaving nothing to waste. Most of the meat he sliced into thin strips and hung over a rack Tom had by the side of the house for just that purpose. Constance came out to help salt it, and soon they were joined by Heather.

"Why didn't you let me know you were back? I was working on a quilt for my mother."

Bret gestured. "Sorry. I wanted to get this done before the sun went down. I didn't mean to be inconsiderate."

Tom looked away so they wouldn't notice his grin. They had to wait two years before they could become husband and wife, yet already they sounded like they were married. Suddenly his grin died and he took a quick step, his breath catching in his throat. "Look!" he blurted.

"Dear God, no," Constance said.

There were five of them, descending to the southwest in single file. Five silhouettes of the riders and their horses. All Tom could tell was that they wore hats with exceptionally wide brims.

"They're comin' down a game trail the deer use to cross from this valley into the next," Bret said. "I've been up there a couple of times, huntin'."

"Only five," Tom said. According to Kit, Vasco Cruz had a lot more men riding with him.

"Maybe the others are comin' another way," Bret remarked.

Tom hadn't thought of that. He spun and scanned the valley but all he saw were cattle. It would be an hour before the five got there, giving them a little time yet. "Finish with the meat," he directed. "Then we'll get everyone inside and see what happens."

"Why wait?" Bret asked.

"Do you have a better idea?" Tom was trying to think if there was anything he had overlooked, anything else that needed doing. He had the nagging feeling there was.

"Let's ambush them," Bret proposed. "I know a good spot. If we do it right, we can kill all five."

Startled, Tom faced him. "And if we do it wrong, we're both dead, and Constance and the others will be at their mercy." He shook his head. "I can think of a dozen reasons why we shouldn't."

"It will work, sir," Bret persisted. "We'll

be well hid and they'll ride right into our sights."

"You hope. But you're forgetting these are bandits. Men who are quite proficient at killing. More so than you or I. They're quick on the trigger and seldom miss what they aim at."

"I don't miss much, either," Bret said, "and you were in the war."

"This isn't the same." Tom didn't try to explain. Only someone who had served would understand. He considered that the end of it; then his wife took hold of his arm.

"I think you should do as he suggests, Thomas." Constance could not believe he had refused. It was a sound idea, in her estimation, and might discourage the rest of the bandits.

"You want me to leave you and the rest here unprotected?" Tom voiced the first objection that popped into his head.

"We'll be fine," Constance said. "I'll lock and bolt the door and shoot anyone who tries to break it down or get in through the window."

"The window!" Tom exclaimed. So there was something he had forgot. "It needs to be boarded up."

"I can take care of that," Constance said.

"I'm not helpless. Or don't you remember all the things I used to do around the farm while you were off in the war?"

"I remember them fine," Tom responded, annoyed that she would take such an attitude at a time like this.

"Then off you go. Shoot to kill, and make it back to us alive."

"I had no idea you were so bloodthirsty," Tom said. She shocked him. She truly did.

"When it comes to protecting my family, I can be as ruthless as anyone," Constance said. She would do whatever it took to safeguard them, and she could not comprehend why he did not feel the same.

"I'll saddle your horse for you, Mr. Waldron," Bret offered, and dashed off toward the corral.

Angry now, Tom gripped his wife by the elbow and led her out of earshot of the rest. "Constance, how could you contradict me like that? As everyone keeps reminding me, I was in the war, not you. I should think I know what is best, and this is too dangerous to try."

"If you can stop those bandits from reaching our doorsteps, it's worth any risk. I would go myself but you're a better shot than I am." Constance studied him intently. "Really, Tom, why all this fuss? It has to be done and that's all there is to it."

It took a few moments for Tom to realize what she was implying. "Are you saying that you think I'm scared?" Any sane person would be, he reflected, but that was beside the point.

"All I'm saying is, we must fight for what is ours. This isn't Ohio, where we could run to the county sheriff for help. I should think that you, better than anyone, would realize what is at stake after what those horrible rustlers did to you."

"They caught me by surprise," Tom said, then drew himself up to his full height. "I see. You don't think I'm capable of protecting you."

"Where did you get that idea from?" Constance asked. She had not said any such thing.

"Very well. Against my better judgment, I will do as you want. If I don't make it back, do what you can for the children and pray Jed shows up before our visitors burn the house down around your ears." Tom left her with her mouth hanging open. She snatched at his sleeve but he shrugged her hand off and went inside for a box of cartridges.

The house was quiet. Tom leaned his forehead against the wall and closed his eyes. Why did life keep doing this to him?

Why must he once again put himself in harm's way when all he wanted was to live in peace? Shaking himself, he went to the cupboard and took down the box. When he turned, she was there. "I didn't hear you come in."

Constance was worried about him. "I've never seen you like this." Her intuition told her he was upset and it had something to do with the bandits.

"I'm fine."

"Sure you are." Constance wrapped her hand around his. "Something is eating at you and you won't tell me what it is."

"You wouldn't understand."

"Try me."

Tom sighed and lightly shook the cartridge box. "It's the killing, Connie. I'm sick to death of all the killing. It's childish, I know. It's not manly. But that's how I feel."

"That's all?" Constance threw herself at him and hugged him close, her cheek on his chest. "Stop being so hard on yourself. If you really don't want to go, then you really don't have to, and I won't hold it against you."

Tom didn't believe her. She would hold it against him. Worse, he would hold it against himself.

"Always remember we love you, and we'll stand by you in whatever you decide to do."

Tom waited for her to let go, then made for the front door. Bret had the horses ready. He embraced Sally and then Heather and climbed into the stirrups. He didn't hug Constance again. He merely nodded and wheeled his horse and rode off to kill some more.

26

There were six of them. Swarthy, dark-haired men with dark mustaches and dark eyes. They were dressed nearly alike in sombreros and short, tight jackets and pants that flared at the bottom. They liked belts with silver circles and wore flashy spurs a third again as big as any Jed had ever seen. Two were leaning on the bar, a bottle between them. Three were playing cards. And then there was the one who had shoved the rifle muzzle in Jed's face and was standing there coldly smirking. This last one had a powerful, stocky body and a pockmarked moon face.

"Pedro, bring the gringo over," said the bandit who had spoken before, the tallest of the card players. He had hawkish features and a thin mouth and eyes that glittered like knives. He said something in Spanish and the other bandits set down their cards.

Pedro relieved Jed of the Morse carbine and motioned for Jed to walk to the table, then touched his rifle to Jed's spine to discourage him from trying anything.

"So." The tall bandit smiled and pushed out an empty chair with his foot. "Have a seat, senor, and we will talk, you and I."

Jed found his voice. "You're Vasco Cruz, I gather."

"You have heard of me?" Cruz beamed and spoke in Spanish and the others laughed. "It is something, is it not, to be famous in one's own time? Since you know of me, it is only right that you tell me who you are, yes?"

The scourge of the border country was not what Jed expected. The courtesy and friendliness were not in keeping with Cruz's reputation as the most murderous bandit in all of Mexico.

"Although I think I already know," Cruz had gone on. "Your uniform, senor. You are the hombre who fought on the losing side during your great gringo war, are you not? Jed Adams, *sí?*"

"How is it you know my name, if you don't mind my askin'?" Jed could bear to be polite so long as Cruz was, too. But worry ate at him like acid; there was no sign of Kit anywhere.

"A man like me, senor, I must know a lot about a lot of things. How else can I stay one step ahead of the *federales* in my country and the *soldados* and Rangers in your country who would love to slip a noose around my neck or put a bullet in my brain."

"You speak very good English," Jed remarked.

Vasco Cruz tilted his head and chuckled. "For an ignorant bandit, you mean? The old priest who taught at the mission school I went to wanted to make scholars of us, I think, but I only went as far as the sixth grade."

Jed had gotten to the fifth grade, himself. As his grandpa liked to say, so long as a body could read and write and count without taking off his shoes, he could get by in the world. "That's more than I did."

Cruz laughed again. For a killer of men, women, and children, he was remarkably carefree. "Why is it you gringos always think a bandit must be *estupido* or else he would not be a bandit, eh?"

Jed had held off as long as he could. "The woman who owns this place, what have you done with her?"

"I raped her and slit her throat and had her thrown out back," Vasco Cruz said.

The blinding rage that seized Jed brought him half out of his chair. He did not care about the rifles and pistols suddenly trained on him, or the rifle barrel that gouged his back. All he cared about was choking the life from Vasco Cruz with his bare hands. But then a familiar voice cried out behind him.

"Jed! No! He's only teasing!"

Jed turned. Kit had come out of the back wearing an apron and carrying a long wooden tray laden with food. He was so happy to see her that a lump formed in his throat and he could not make his vocal cords work.

"I was fixing a meal for them," Kit explained. "Senor Cruz had promised me that so long as I behave, neither he nor his men will harm me in any way."

"That is correct, senorita," the bandit leader said graciously. "And the same will go for Senor Adams, provided he sits back down and does not commit suicide."

Jed swallowed and slowly sank into the chair. The barrel gouging his back was withdrawn and the two men at the bar holstered their pistols. "I thought you were serious," he said softly.

"Life is too short for serious, senor," Cruz remarked. "We must enjoy ourselves while we can. Make the most of it, as you *norteamericanos* say."

Jed looked at him. "You are not all what I expected."

"Ah." Vasco Cruz nodded, then glanced at one of the men at the bar and addressed him in Spanish and the man brought over the whiskey bottle and filled Cruz's glass. "You have heard the stories about me. How terrible I am. How vicious. How mean."

"I've heard a few," Jed said.

"And they are true, senor. Every one of them. I have killed many people, your kind and mine. I have shot old men who were begging for their lives and shot women who displeased me and bashed the head of a baby with a rock."

Jed remarked, "I can't tell when you're teasin' or tellin' the truth."

Cruz swallowed some whiskey and sighed. "I do not live by the rules others do, senor. Laws mean nothing to me. I do as I want when I want. If I want to kill someone, I kill them. If I want to spare them, I spare them. It is as simple as that."

"And which group do I fall into?" Jed asked. If the latter, he would die then and there, taking as many of them with him as he could before they brought him down.

Vasco Cruz pushed his sombrero back on his mop of black hair. "I have heard of this valley of yours, senor. Of you and your sons. Of the Yankee gringo and his wife and daughters. Of the cattle you have."

"And you plan to kill us and help yourself to our herd," Jed guessed.

"I could," Cruz conceded, then fell silent as Kit passed out plates heaped with thick slabs of beef and potatoes.

"I'm afraid I don't know how to cook Mexican dishes, Senor Cruz. This was the best I could do on short notice."

"It will be fine, senorita," Cruz said. "We are starved, my men and I. When you are on the run, you do not get to eat and sleep as you would like."

Jed was amazed at how calm Kit could be. She was treating the notorious killer as if he were just another customer.

"Which brings us back to you, senor," Cruz said. "But first, you will join us at our meal, eh?" To Kit he said, "Bring a plate for your friend, and you may join us, too, if you like."

For the life of him, Jed could not see why the bandit was being so friendly. "I am hungry," he admitted. He had only eaten one meal since leaving the Bar G.

"Tell me of this valley of yours, senor."

Jed did not hold anything back. He told about their families and their cattle and the cabin and the ranch house under construction and the stream that ran year-round. "But I haven't told you anything that the men you have spyin' on us haven't already told you."

"You know about them? Domingo has been careless. I must have a talk with him when next we meet." Cruz's mouth creased in an odd little smile; then he forked a piece of beef into his mouth and chewed hungrily. "But you are mistaken, senor. I sent them, yes, but I have not seen them since. What I know of you I learned from someone else."

Jed remembered the silver crucifix. "From the parson? What happened to him? Is he still alive?"

"We had a long talk, senor, that parson and I," Vasco Cruz said, "about God and the devil, heaven and hell, and what he called the wages of sin. In his eyes I was a *muy grande* sinner. Heaven was too good for vermin like me. Vermin. That was the word he used."

"That's all you did? Talk?" Jed said after Cruz ate a piece of potato and swallowed whiskey and did not seem inclined to say more.

"He was a great talker," the bandito chief said. "Telling me how there is right and there is wrong and he was right and I was wrong. So I would go to hell and he would go to heaven, and he would look down on me from up there and shake his head in pity."

Jed waited.

"He could not wait to get to heaven. He had been looking forward to it his whole life, he said. To his reward. To going through the pearly gates and being greeted warmly by God himself." Cruz smiled thinly. "Who was I, a terrible sinner and vermin, to deny him that which he wanted more than anything else?"

"You didn't," Jed said, although he knew perfectly well Cruz had.

"For a man of God, he did not die well. When I shot him in the knee he cursed me. Such language even I rarely use. When I shot him in the other knee, he stopped cursing and started whimpering." Cruz paused. "That is the word, yes? Whimpering? Sometimes I do not get them right."

"That is the word."

"Well, he did much whimpering. I shot him many more times, twelve to be exact, once for each of the apostles, and when I was done, he was crying and begging and saying he did not really want to die, after all. It was quite pitiful, senor. For a man of faith he had very little."

334

"Then you finished him off," Jed said.

"What do you take me for? We left him lying there to make his peace with the God he loved so much. I think he was a long time dying. Unless the coyotes or the buzzards found him first." Vasco Cruz laughed.

Any lingering doubts Jed had about the truth of the stories he had heard about the bandit leader vanished. Cruz was a wolf among sheep, a rabid wolf who could kill in the blink of an eye as the whim moved him. Cruz was smart, too, as his next comment proved.

"So now we understand one another better, *sí*? And you will not do anything to upset me, and you will listen to what I ask of you?"

"*You* want something from *me*?"

"In a manner of speaking. I have not come all this way for nothing. When the parson told me about you and your valley —"

"Hold on there," Jed interrupted, and then realized the risk he had inadvertently taken. He quickly said, "Sorry. But how is it the subject of me and the valley even came up?"

"A good question. He traveled widely, that parson. Saving souls. Visiting every settlement, every homestead. He mentioned yours in passing."

Jed sensed there was more to it but he did not voice his hunch.

"Anyway, your valley gave me much to think about. Very much indeed. You see, I am in need of such a place. A place where my men and I can sit out the winter. Hole up — is that how you gringos say it? We have been on the run so long that it would be nice not to run for a while. We will rest and relax and in the spring head south of the border."

Jed said grimly, "So that's it."

"I do not plan to kill you or your family. Or the Yankee gringo and his. Or the lovely senorita here. Or that old man out in the shed who is so drunk, my men could not wake him. I have no desire to kill any of you."

It was a lie. As surely as Jed was sitting there, he knew the bandit would not let them live. Oh, Cruz might promise to, but anyone who could do what Cruz had done to the parson was not someone to whom honor meant much.

Kit had not spoken since she sat down but now she asked, "What is it you want, Senor Cruz?"

The bandit chief set down his fork. "In return for my promise not to harm any of you, you must, in return, give me your word that you will not tell anyone about my men and me."

"That's all?" Kit said.

"It is no small thing, senorita," Vasco Cruz said. "We will be here two or three months, perhaps longer."

An obvious question occurred to Jed but he was not about to bring it up and give Cruz ideas. Once again he underestimated the bandit leader.

"I know what you two are thinking. Why do I not kill all of you? It is a surer way of silencing your tongues, no?" Cruz drained his glass and set it down with a contented smack of his lips. "You must put yourself in our place. The Rangers are looking for us. Your *soldados* are looking for us. I prefer they not find us." He looked at Kit. "Many people stop here, senorita. Many people know you. They would wonder where you were. Word would reach those with badges and uniforms, and I would be on the run again."

Jed was beginning to see what Cruz had in mind.

"As for you, senor, and the other gringo, you have relatives, yes? You have friends? Perhaps some will come to visit, and if you are missing, what then?"

Jed had no one who would come looking for him but he did not tell Cruz that.

"If you are left alone, senorita, and the people in the valley are left to go about their affairs as they wish, no one will suspect to look for me here. My offer, then, is this. My men and I will not touch a hair on your heads, and in return you will not tell anyone about us. Anyone at all. Simple, *sí?*"

"Simple and crafty," Kit said. "You'll be hiding in plain sight, right under the noses of those who are searching for you. I've heard you were clever but I had no idea."

Cruz indulged in a smile. "Whether your flattery is sincere or not, I thank you. A man in my position must be crafty or he does not stay in my position very long." He looked at Jed. "What do you say, man in gray? Will you and the others in your valley agree to my terms?"

"I can't speak for Tom Waldron," Jed said. "He's my partner but he makes his own decisions. All I can do is ask him for you."

"Then you may leave as soon as you want," Cruz said. "But keep two things in mind, senor. First, I will always have a man or two here with the senorita, and if you try any tricks, it will bring much unpleasantness down on her. Second, and this is more important, I will keep my promise not to harm any of you only so long as you do not harm any of us. Is this understood?"

"It sounds reasonable to me," Kit said.

"I hope you are not just saying that, senorita. I hope that you and Senor Adams and those in the valley do not betray me. It would make me *muy* mad, and you do not want to do that. I am not a nice person when I am mad."

27

It was no wonder Tom Waldron did not like waiting. During the war his company would wait around in camp for orders to move out. Then they would march to where they were supposed to go and either form up and wait for the enemy to appear or sit around waiting for orders to go somewhere else. As someone once said, military life consisted of waiting, waiting, and more waiting.

So now, lying on his belly behind a log in timber that bordered the game trail the five bandits were descending, Tom chafed at how long it was taking them and anxiously ran his hand along the cool metal barrel of his Sharps. He glanced across the game trail at the spot where Bret Adams had taken cover, but did not see him. The boy had an uncanny knack for blending into vegetation.

They had been there for more than an hour. Tom expected to hear the thud of approaching hooves any moment. Actually, he had been expecting it for some time and was puzzled by the bandits' failure to appear.

It didn't help Tom's mood any that the day had turned cloudy and brisk. Winters in Texas were not as snowy as those in Ohio but they could be as cold. The temperature had been steadily dropping. Ten degrees since they got there, he figured. His Union overcoat helped but he still would rather be back at the ranch house in a chair in front of a crackling fire in the stone fireplace Jed had helped him build.

Thinking of Jed brought Ruth Kittle to mind, and Tom wondered when they would get around to announcing they would marry. So far they acted as if they were good friends and no more, but they weren't fooling anyone, certainly not Constance, who could not stop going on about how it sweet it was, and how fitting, that Jed and Kit had found each other, and they were a perfect couple — didn't Tom think so? It was more of that "everyone had a special someone" bunk Tom wouldn't accept. He once pointed out that her true love idea had a flaw; wives were often left widows and husbands were often left widowers, and many went out and found someone new to marry. Her response? That when a person's first true love died, God, in His infinite wisdom, provided another.

Tom never ceased to be amazed at the workings of the minds of females. Their logic was beyond him. He might as well try to decipher the meanderings of the stars.

Suddenly the brush across the trail parted and out came Bret. He gazed up the mountain, then came over and squatted by the log. "I don't think they're comin', Mr. Waldron."

Stiffly rising, Tom sat on the log with the Sharps between his legs. "You could be right. Where the blazes did they get to?"

"Beats me. It's the only trail down that mountain. They must have turned back and we couldn't see them for the trees."

"But why?" Tom said.

"The only thing I can think of is that they spotted us and didn't want to ride into our gun sights," Bret speculated.

Tom said confidently, "I seriously doubt they know we're here."

A voice out of the woods disagreed. "But we do, gringo, and unless you and your young friend want to die, I suggest you stand up with your hands where we can see them. *Por favor.*"

Tom's first instinct was to jump to his feet and turn and shoot but the bandit had said "we," so all five must be out there and he would be riddled before he got off a shot. He saw Bret tense and said quickly, "Don't. We won't do Constance and Heather and the rest any good if we're dead." Moving slowly, he rose and raised his hands as he had been instructed.

After a few moments Bret followed suit but he scowled and whispered, "I hope you know what you're doin', Mr. Waldron."

So did Tom.

Spurs jingled lightly and shadows detached themselves from other patches of shadow. Four bandits came from four different points of the compass with drawn revolvers. The fifth bandit, the one behind Tom, came around in front and chuckled.

"The hunters were the hunted, eh?" He was of middling height with curly black hair and a thick mustache and shoulders as broad as a bull's.

Since the bandits did not seem disposed to kill them where they stood, Tom asked, "How did you know?"

The one who was smirking reached inside the vest he wore and pulled out a small folding brass telescope. "With this I have the eyes of an eagle, gringo. I saw you sneak to this spot and decided we would do sneaking of our own." He apparently translated for the others and they all laughed. Then he bobbed his sombrero and said, "I am

Domingo. Perhaps you have heard of me?"

"Can't say as I have, no," Tom admitted.

Domingo's mouth drooped in disappointment. "I ride with Vasco Cruz. His right-hand man is how you gringos say it."

Bret kept shifting his weight from one leg to the other and glancing at his rifle, and Domingo noticed.

"I would not, were I you, young one. Ramon, Felipe, Emilio, and Pablo would shoot you dead before your fingers touched it."

"So?" Bret said. "You're fixin' to kill us anyway."

"Not true," Domingo said. "We only watch and wait for Vasco. He will come soon, I think, now that the one in gray has gone down to Vinegar Flats. He is your *padre,* is he not? Your father?"

"How do you know that?" Bret asked.

"We have been watching your families. Only watch, Vasco told us, but let them know they are being watched."

Tom digested that mentally. "Am I to take it you deliberately left tracks where we would be sure to find them?"

"*Sí,* gringo. What better way to send the one in gray rushing to the pretty senorita he cares for?"

"My pa rode into an ambush?" Bret

tensed and was set to spring but the click of a revolver hammer dissuaded him.

"Por favor, niño," Domingo said. "Do not be in so great a hurry to die. Nothing will happen to your *padre*. Vasco only wants to talk to him. Then, if all goes well, they will come here and he will talk to you." That last was directed at Tom.

"I don't understand any of this," Bret said.

Tom decided to put Domingo's statements to a test. "Is it all right if we lower our arms?"

"Sí, gringo, and you may pick up your rifles. But do not do anything stupid. Vasco does not want you harmed, but if you try to shoot us, we can do as we please. We are quite quick with our *pistolas,* gringo, and when we shoot at someone, we hit what we aim at." Domingo twirled his revolver into his holster. He wore another on his other hip but on a separate gun belt so that the two belts crossed below his waist. Bandoleers filled with rifle cartridges crisscrossed his broad chest.

"What now?" Tom asked.

"Since you know about us," Domingo said, "we have no reason to hide. We will follow you to your *casa* — your house — and wait there for Vasco and your friend in gray. *Con permiso, por favor?* With your permission?"

Tom did not know who the bandit thought he was kidding. They were prisoners, nothing more. "Let us ride on a ways ahead. My wife might get the wrong idea and take a shot at you."

"By all means, gringo," Domingo said. "Talk to your *mujer* — your woman. But remember, if any of you shoot any of us, all of you die."

As soon as they were far enough ahead, Bret twisted in the saddle and asked resentfully, "How could you give in so easily?"

"What else would you have me do?"

"Jump them when we get the chance," Bret said. "We'll hide around the next bend and shoot them as they ride up."

"Look behind us," Tom directed, "and tell me how many you see."

Bret twisted and stiffened. "Only three. Where did the other two get to?"

"Oh, they're there, waiting for us to pull a dumb stunt like the one you want to pull." Tom shook his head. "For now we play along with them."

"I still don't like it," Bret groused.

"And you think I do?" Tom glanced back at Domingo, who grinned and gave a little wave. "Your father said you were to listen to me, remember? So keep your rifle in its scabbard."

Bret fell silent but he wore his feelings on his face the rest of the ride, and when they came in sight of the ranch house, he galloped on ahead to break the news.

Tom took his time. When he came to the clearing, he looked back again. The bandits had reined up well out of rifle range to await developments.

Constance rushed out to meet him, all flustered. "What's this Bret just told me? We're not to lift a finger against them?"

"That's the general idea," Tom said as he dismounted, "unless you don't care if Kit and Jed and Three Fingers Bob are added to the long list of people Vasco Cruz has killed."

Constance stared at the three bandits and saw two more join them. She agreed her husband had done the right thing but part of her was disappointed that he hadn't taken care of them as he was supposed to. "How did all this come about?" she asked, and after Tom explained, she said without thinking, "How could you let them sneak up on you like that?"

To Tom her question was akin to being kicked in the groin. She was implying that all this was his fault, that if he had been more alert, the bandits would not have gotten the drop on them. "They caught Bret by surprise, too."

"But he's just a boy. You were a soldier. You saw combat."

Resentment flared, and Tom said testily, "That's right. Blame me. The fact you don't have any idea what you are talking about is irrelevant."

"Thomas, please —"

"Don't talk down to me, Connie. I'm not one of the kids. And yes, I was in the war, but I wasn't a scout or a guerrilla. I was in the infantry. We marched, we shot at the Rebs, we marched some more. I wasn't taught how to have the eyes and ears of a Comanche."

"Simmer down," Constance tried again, but he wasn't listening.

"I could have resisted. I could have killed one or two. But that would leave the rest alive to come after you and the children. Maybe I'm irresponsible, but I would rather be here to protect you than lying dead in the woods." Tom stopped and took several deep breaths to steady himself.

"You are forever putting words in my mouth," Constance chided. "But I didn't mean it as an insult. I know you always do your best. It's one of your traits I admire most."

Tom was beginning to wonder if he had *any* traits she admired. Just then Bret and Heather came out of the house, giving him an excuse to hurry past Constance. "Heather, get back inside!" he said sternly, putting himself between her and the bandits to block their view. He didn't succeed. One of them whistled loudly and another made a comment in Spanish that resulted in lusty mirth.

"I just wanted a better look," Heather said.

Tom sighed. "You gave them one." Not that it made a difference. They had seen her through the telescope; they knew how pretty she was.

Bret had the stock of his rifle halfway to his shoulder. "Say the word, sir, and I'll drop one."

"And have them lay siege to the house?" Tom shook his head. "We'll behave ourselves until your father returns."

Domingo and the other bandits moved off into the timber and presently tendrils of smoke rose from the trees.

"They've started a campfire?" Constance said in surprise. It wasn't the fire that upset her; it was how close to the ranch house the bandits had camped.

"I should go keep an eye on them," Bret suggested.

"I'd rather you stay here," Tom said. "We don't want to antagonize them until we know what is going on." He added as extra persuasion, "I'm sure Heather will want you with us, too."

The mention of his beloved sent the young Southerner hurrying after her.

Tom went in last, after casting a glance at the trees. A bandit was watching them, thumbs hooked in his gun belt, the portrait of insolence. Tom closed the door and leaned his forehead against it, struggling to control an upwelling of fear for his family and of helplessness.

Tom noticed Sally and Pitney over by the fireplace, sitting on the floor, Sally with her chin on her knees and her spindly arms wrapped around her legs, Pitney with his squirrel gun across his legs. Tom went over. "Are you two all right?"

"I won't let them hurt her, sir," the boy said.

Sally raised her head. "I heard Mother and Bret and Heather talking. Do they really have Mr. Adams and Kit?"

"We don't know yet," Tom tried to set her at ease. "Until we do, neither of you are to leave the house without telling your mother or me. I mean it, Sally Ann. This isn't make-believe. None of your games like the time you hid from us back home and we had to search for you for hours, with your mother worried sick the whole time." Tom had been worried sick, too.

Pitney said, "Bret told me they might have killed my pa. Is that true?"

Tom decided to have a talk with the older boy later. "Might have and did are two different things."

"And if they have?" Pitney persisted.

"I will avenge him, I promise." Tom would try, anyway. But if the bandits made it south of the border, he would need a regiment to ferret them out. He patted Pitney's head, then walked over to his wife. She had opened the door and was staring out at the bandit. "Do you think that's wise?"

"It's not as if they don't know we're here," Constance said dryly. "We should keep an eye on them in case they were lying to you and intend to sneak up on us when our backs are turned."

"That's the spirit," Tom complimented her.

"Spirit, nothing. I just want to live to a nice old age" — Constance lowered her voice so no one else could hear — "which is looking less and less likely."

28

Jed Adams' nerves were frayed. A month and a half had gone by since he had sat down with Vasco Cruz and Tom and Constance out in the open near their ranch house. In the open, no doubt, so the eight banditos with Cruz could better protect him should there be treachery. Not that Jed would dare try anything when two more bandits were down at Vinegar Flats keeping an eye on Ruth Kittle and Three Fingers Bob.

Cruz had been brief and to the point. He repeated everything he told Jed at the emporium and then asked Jed and the Waldrons to decide.

"Do we have an agreement or not?"

What choice did they have? Jed angrily reflected. Either they accepted or they suffered the fate of the bandit leader's many other victims. So they told Cruz they would go along with him so long as Cruz kept his word.

Afterward, the bandits rode off whooping and laughing. Jed expected Cruz to have men watch his cabin and Tom's ranch house but he never caught sight of them. Nor any of the others. The bandits kept to themselves.

Two were always at the emporium, keeping an eye on Kit. Never the same two, Jed noticed, each time he paid her a visit. Kit was never bothered. The bandits drank and played cards and watched her closely when riders or wagons stopped at the store. Jed figured they were afraid she would slip a note to someone to get word to the Rangers or the army.

Since many Texans were of Mexican descent and Mexicans often came north of the border, the presence of two at the emporium did not arouse suspicion.

Jed constantly worried about Kit. He wanted to stay with her around the clock but she would not hear of it.

"Your boys need you more than I do. And Bob is always here."

The old Ranger was there, all right, but he was next to useless in his perpetual drunken state.

One evening Jed went out to the shed Bob was sleeping in, taking a pot of coffee along, and tried to sober him up. Bob took one sip and threw the cup to the ground.

"Leave me alone, damn it. I don't tell

you how to live your life. Don't butt into mine." Bob slurred every word. His eyes were terribly bloodshot, his clothes rumpled and smelly.

"Why are you doing this to yourself?" Jed had asked.

"What do you know? What do any of you know?" Then Bob had given Jed a push and picked up a half-empty whiskey bottle and sucked on it greedily.

Jed asked Kit to try to get the old man to stop drinking but she had no more luck than he had. Kit told him Bob got this way now and again, so deep in booze he was deaf and dumb and blind to all that went on around him, and there was nothing anyone could do to snap him out of it.

Jed hated leaving her there alone. Each ride up to the valley tore at his insides. So did each ride down. When he was at the emporium, he worried about his sons and the Waldrons. When he was at the Bar G, he worried about Kit.

Jed wasn't fooling himself. The bandits would turn on them eventually. After enough time passed and the army and the Texas Rangers weren't searching quite as hard and Vasco Cruz deemed it safe to return to Mexico, then Cruz would show his true nature.

Tom Waldron and Constance were holding up well. Jed visited them often to talk over the situation. They had considered taking Kit and sneaking off in the middle of the night but the risk of Cruz overtaking them was too high.

Constance wanted Tom or Jed to go for help alone. To find the Texas Rangers or any army patrol. But that could take weeks, and Cruz was bound to notice one of them was missing

So Jed and Tom did nothing. It rankled them to be so helpless. Cruz had let them keep their weapons but that only made them feel worse, for it showed that, in Cruz's eyes, they were no threat whatsoever.

The children were holding up well, too. Sally and Pitney, anyway. The two younger children went about their daily chores with their usual trusting innocence, taking it for granted their parents would protect them and things were not as bad as it seemed. Heather was a bundle of nerves. But Bret was worse.

Jed was concerned for his older boy. Bret wanted to drive the bandits from the valley or wipe them out. Never mind that there were eleven of them. Eleven heavily armed, vicious cutthroats — renegades who could ride like the wind and shoot as well or better than most other men.

Whatever else might be said about the bandits, no one could deny that Vasco Cruz and his men were experts at what they did — masters at the art of self-preservation, ten times as deadly as the rustlers Jed had dealt with down in the Nueces River country.

None of that mattered to Bret. "We can do it!" he insisted one night at the Waldrons'. "All we have to do is find out where they're camped and get close and shoot them as they climb out of their blankets."

"Would that it were that easy," Tom said.

Cruz never camped in the same place twice. The wily devil always stayed on the move. One night the bandits might be at the north end of the valley, the next night at the south end. Occasionally the smoke from their campfires could be seen. Other times, Jed came on their camps well after the bandits were gone.

"Cruz is bound to have sentries," Jed had argued. "We would never get close enough." If, by some miracle, they did, their first volley would not account for all the bandits, and the others would not rest until both the two families were dead, dead, dead.

Jed made Bret promise not to do anything, to go along with the arrangement until Jed said otherwise. Bret gave in, but he was a keg of black powder primed to explode, and Jed had to keep a constant eye on him or have Tom and Constance do it when he was down at Vinegar Flats.

Then, one afternoon, Jed rode over to the ranch house with Bret and Pitney along to talk to Tom about their cattle. "As near as I can tell," Jed said while seated at their table with a pastry in front of him, "Cruz is helpin' himself to a longhorn a week."

Tom frowned. "By spring we'll be twenty head short. But we should have plenty of calves to make up the loss." He cupped his coffee in both hands and sipped. His pastry went untouched. He did not have much of an appetite these days.

"Yes, if we still have a herd," Jed said. "Cruz won't pass up that much money on the hoof."

"I've thought of that," Tom said. "So long as he leaves our families alone, I don't care what he does with the cattle. We can always get more."

Jed remembered the heat and the long hours and the danger. "I reckon so, but I'd rather not go through that again so soon if

I can help it." He lowered his voice. "We're only foolin' ourselves. Cruz won't head for Mexico until after he's dealt with us and ours."

"Any idea how we can turn the tables on them before that happens?" Tom asked. He was at a loss, short of engaging in a gunfight they were bound to lose.

"Not yet," Jed said. But sooner or later the bandits would make a mistake. He was sure of it.

Constance came from the kitchen with a bowl of sugar and a spoon and took a chair. "Here you are, Jed, for that sweet tooth of yours."

Jed thanked her and spooned sugar into his cup. "How are you holdin' up."

"I could lie and say I'm doing fine but I wouldn't be fooling anyone," Constance said. Her mirror never lied. It had gotten so she could hardly bear to look at the lines in her face that had not been there before, at the dark bags under her eyes. Anxiety was wearing her down. A few more months and she would look like an old woman.

Suddenly there was a commotion outside, a loud outcry and then the front door flew open and Sally hollered, "Come quick! Something has happened to sissy!"

They rushed from the house. Heather was in Bret's arm, crying, her face pressed to his shirt, her fingers clenching and unclenching. At their feet lay a bucket on its side.

Constance rushed over. "What's wrong? What happened to you?" Heather's dress was intact and she wasn't bruised or bleeding.

"Oh, Mother!" She threw herself at Constance. "They were brutes! The both of them! They just stood there laughing and laughing."

"Now, now." Constance stroked Heather's hair to calm her. "Who did? Tell us all about it."

"I went to the stream for water," Heather said between sniffles. "I was at the big pool, the one we go to all the time. I was thinking how long it had been since I had a bath, and how nice it would be to take a swim."

"You didn't," Constance said.

Heather drew back. "Why not? It's the warmest day we've had in weeks." She swiped at her eyes with the end of her sleeve. "But when I was half undressed, I heard someone laugh. Two of those bandits were watching me. So I put myself together and ran home."

"That's all?" Tom said. Here he thought her virtue had been violated or something equally horrendous.

"Isn't that enough?" Heather rejoined. "Don't you understand. They were *looking* at me!"

"You shouldn't have done it," Constance said. "Going there alone is bad enough. But to take a swim!"

"How can you blame me?" Heather squealed, and turned to Tom. "You'll do something, won't you? Make them go away? I can't stand it anymore! I just can't!" Of all of them, she was enduring the strain the worst. Where formerly she had been as pretty and vital as any girl could hope to be, now her face was worn and tired, and she constantly complained that she couldn't get a decent night's sleep.

"Where are the two who were watchin' you?" Bret demanded. "I'll go do what we should have done long ago."

"You're going nowhere," Jed said. "Harm them and the rest will be on us like starvin' wolves."

"They ogled her, Pa!" Bret practically shouted. "We can't just sit here and do nothin'!"

Constance intervened, saying, "If all they did was stare, and she still had most of her clothes on, no real harm was done."

"Mother, how can you say that?" Heather was horror-struck. "I'm your own daughter."

"And you!" Bret said to Jed. "If it were Ma, you would be out for their hides. I still remember that time in Charleston when a man whistled at her and you beat him within an inch of his life."

Jed had been about to demand that his older boy start acting his age, but his son had a point. He never stood for anyone, anywhere, anytime treating Melanie with anything less than the respect she deserved.

"Listen to me, both of you," Tom addressed his daughter and the boy she was again clinging to. "We understand how you feel. But we're not in a position to do anything about it right this moment."

"When will we be?" Bret angrily asked.

Tom focused on Heather. "You've been saying all along that you feel like the bandits are always watching you. Why then, in God's name, would you decide to take a dip in the stream?"

"I just wanted —" Heather said softly, her lower lips quivering. She broke out in more tears, her arms rising around Bret's neck.

Constance put a hand on her shoulder.

"I'm sorry. I truly am. But what you did was irresponsible and could have gotten all of us killed."

Stemming the flow of tears, Heather looked up. "What are you talking about, Mother?"

"Think it out, dear," Constance said. She had, and it scared her breathless. "If you had stripped naked and gone into the water, what might the bandits have done? And after they had their way with you, what would they do? Probably kill you so you couldn't accuse them of the rape. Then what? We would find your body. Your father would want to avenge you and one thing would lead to another, and we'd all be dead."

"You would avenge me?" Heather asked Tom.

"What kind of silly question is that? Just because I've had to go along with Cruz and his demands doesn't mean I like it. I would love to line him up in the sights of my Sharps." Tom grew red with resentment. "I would go do it right this minute if it wouldn't bring the rest of the bandits down on the rest of you."

"Patience. That's what we need," Jed contributed his two bits. "We must bide our time or none of us will get through this alive."

Bret made a savage gesture. "I don't agree, Pa. I say we do somethin' now. We can't let them get away with this."

"I'm sorry, son, but we're not liftin' a finger against them until Tom and I agree we should."

Bret and Heather walked off, Heather's head on his shoulder, and sat on a log at the edge of the trees.

"I'm sorry," Jed said to the Waldrons. "Ever since he was in diapers he's had a stubborn streak."

"No need to apologize," Tom said. "Heather is the one to blame."

"I'll try and talk some sense into Bret when we get home," Jed promised. Later that evening he did. Bret listened attentively but did not say much until Jed rose to help Pitney with the dishes.

"Don't worry, Pa. I was mad today. I wanted to rush off and punish Cruz and his banditos. But I know better now."

"I'm glad to hear that, son."

For several days all was well. Bret behaved, and Jed figured that was the end of it. Then, shortly after noon four days later, Jed and Pitney were at the cabin and Jed was chopping wood when he spied Tom Waldron galloping madly toward them.

"He sure is in a powerful hurry, Pa,"

Pitney commented. He was holding the carbine for Jed while Jed worked. "What do you reckon has him so flustered?"

"We'll soon find out."

Tom leaped from his saddle before his horse came to a stop and ran up to Jed and gripped him by the shoulders. "Heather and Bret are gone!"

29

Damn him, Jed thought. Bret was his flesh and blood, but damn him, anyway. Jed lashed Hickory with the reins, pushing the horse hard, as he had been since leaving the Bar G the day before. He had to catch them. He had to stop the two young fools from making a mistake that could cost all of them their lives.

Jed had to hand it to them, though. Bret and Heather had worked it out and tricked everyone but good. The note he'd found the previous morning from Bret saying that Bret would be over at the Waldrons all day had not given him cause for concern. Bret went over to visit Heather every chance he got. It wasn't until Tom showed up that the truth came out.

As best they could reconstruct how it happened, Bret actually sneaked off at midnight and went straight to the ranch house for Heather, taking an extra horse along. She had slipped out and was waiting for him, after leaving a note of her own explaining that she had left for Vinegar Flats at sunup with Jed and the boys. Tom and Constance did not think much of it since the girl had accompanied them a few times before.

Later in the day Tom discovered two of his horses were missing, which seemed strange, since Heather only needed one. He wasn't much of a tracker but he was able to tell that Heather had saddled one of the horses and led both away from the house so as not to awaken Constance and him. Tom found where two fresh sets of hoofprints came from the direction of the Adams cabin. He literally put two and two together, and rushed over to Jed's to let him know.

Now Jed was riding hell-bent for leather to try to stop the young idiots. He was mad that they were so rash, but more than that, he was severely disappointed in his son. Bret should have known better. He should have known how Vasco Cruz would react if Cruz learned they were gone. Bret and Heather had to be stopped.

Poor Constance was devastated. "Where can they be going?" she'd asked with tears in her eyes. "What can they be thinking?"

Jed partly blamed himself. He should have kept a closer eye on his older son. He had forgotten how it felt to be that age and to be in love. He had forgotten how it was when he fell in love with Melanie. How he had pined for her day and night. How every moment spent in her company was bliss. How he would bristle at the thought of her being insulted or hurt. How he would do anything to make her happy.

So how could he find fault with Bret for doing what he would do if their situations were reversed? He had no idea what the two were up to. Were they running away? Bret had never shown a streak of yellow but he might do it for Heather's sake. Were they going after the Texas Rangers or did they intend to contact the army? If so, didn't they realize the bandits would be long gone when help got there?

On Jed rode, as grim as death. He camped that night at a spot he used on every trip to and from the emporium. By sunrise he was back in the saddle. He didn't rest again in order to reach Vinegar Flats that much sooner.

Jed had taken it for granted his son would stop there. It was the logical thing to do. The young lovebirds would need a few supplies and however much ammunition they could afford.

At long last the buildings sprouted from the baked prairie. Jed's happiness at arriving was tempered by his discovery that the horses the pair had taken were nowhere to be seen — not at the hitch rail, not in the corral, not anywhere. He came to a stop at the rail and quickly swung down and looped the reins around it.

After the glare of the bright winter sun, the interior of the emporium was as dim as a cave. The first thing he saw was Kit folding clothes in the dry goods section. The second thing was two bandits at a table near the bar, one of whom was Domingo. The other, he believed, was Felipe.

"Jed! This is a surprise!" Kit spread her arms wide and warmly clasped him to her. "I wasn't expecting you until next week."

"I came early," Jed said. He did not dare tell her the truth, not with the bandits eavesdropping.

"You missed me that much?" Kit asked, grinning in delight. "I'm flattered, you handsome Rebel, you."

"Is anyone else here?" Jed inquired.

"Just Bob. Drunk as a coot, as always." Kit's eyes narrowed and she asked, "Why? Is anything wrong?"

"Only that I've been here a whole minute and you haven't offered me a drink yet," Jed teased.

"I didn't realize you were that fond of liquor." Kit escorted him to the bar. "But I imagine you need to warm your insides after that long, cold ride. How is everyone at the Bar G?"

"Never better." Jed placed his carbine on the bar and leaned on an elbow. He nodded at the bandits but neither had the courtesy to acknowledge his greeting. "Constance and Tom send their regards, and Sally wants to know when you're gettin' in more peanut brittle."

Kit grinned and filled a glass halfway and set it in front of him. "On the house but only because I'm fond of men in uniform. Well, one man in one gray uniform, anyway."

Jed laughed and took a gulp and winced as the whiskey burned a path down his throat to his gut.

"Whoa there," Kit bantered. "Keep that up and you'll be keeping Three Fingers Bob company out in the shed." Again her eyes narrowed. "Are you sure something isn't the matter?"

Jed was flattered she knew him so well but he wished she would stop asking. He swallowed more whiskey and said, "Any chance I can get a bite to eat?"

"I have just the thing."

Kit whisked off and Jed collected his thoughts. Obviously Bret and Heather had not been there or she would have mentioned it, which meant they had skirted the emporium and struck off across the prairie to God knew where, and they were so far ahead of him, he didn't have a snowball's chance in hell of catching up, not when they had those extra horses.

Outwitted by his own son. Who would have thought it? But Jed smiled.

Spurs jangled, and a hand tapped his shoulder. "A moment of your time, *por favor,* gringo?"

The blood in Jed's veins chilled to ice. Forcing a smile, he shifted and said, "Domingo, isn't it? Haven't seen you in a while."

The bull-shouldered bandito was nursing a glass of tequila. "Vasco likes us to stay away from you gringos except when we come down here to rest and drink."

"He's a smart man," Jed commented for want of anything better.

"Vasco is a fox. He is always thinking, that one. Always one step ahead of those who would do us harm." Domingo adjusted the strap to his sombrero. "How are you gringos holding up?"

"Sorry?"

"That is how you say it, is it not? Holding up? We are doing our best not to upset you in any way, as Vasco promised."

"He is a man of his word," Jed said, not without a trace of sarcasm.

Domingo was raising the tequila to his mouth, but paused. "That he is, gringo. He always does as he says he will. I hope you and the others remember that. Betray him, and you will be *muy* sorry."

The veiled threat made Jed wonder if Domingo suspected something. "How stupid do you think we are? We have the children and Constance to think of."

"*Sí,* you do," Domingo said. "But gringos never seem to listen. Gringos always know better than us chile peppers, eh? You look down your noses at us and then are surprised when we cut your noses off."

"We've held up our end of the agreement, haven't we?" Jed responded. "We haven't given you any trouble."

"Because we do not give you the chance," Domingo said. "But it is my hope that you will."

"You're hopin' we'll break the truce?"

Sneering raw malice, Domingo leaned forward. "*Sí,* gringo. I hope you or your friend give us an excuse, any excuse, to do to you as we should have done at the start. I do not like your kind. I do not like *gringos*. As your people like to say about Indians, I say about you. The only good gringo is a dead gringo."

Jed felt his temper surge but he controlled it and said calmly, "I'm sorry to hear you feel that way."

"Sure you are," Domingo scoffed, "as sorry as I will be when I put a bullet in your head" — his sneer widened — "or when I help myself to that *bonita* Senora Waldron. Or her older daughter."

"What would Vasco Cruz say if he heard you talkin' like this?"

"Vasco says what he wants. I say what I want. But I do as Vasco wants, always, which is why he trusts me more than any other."

Jed took a gamble. "Misplaced trust, if you ask me. A coyote like you is bound to stab him in the back one day."

Domingo swore in Spanish and raised a fist to strike but the blow did not land. Instead, he smiled and said, "Very clever, gringo. You make me angry so I will do what Vasco does not want. But it did not work. I am not so easily fooled." He started toward the table but stopped after a few steps.

The front door had opened and in staggered Three Fingers Bob. His clothes were a filthy ruin but he was worse off. He had not shaved in weeks and his hair was a matted mess. His eyes were a vivid red. Thirstily smacking his lips, he teetered toward the bar, calling out, "Kit! Kit! I need a new bottle! I'm plumb out of coffin varnish!"

Jed intercepted him and placed a hand against Bob's chest. "Hold on there, friend. What in hell has gotten into you? You look terrible?"

The old Ranger pushed Jed's hand aside. "So what if I do? I'm not botherin' anyone, am I?" He smacked his lips again and ran his dirty sleeve across his mouth. "Out of the way, Reb. I need a drink and need it bad."

"Why, Bob?" Jed asked. "Why do this to yourself?"

"Why not?" Then Three Fingers Bob steadied himself and met Jed's firm gaze. "I'm tired, sonny, as tired as a body can be and still be breathin'. I've seen it all and done it all and it's caught up with me."

"But you were sober down on the Nueces."

"I did it for you, sonny, you and the Yankee. My good deed for the decade, you might say. Now I'm back to being me and that's how I want to be." Bob moved to go around Jed. "Don't look at me like that. I don't want your pity. I'm a grown man and I make my own bed." He reached the bar and pounded the counter. "How about that bottle, Kit?" He glanced around. "Where in tarnation did that woman get to?"

Domingo was staring at the old Ranger in open contempt. "To all you stinking gringos," he said in a mock toast, and downed some tequila.

Three Fingers Bob faced him. "Look who's talkin'. Why don't you crawl back up your ass where you belong?"

"What did you say?" Domingo's jaw muscles twitched.

"You heard me," Three Fingers Bob said. "Or are your ears plugged with tacos?" He pounded on the bar some more. "Kit! Kit! Come on, darlin'! I can't take much more of this."

Domingo set his glass down and slowly backed away a few steps. "You will apologize, old man."

"Like hell." Three Fingers Bob gripped the counter and his body shook from his hat to his boots. The spasm lasted about ten seconds; then he sucked in a deep breath and looked at the bull-shouldered bandit. "I've seen your kind before. White or Mex or Injun, you're all the same: scum who hate for the fun of hatin', polecats who kill for the thrill of killin'."

"Apologize," Domingo repeated.

"Not on your life." Three Fingers Bob winked at Jed. "Listen to him. The big, bad pistolero threatenin' an old man who isn't even armed. Mighty brave, ain't he? What do you reckon he'll do next? Beat the first old lady who happens by?"

"I mean it, gringo," Domingo growled. "I am not someone you can insult."

Three Fingers Bob laughed. "You've got me tremblin' in my boots. Why, if I had a switch, I'd take you over my knee and learn you some respect for your elders."

Felipe spoke from his chair. "Pay the old fool no mind, amigo. Vasco has given his promise, remember? Let us play our game. I want to win my money back."

Domingo did not answer him.

"Do as he says," Three Fingers Bob taunted. "If you get me riled, I'm liable to stomp on you." He chuckled and glanced toward the rear. "Kit, consarn it! Where are you?"

Jed saw Domingo's eyes blaze with fire and he sprang between them, leveling his carbine. "No! Shoot him and our deal is off."

"Domingo, *por favor!*" Felipe urged.

The stocky bandito slowly uncoiled. Without another word, he wheeled on the high heels of his boots and jangled out the door. Felipe hastened after him, calling out in Spanish.

"I knew he was worthless," Three Fingers Bob grinned. "His kind don't have enough sand to fill an hourglass."

"You shouldn't have done that," Jed said.

"Hell, sonny, in my prime I ate curs like him for breakfast. My sister could whip him with one hand tied behind her back."

"That's the booze talkin'."

"What booze? I'm as dry as the desert." Three Fingers Bob lit up as Kit came hustling over and set a tray with a bowl of soup on the counter and then moved behind the bar.

"Goodness gracious, Bob. I heard you bellowing clear in the back. Here's your darned whiskey."

Bob clutched the bottle and caressed it. "I'm obliged. Now if you two fine folks will excuse me, I have some serious drinkin' to catch up on." He cackled and staggered out.

"I wish he wouldn't do that to himself," Kit said.

Jed was about to agree when three pistol

shots cracked loud and sharp. He ran out with Kit close after him, and there was Three Fingers Bob, lying halfway to the corral, his arms flung out, the whiskey bottle in the dirt at his side. Three holes between his shoulder blades were leaking blood.

Jed was frozen in shock. Then the drum of galloping hooves penetrated his daze, and he whirled. Domingo and Felipe were racing to the northwest, Domingo with a smoking pistol in one hand, whooping in savage glee. Instantly, Jed jerked the carbine to his shoulder and centered the sights on Domingo's broad back.

30

Jed was not thinking of the consequences. He was not thinking of Pitney or Constance or Sally. He was thinking of the old Ranger lying dead in the dust in a spreading pool of red, and he yearned to send lead smashing into the back of the bandito responsible. A small voice deep in his mind screamed at him not to, but he tightened his trigger finger anyway.

At the same instant, a much louder and shriller voice cried, "No, Jed!" and Ruth Kittle grabbed the carbine's barrel and jerked it down.

Off to the northwest, Domingo suddenly twisted in the saddle as if he had been pushed, and slumped forward. But he did not fall off or slow down, and soon he straightened and he and Felipe dwindled in the distance until they were specks.

"I wish you hadn't done that," Jed said grimly.

"Don't you realize what you've done?" Kit asked, as pale as the sheets on her bed.

Jed pointed at Three Fingers Bob. "How

378

about what Domingo has done? Or don't you give a damn that he gunned down that kindly old man in cold blood?" He had never sworn at her, never swore at any woman, but he was seething mad and he could not stop himself.

"Aren't you forgetting something?" Kit countered. "The Waldron boys and your girls and Tom and Connie? Vasco Cruz won't turn the other cheek. You've shot one of his men and he will make you pay."

Jed was staring at Bob. Walking over, he sank onto his right knee and gently rolled him over. There was no doubt Bob was dead but he checked for a pulse anyway. "I liked this old coot," he said softly.

"So did I." Kit was at his elbow and she tenderly squeezed his shoulder. "But you've just unleashed a pack of rabid wolves on us."

"Hold this." Jed gave her the Morse carbine and went to the tool shed and returned with a shovel, which he also had her hold while he carried Three Fingers Bob on around the emporium to a spot twenty yards from the building. "Will this do?"

"Anywhere is fine," Kit said. "But shouldn't we be making plans? Cruz will come after your families. After me, too, when he gets around to it." She gazed for-lornly in the direction of the Guadalupe Mountains. "May Domingo burn in hell for what he's done."

"We have time," Jed said as he placed the tip of the shovel on the hard earth and kicked at the top with his right boot. "It'll take Domingo three days to reach the valley. More, if he takes his time. He won't be in any hurry to tell Cruz how he got shot. Not when he's the one who lost his head and gunned Bob first."

"Domingo will lie," Kit said. "He'll claim Bob and you were shooting at him and he shot Bob as he was getting away."

Jed flipped some dirt to his right and set-tled into a rhythm. "No. Domingo is as loyal to Cruz as loyal can be. He would never lie to him. But that's neither here nor there. While I'm digging, I want you to pack whatever things you want to bring. I'm takin' you to the Bar G, and don't think of refusin'. I'm not leavin' you here alone."

"Whatever you want, darling."

A warm feeling spread through Jed and he had to cough to say, "Before you go, have you seen any sign of Bret and Heather?"

Kit shook her head. "Why? Are you

saying they're missing?"

Jed explained about the incident at the stream and the notes. "I reckon my older boy decided enough was enough, and he was gettin' her out of there whether I liked it or not."

"He loves her, Jed."

"I know, I know. And at his age you don't think straight when your heart is involved." Jed paused in his digging to scan the prairie. "I just wish I knew where they were goin'. There are Indians out there, and a lot of men just like Cruz, or they might run out of water or not have enough food or —" He stopped and bowed his head. "Part of me will die with him."

"Give Bret more credit, will you?" Kit smiled encouragement. "He's cut from the same cloth as his father, and his father has survived a war and a Comanche war party and rustlers."

"That's awful kind. But he's still a boy, and if he had a good head on his shoulders, he'd have thought it through before he ran off on us."

"So that's it. You're taking this personally."

"How else?" Jed responded. "He's bein' selfish. We need his rifle when the attack comes, as we've always known it would. Heather would be of help, too. Now it's

Tom and me and you women and the little ones."

"Speaking for Constance, we'll be right at your sides, reloading for you or shooting if we have to." Kit said the next quietly: "And it's not as if I've never killed anyone."

"Go pack and get ready to lock up. We'll take all your horses, so load however much you can. Ammunition and food are what we need most."

It took more than an hour to bury Three Fingers Bob. The ground did not yield easily, and Kit wanted to read a passage from the Bible. She chose psalm twenty-three. Then she hung a sign in the door that read CLOSED, and they mounted and headed for the high green valley that had become more a prison than a home and might soon be a battleground.

On the afternoon of the second day, with a cold wind from the north howling in their faces, Jed broke hours of silence by saying, "When this is over, you can be my wife if you want."

Kit laughed lightly. "Is that your idea of a proposal? I was hoping for flowers and a ring."

"I'll do it proper when the time comes," Jed promised. "I only wanted you to know it's on my mind."

"Honestly, Jedidiah, I've known that from the moment you kissed me."

Jed made a show of studying the sky and then could not stand the suspense any longer. "What will your answer be?"

Kit grinned. "I'd say the omens are favorable. But are you sure you want to? I can never replace Melanie. She was your first and the first ones are always special."

"I won't love you any less," Jed said. "It's root hog or die, in romance as well as real life."

Kit affected a Southern accent. "I do declare, sir, you have a most marvelous way with words. A woman would be swept off her feet if she wasn't careful."

The temperature continued to drop. By nightfall it was bitter cold, made worse by the wind. They were in the hills and Jed made a fire in a hollow and they cuddled under the blankets next to it to stay warm.

The next morning Jed was the first to awaken. The fire had gone out and he sleepily sat up to rekindle it. Something white and cold and wet slid off his shoulder and under his shirt and made him shiver. "Snow!" he blurted. An inch of white fluff had fallen overnight, the first snow he had seen in years, and he scooped up a handful in delight. Bending over Kit, he let some trickle onto her neck, and when she abruptly sat up, blinking and shivering, he laughed. "Mornin', beautiful."

"Having fun, are we?" Kit pulled the blanket tight around her. "Now I know where Pitney gets it from." She pinched his arm, then regarded the slate gray sky. "It will be deeper higher up."

"But not deep enough to stop us, I reckon."

Jed was proven right. By the time they reached the Bar G, the snow was only four inches deep. Drawing rein, Jed sat back and exclaimed, "My God, that's grand!"

A white mantle covered the valley from end to end except for the brown and green of the tall timber and the reddish-brown of the high cliffs and the blue-green of the stream. Cattle sprinkled the valley like pepper on a white plate, unaffected by the wintry weather. They were hardy brutes, those longhorns.

Smoke curled from the stone chimney atop the Waldron ranch house. Someone saw them winding up the valley because when they reached it, Tom and Constance and Sally and Pitney were outside to welcome them.

"Bret and Heather?" Constance anxiously asked. She had been worried sick and could neither eat nor sleep.

Jed shook his head as he alighted. "They're long gone. Your guess is as good as mine where." He stepped over to his younger son. "Did you miss me?" Jed wanted to hug him but of late Pitney had been saying that hugging was for kids, and he wasn't a little kid anymore.

"You know I did, Pa," the boy said and came into Jed's arms on his own. "Why did Bret do it, Pa?" he asked, his voice breaking. "Why did he leave us?"

"He did what he thought was best," Jed said. Later, he would try to explain it more fully, as best he was able, but for now he had other tidings to share. "I'm about froze. Kit, too. We could sure go for some coffee."

A pot was already on the stove. Jed and Kit sat on one side of the table and Tom and Constance on the other.

They took the news hard. "I liked that old cuss," Constance said, her eyes moistening. "He was always nice to the children, and he helped us when we needed it most."

"It's the bandits we need to think about now," Tom said. "They'll be coming after us before too long."

Constance glanced at him sharply.

"What?" Tom said. "I'm as sorry about Bob as you are. When he wasn't drinking, he was a fine human being. But he's gone now, and I don't want any of us to join him. We must deal with the bandits."

For the rest of the day and long into the night, they discussed their predicament.

At eight Jed tucked Pitney under blankets in a far corner of the main room. Shortly after midnight he sat down on his own blankets to take off his boots and was mildly surprised to notice his son was awake and watching him. "Can't you sleep?"

"I keep thinkin' about Bret, about him goin' away without tellin' us. Doesn't he care for us anymore, Pa?"

"Sure he does. But he's in love with Heather, and when men are in love, they do things they wouldn't do if they were in their right mind."

"Love makes folks crazy?"

"You could say that," Jed said. "It's a strange sort of craziness, son. Your head hurts sometimes and you have an ache in your chest, and when you try to think, your mind is as mushy as oatmeal."

"It sounds like havin' a cold," Pitney said, "only without the runny nose. Why would anyone want that?"

"There's no greater feelin' in the world."

"But you just said —" Pitney began.

"I know," Jed said, "but there's more to

it. You see, most of the time you feel just fine. Finer than you ever have. So fine, you think you must be dreamin'. Life is warm and wonderful and everythin' is right with the world."

"That doesn't make any kind of sense."

"I suppose it doesn't. You have to be in love to understand it. It's a mystery how it works. Folks have been tryin' to make sense of it since Adam and Eve and no one has figured it out yet."

Pitney said, "I hope to God I never fall in love."

"Don't take the Almighty's name in vain. And I don't know how to break this to you, but odds are, you will. Cupid hits everyone sooner or later, and once he does, you're a goner."

"Who?"

"Cupid is a little gent with wings who flies around shootin' little arrows into people. Invisible arrows we can't see that go right into our hearts and make us grow to love someone."

"You're makin' this up, aren't you, Pa?"

"As God is my witness." Jed grinned and set his boots to one side. "Don't fret yourself about it. One day your turn will come. Until it does, don't pay girls no mind."

"I won't, Pa," Pitney said, "but I sure do

like Sally a lot. She's not like most girls. She likes catchin' snakes and such. And she hates to take a bath as much as I do."

"Imagine that." Jed turned in and lay on his back with his hands folded on his chest. Soon his son was breathing deeply but Jed could not do the same. He had too much on his mind: Bret and Heather, the bandits, the welfare of his family and friends. Sleep claimed him, although he was not conscious of drifting off, and the next he knew, he was awake and sitting up. A few of the logs in the fireplace blazed red but the room was cold. Soon he had the fire going again.

Slipping outside, Jed stretched, then made a circuit of the house. The horses in the corral had not been disturbed. Nor were there any suspicious new footprints in the fresh snow.

"Wouldn't it be funny if after all this worry the bandits don't show?" Jed asked himself. Silently closing the door, he put coffee grounds in the coffeepot and filled the pot with water and placed it on the stove. No one else was up yet, so he hunkered by the fireplace with his hands to the flames.

Sally stirred before the rest. She came shuffling over with her eyes half shut and her hair hanging down her face. "Morning, Mr. Adams."

"When will you start to call me Jed like I've asked?"

"My mother says a lady should always be polite and I'm a lady whether I want to be or not." Sally scratched her head and her side and her shoulder. "How long will you be staying with us this time?"

Distracted by a burning log that was sliding toward the floor, Jed absently answered, "For as long as it takes." He used the poker to push the log in place.

"Until we kill all those bad men, you mean? Pitney says we should sneak up on them in the dark and bash their brains out with rocks."

"He does, does he?" Jed's younger son had never mentioned that to him.

"Can I go look at the snow?" Sally asked. "My mother and father aren't up yet and I always have to ask first."

"I'd better go with you," Jed said. He walked to the door and waited while the girl donned a shawl. Then he opened the door for her and said, "After you."

Sally stepped to the doorway, then froze, her face a mask of terror. "Mr. Adams!" she bleated.

Jed knew who he would see before he looked up.

It was Vasco Cruz.

31

The bandit leader had reined up by the woodpile and was dismounting. He saw Jed and Sally in the doorway and smiled. Hooking his thumbs in his crisscrossed gun belts, he jingled toward them.

Jed Adams had left his carbine by the fireplace. He had an overpowering urge to run over and snatch it up but he stayed where he was. Out of the corner of his mouth, he whispered to Sally, "Get over by Pitney and stay there." She looked at him, then turned and did as she had been told without arguing.

Cruz stopped ten feet out and beckoned. "A word with you, Senor Adams, *por favor.*"

Jed had to fight another urge — the urge to slam the door in the bandit's face and bolt it. But he did not see the other bandits, and Cruz was behaving friendly enough. Jed told himself that maybe, just maybe, the bandit leader did not know about the gunfight at the emporium. His mouth as dry as sand, he walked out, leaving the door partway open behind him. "This is a surprise," he said by way of greeting.

"I have kept my word to leave you alone, have I not?" Cruz surveyed the log ranch house and the cleared ground. "Senor Waldron has put a lot of work into his new home, eh?"

"Buildin' a ranch takes a lot of sweat," Jed said. He gazed past Cruz into the timber. If the bandits were there, they were well hidden.

"So does doing what I do. It is not an easy life. To sleep with a roof over our heads is a luxury." Cruz's smile faded. "But I did not come here to make small talk, as you gringos have it. I came because I am puzzled."

"Puzzled?" Jed said, regretting he had not brought his carbine.

"*Sí. For instance, I have been down to Vinegar Flats and the pretty senorita is gone. You wouldn't happen to know where she is, would you?*"

"Right here," Jed said. "Payin' us a visit. She does that from time to time, you know."

"*Sí,* I do know. But usually she leaves the old drunk to watch over her store. He was not there, so I looked around. Imagine my surprise to find a mound of dirt that had not been there before. Imagine my bigger surprise, senor, when I had my men dig into the dirt and we found the old one with bullet holes in what was left of his body."

Jed was confused. By now Domingo should have told Cruz about the shooting. Then it hit him. Domingo must be keeping quiet so Cruz wouldn't learn what he had done.

"You wouldn't happen to know anything about that, would you, senor?" Vasco Cruz asked.

"Maybe you should talk to Domingo," Jed suggested, in case Cruz did know and was testing him.

"I already have. You see, last night we were sitting around the campfire, talking and telling tales, as men do. I clapped Domingo on the shoulder, as men do, and it caused him great pain he could not hide."

Off in the trees something moved — an arm or a leg, Jed wasn't sure.

"I was curious. So I asked him what was wrong and he said his horse had thrown him." Cruz laughed a laugh without warmth. "Domingo! Who could ride before he could walk! I made him take his jacket and his shirt off, and do you know what I found, senor?"

"What?" Jed said. He spied the crown of a sombrero in a patch of thick brush, and his palms broke out in sweat.

"A bullet hole. He had been shot in the back but the bullet went through and he was not too badly hurt."

"Did he tell you who shot him?"

"Why, yes, senor, he did." Vasco Cruz's dark eyes glittered. "He says that you shot him. That he and the old one argued, and the old one pulled a gun and Domingo had to shoot him, and then, as Domingo and Felipe rode off, you ran out and shot Domingo in the back." Sudden hatred twisted Cruz's features. "You gringo bastard."

Jed saw a rifle barrel poke from behind a pine, and another from behind a madrone. But they couldn't shoot with Cruz in the way. "Your man lied. Three Fingers Bob did not have a gun."

"So you say. But am I to believe you or Domingo, who has been like a brother to me all these years? Domingo, who has saved my life more times than you have fingers and toes? Domingo, my most trusted and loyal follower?"

"If he's so loyal, why didn't he tell you

he was shot?" Jed asked. "Why did he keep it a secret?"

"For my sake. He knew how mad I would be that you gringos had not lived up to your promise."

"So naturally you take his word over mine."

"Did you not hear me? He is the brother I never had. As close to me as this." Cruz held up his left hand with two fingers entwined. "I would never doubt his honesty."

"Then you're a fool," Jed said flatly, knowing doing so was a mistake but unable to stop himself.

"One of us is," Vasco Cruz said. Then he went for his pistols.

Jed was expecting it. He figured Cruz thought he would turn and run and be easy to gun down but instead Jed sprang and slammed his right fist against Cruz's jaw. Cruz stumbled, half stunned, and Jed grabbed him by the front of his jacket and swiftly backpedaled, using him as a shield. He saw five or six bandits rise from concealment but they held their fire.

Jed was almost to the door when Vasco Cruz abruptly straightened up and tore free and dived to one side, shouting a command in Spanish. Whirling, Jed threw himself through the doorway as the woods erupted in a thunderous volley. Lead bit into the jamb and the door and the floor. Flying slivers stung Jed's cheek. He landed on his stomach and kicked out, shutting the door with his foot.

Tom Waldron was startled out of a deep sleep by a blast of gunfire. He heaved up out of bed, blurting, "What in the world?" Lead was splatting against all four sides of the house. He heard Sally scream. Grabbing the Sharps from the corner where it was propped, he ran from the bedroom.

"Get down!" Jed shouted, as much for Tom's benefit as Pitney's and Kit's. His younger son was on his hands and knees, crabbing toward his squirrel rifle, and Kit had sat up over in the far corner. "Everyone stay down!"

The walls and the door resounded to thud after thud. So did the boards nailed over the window. The bandits emptied their rifles, some yipping and yelling as if it were a game.

Constance came crawling from the bedroom, frantic with fear for her daughter and her husband. Seeing them safe, she crawled to Sally, who scrambled into her lap.

The firing ended and silence fell.

Jed reached his carbine and fed a cartridge

into the chamber. Rising into a crouch, he moved over near the door and was joined by Tom. Briefly, Jed related what Cruz had said.

"It was bound to come to this sooner or later," Tom said. "Cruz should have jumped us when we were outside. We can hold out a good long while in here." The log walls were thick. They had plenty of food and water and enough firewood to last them a month.

"Maybe I should try to talk to him," Kit suggested, "tell him I saw the whole thing, and Domingo is the one who broke their word."

"He'd never believe you," Jed said. Worse, Cruz might take her hostage to force them to give up.

A tense hour passed. Whenever they moved about, they made it a point to stay low to the floor. Constance gave each of the adults cups of coffee. Sally and Pitney were happy with bread smeared with butter.

"I hate this waitin'," Pitney said. "Why don't they do somethin'?"

As if in answer, Vasco Cruz hollered, "Can you hear me in there, gringos?"

"We hear you!" Jed shouted. He was at one of the gun slits. Only two inches wide and three inches high, it did not afford much of a view.

"You think you can wait us out in there. But you are not as smart as you think you are. My men and I could burn the house down with all of you in it."

Tom glanced at Jed. Fire was the one thing they could not defend themselves against. The flames would drive them out, straight into the waiting rifles of the bandits.

"But that is not how I want your end to be," Cruz had continued. "I want to kill you myself. I want to hear your screams. I want to see your blood and feel it on the palms of my hands."

"I'm scared," Sally said.

Cruz wasn't through. "We can wait until you run out of food, gringos, but that could be days. Perhaps weeks. And why bother when I can kill you anytime I please? I should thank you for making it so easy for me."

"What does he mean?" Tom asked.

"I like the idea of you living in fear, of not knowing when I will come again. Think of me, gringos. Think of me every second you are awake. See me in every shadow. Hear me in every sound." Vasco Cruz laughed, then spoke at length in Spanish. Hooves drummed, and the bandits called out to one another.

"What are they up to?" Tom wondered. Something was happening at the rear of the house. A loud whinny provided the answer, and he lunged toward the door. "They're stealing our horses!"

"No!" Jed seized him by the arm and held fast. "That's exactly what they want you to do."

"But the horses!" Tom exclaimed, trying to break free. Without them, they were at Cruz's mercy. Then he saw the panic mirrored on Sally's face, and realizing he was to blame, he sank back down and said as calmly as he could under the circumstances, "You're right. It's not worth being shot."

Cruz's laughter taunted them. "What will you do now, gringos? Will you run away? How far will you get on foot in this cold and the snow, with your little ones at your side?"

Tom swore luridly.

"I leave you now but I will be back. Count the minutes. When next you see me, your lives will end."

Shouting and yipping, the bandits rode off. After a while, Pitney fidgeted and asked, "Do you reckon they're really gone, Pa?"

"I don't know, son," Jed answered. "It could be they want us to think they are but some of them are waitin' for us to poke our heads out. We'll do some waitin' of our own until we think it's safe."

The rest of the day crawled by. Morning became afternoon and afternoon gave way to night. Constance wanted to light a lantern but Jed said they should hold off a bit. "The light will give me away when I go have a look-see."

"Why you?" Tom asked. "We should flip a coin."

"Next time, pard." Jed was at the door. "I'm the one who shot Domingo. It's on my shoulders." He quietly worked the latch and eased the door open a crack. Brisk air fanned his cheeks. With a glance at Pitney, he jerked the door open wide enough to slip outside. Instantly closing it behind him, he sidestepped to the right, his back to the logs, braced for the blast of gunfire, for the darkness to flare with the flash of rifle muzzles. But there was only the wind and the slight crunch of his boots on the snow's hard crust.

At the corner Jed paused. He was sure it was a trick. Some of the bandits were still out there or else had circled back. Tucking at the knees, he sprinted to the corral.

Once again no shots rang out.

The corral was empty. All their horses were gone. Jed started to turn, then sensed he was not alone. A shadow was slinking toward him from the front of the house. He raised his carbine.

"Jed, it's me!" Tom whispered. "I couldn't let you do it alone." Not with Kit looking at him in unvoiced reproach.

"You almost got yourself killed!" Jed hunkered, secretly pleased Tom thought enough of him to come after him.

"Any sign of —" Tom began.

They both heard it. The *clomp* of a hoof in the trees beyond the corral. Two figures came warily stalking along the fence.

"It's them!" Tom snapped his Sharps to his shoulder but as he touched his finger to the trigger, the second figure took a step away from the fence and was silhouetted against the snow. The figure was wearing a dress.

"Father, is that you?" Heather asked and hurried up, her hand in Bret's. "We thought it was but we couldn't be sure."

Tom was too overjoyed to take her to task. He hugged her, and she said in his ear, "I'm sorry. We're both sorry. It was a dumb thing to do."

Jed gripped his older son's shoulder and

smiled. "You came back to us. I can't tell you how proud I am, son."

"I talked her into it, Pa," Bret said. "I wanted her safe. As far from here as we could get. But we couldn't go through with it. We couldn't desert our own kin. So here we are."

"The bandits?" Jed asked.

"We saw them ride off but I wasn't sure it was all of them, so we laid low. They made camp a couple of miles down the valley. You can see their campfire from over yonder."

Tom said, "If any were still here, they'd have shot at us by now. Bring your horses around front." He pecked his daughter on the temple. "As for you, young lady, your mother has been sick with worry. You owe her an apology. Go in and set her mind at ease."

Heather hastened away, and Tom faced Jed Adams. "My commanding officer used to say that the key to winning a battle is the element of surprise. Well, Cruz thinks he has all our horses. The last thing he'll expect is for us to pay him a visit." Tom grinned. "What do you say, Reb?"

Jed responded, "You took the words right out of my mouth, Yankee. I say we pay those coyotes a visit."

"Count me in, Pa," Bret said.

Ordinarily, Jed would have refused. But his older boy was a man now, or close to it, and three guns were better than two when they were up against eleven. "On one condition, son. You do exactly as I tell you. No guff, no sass, no thinkin' you know better than me."

"I'll do whatever you want," Bret promised. "All I care about is killin' those sons of bitches."

Tom Waldron patted his Sharps. "That makes three of us."

32

The fire had died low. Only a few small flames licked at charred limbs. The three sleeping forms ringing it were bundled deep in their blankets. They had not posted a guard. Their horses, and the animals stolen from the corral, were tethered nearby. Several of the animals pricked their ears and raised their heads but did not whinny or stamp their hooves, which was fine by Tom Waldron. He was on his belly, snaking through snow, wet and cold but not caring.

Jed crawled toward the bandits from the south. He could just see Bret to the west. They had worked it out in advance, and when Jed was close enough, he quietly rose and stalked to the nearest bandit. "Rise and shine, you no-account scum."

The man's head snapped up and his arm moved under his blanket, and Jed did the only thing he could; he squeezed the trigger.

Tom had another bandit covered. The plan was to take one alive and find out where Cruz had gone but the second bandit was as reckless as the first and rolled out from under his blankets with a pistol in his hand. At that range the Sharps made a hole the size of a pear.

That left the third bandit, who was as quick as a rattler. He jumped up with his blanket hanging from around his shoulders and made a break for cover. Bret fired and the blanket whipped as if in the wind but the bandit was not in it.

The man had thrown the blanket to the left and gone right, toward the horses. He launched himself onto the bare back of a grulla. A swing of his arm and a slap of his legs and the tether rope was gone and the grulla bolted into the night with the bandit bent low, holding on to its mane.

Jed drew his revolver and fired but he was hasty and knew he missed. His son ran to another horse to give chase, and Jed shouted, "Forget it! We can't catch him in the dark." Left unsaid was his concern that the bandit might lie in wait for them out in the dark and pick Bret off.

Tom said, "We got two of them, anyway. Where do you think the rest got to?"

"We'll find out once it's light enough to follow their tracks." Jed checked each of the bandits to ensure they were dead, then stripped them of their revolvers and gun belts and knives. "We'll take these to Kit and Constance and the horses to the corral and head out at daybreak."

"I'm sorry, Pa," Bret said.

"For what?" This from Tom. "In battle nothing ever goes as it should. It wasn't your fault."

Jed thought it awful kind of his partner to say that. "Fetch our horses, son." When Bret jogged off, he stated the obvious. "We can't surprise Cruz now. It's not too late to change your mind and take Constance and the kids to Fort Bliss."

Tom swept an arm at the snowy landscape. "It's the dead of winter. It would take weeks. Across country infested by outlaws and hostiles. No, thanks. Connie and the kids are safer here." He paused. "Besides, it wouldn't be right to let you face Cruz's pack of wolves alone."

"Bret will be with me."

"He's brave enough," Tom said. "But you saw how he let that bandit get away. There's no substitute for experience." He grinned as he added, "You're stuck with me, Reb, whether you like it or not."

"Typical Yankee," Jed joked. "Always tellin' us poor Southern trash what to do. Just don't blame me if they blow out your wick."

They buried the bodies in shallow graves. Tom was all for letting them rot, but Jed pointed out that it might not do to have Sally or Constance or Kit ride by one day and see the skeletons. "Why remind them of what we've been through?"

"Sounds to me as if you expect Kit to make her home at the Bar G one day," Tom remarked.

"I hope to God, yes," Jed said and felt a tweak of remorse. *Melanie, please forgive me*, he thought.

By the time they placed the horses in the corral and had a cup of coffee, dawn painted the eastern horizon in vivid pinks and yellows.

"You make it back to me, Thomas Waldron," Constance said as she handed him his saddlebags. "I didn't come all this way to be made a widow."

Jed squatted in front of Pitney and touched his son's chin. "While we're gone, you're the man of the house. I expect you to help Connie and Kit with whatever needs doin'."

"I will, Pa. And I won't let anyone hurt them, neither."

"That's my boy." Jed pecked his younger boy on the forehead and turned to fork leather. Only Kit was between him and

Hickory. "I just gave you a hug, woman. Do you want another?" Without answering, she kissed him full on the mouth, long and hard, and when she stepped back, they were both breathing heavier than they had been. "What was that for?"

"Incentive," Kit said.

Tom was taken aback when his wife kissed him in the same lingering manner. "Was that my incentive?"

"A promise of things to come."

Thanks to the snow, the trail was as plain as if the bandits had left signs pointing the way. It led out of the valley and down through the mountains and wound through the foothills to the prairie, where only patches of snow remained.

"They're headin' for Vinegar Flats," Jed said.

"Why there, of all places?" from Bret.

It was Tom who answered. "All that liquor, all that food. With Kit gone, they can get in out of the cold and help themselves. Not many travelers come by at this time of year, so they're safe enough. And since Cruz took all our horses, he figures he doesn't have reason to worry about us."

"But now he'll know better because of that bandit who slipped away," Bret said in self-reproach.

"Don't be so hard on yourself, son," Jed said. "Things have still worked out better than we could have hoped." He rattled off why. "We have horses, thanks to you. We've whittled the odds, thanks to you. We're takin' the fight to Cruz instead of waitin' for him to bring it to us, and we have you along to help."

Tom nodded. "Best of all, the women and the girls are safe. We owe it all to you, Bret. If you hadn't come back when you did, your father and I were staring at early graves. And I don't need to tell you what Cruz had in store for my wife and Kit, do I?"

"Thanks. Both of you," Bret said. "I feel a little better."

That night they camped a half mile from the emporium. They did not dare a fire, and it was bitterly cold. The wind howled out of the northwest and clouds scuttled across the sky like a swarm of hungry locusts. A few snowflakes fell, but only a few.

An hour before sunrise Jed rose and stretched. He had not slept much. He was a bundle of nerves, as he had often been during a campaign. Sleep came hard when a man might die the next day. Thankfully, the wind had slackened and the clouds were gone. He could use a cup of coffee but it had to wait.

Tom threw off his blankets. "It's nights like this that make a man appreciate a bed." He donned his blue cap and glanced at Bret, who was snoring blissfully. "You can do the honors."

The night before they had worked out their plan of attack. Jed rode off first, heading north in a wide loop that would eventually bring him up on Vinegar Flats from the east. Tom and Bret waited a half hour, then mounted and rode briskly toward the buildings. They had to be in position before the sun came up.

"Do you think it will work, Mr. Waldron?" Bret anxiously asked.

Tom tried to sound more confident than he felt when he said, "Combining infantry and cavalry tactics? It worked for Grant and Lee."

"But they had whole armies. There are just the three of us."

"The bandits don't have an army, either," Tom said.

Two hundred yards out they slowed to a walk. At one hundred yards Tom drew rein and swung down. They advanced on foot, skirmish style. Tom had told the boy to do exactly as he did, so when he tucked at the knees and wedged the Sharps to his shoulder, Bret imitated him. They angled slightly south of the main building so Tom could take up position behind the shed near the corral and Bret behind the shed near the pump. They were far enough apart that they could cover the front door and the window, and both corners.

The eastern sky brightened rapidly. Another few minutes and a sliver of gold crowned the horizon, growing in size as the sun rose to reclaim the vault of sky.

No sounds came from within the emporium but Tom suspected it wouldn't be long before the banditos were up and about. Their horses lined the hitch rail and were tied to posts at each end of the overhang, saddled for a quick getaway should the need arise. Vasco Cruz was not one to be caught unprepared but he had made a mistake this time, and if Tom had his way, it would be his last.

Suddenly the front door opened and out came a bandit whose name Tom did not know. The man was short and stocky; he blinked sleepily. Scratching himself, he moved slowly toward the pump, a bucket swinging by its handle from his left hand.

Tom saw Bret lean his rifle against the pump shed and draw his long-bladed knife. He wanted to signal the boy not to try it but the bandit might notice. All he could do was crouch and watch as the bandit came to the pump and set down the bucket and reached for the handle. Only half awake, the bandit rubbed his eyes and shivered in the morning chill.

Bret was on him in a rush, the blade gleaming in the sunlight. He buried it to the hilt in the bandit's armpit. As Tom had been taught during bayonet training, it could incapacitate a man in seconds, although how the boy knew that, Tom had no idea. Bret jerked the knife out and blood spewed in a geyser. The bandit had stiffened and now clumsily clawed for a pistol with his other arm while opening his mouth to shout a warning to his friends inside. Bret was a shade faster. He swung the knife in a crimson arc that opened the bandit's throat from ear to ear. More blood gushed, and Bret had to spring out of the way to keep from being drenched as the bandit slowly sank to his knees and then pitched face-first to the dust.

Quickly, Bret wiped his knife clean on the man's jacket, then sheathed it, grabbed the bandit by the shoulders, and dragged him behind the pump shed. Bret glanced at Tom and grinned.

Tom smiled and nodded. His prospective son-in-law had done amazingly well. Evidently Jed had taught him a thing or two.

They settled down to wait. Tom gazed eastward but did not see Jed. He hoped nothing had happened to him. If Jed didn't show at the crucial moment, all was lost. He was surprised Cruz hadn't posted a lookout. The bandit who escaped up in the valley must have reached Vinegar Flats the night before, so Cruz had plenty of warning. Or maybe, Tom reflected, the bandit who just came to the pump had been the lookout, and had fallen asleep.

For the longest while, the store was quiet. The sun was almost above the horizon when another bandit opened the front door and stepped outside. This one was tall and thin. Emilio was his name, and he wore two Remingtons high on his skinny hips. His hands on their grips, he moved to the edge of the overhang. "Ramon?" he called, his face screwed up in puzzlement. He looked right and then left and then toward the outhouse. "Ramon?"

When he received no answer, Emilio took a couple of steps, then abruptly stopped, a wariness about him as he intently scanned the outbuildings and the corral. "Ramon?" he shouted, adding something in Spanish.

Tom had one eye to the corner of the

shed, careful not to show more of himself. He could see the pump shed. Bret was easing his rifle past the corner to take a shot. The boy had the right idea but he should have waited for the bandit to come farther out.

Suddenly Emilio gave a start. The Remingtons leaped clear of their holsters and Emilio fired four swift shots at the pump shed while backpedaling toward the emporium. His aim was good. All four slugs bit into the shed within inches of the rifle barrel, and Bret had to duck back.

Emilio was under the overhang, almost to the door, and he fired twice more. By then Tom had the sights of his Sharps centered on the bandit's chest above the spot where Emilio's bandoleers crossed. He had the hammer thumbed back and he pulled the rear trigger to set the front trigger and then ever so gradually he applied pressure to the front trigger until the big rifle boomed. The impact smashed Emilio against the jamb and he hung suspended there an instant before his legs gave way and he oozed down into a sitting position. Tom figured he was dead, but Emilio suddenly twisted and pushed on the door and vanished inside.

Shouts filled the emporium. Boots thudded on the floorboards. The new glass in the store window filled with swarthy, mustachioed faces.

Tom hoped Kit would forgive him. He had reloaded, and sighting on one of the faces, he fired. Whether he hit the bandit or not he couldn't say, but half the window shattered and dissolved in a shower of shards.

Bret fired, too.

Then pistols blasted, from the doorway and the window. Tom had to jerk back as lead struck the shed and sizzled in the air. He ejected the cartridge and fed in another.

Someone was yelling. It sounded like Vasco Cruz. The firing stopped and the bandit leader called out, "You are a dead man, Yankee gringo! You and the young one!"

Tom did not answer. There were eight of them left. Still a lot but he had gone up against worse in the war.

"Where is the other one?" Cruz shouted. "Senor Adams, the Rebel? He is out there, I know, and we will kill him as surely as we will kill you."

Bret cupped a hand to his mouth. "Big talk, mister! We've got you trapped in there! Your days of robbin' and murderin' are over!"

Foolish, Tom thought. The words had accomplished nothing. But the young ones always liked to make themselves heard in battle. It was encouraged by their officers. Battle cries lent courage to the timid and the scared.

"You think so, do you, boy?" Vasco Cruz responded, then laughed. "This is what I get for not burning you out when I should have! For playing cat and mouse and letting the mice live a little longer!"

Tom was glad the emporium did not have a back door. He had asked Kit about that once and she said her husband only wanted one way in and out so if they were ever beset by hostiles, the Indians could only get at them from the front, making the store that much easier to defend.

Cruz was in a talkative mood. "Do you hear me, Senor Waldron? Why do you not speak? Are you wounded, perhaps? It serves you right for turning against me."

Tom could not let that pass. "Who are you trying to kid, you bastard? Even if Jed hadn't shot Domingo, even if we had done everything you asked, you had no intention of letting us live. Come spring, you were going to slaughter us just like you did those people on the wagon train."

"Sí," Vasco Cruz candidly admitted, "but that would not be for a month or two yet. Now you will die that much sooner."

Tom suspected Cruz was stalling. The bandits were up to something. He could hear muffled noises, hear them moving around. Then a bundled blanket came flying out the front door and landed in the brown earth past the overhang. Another followed it, and yet a third. More came sailing through the window, along with shirts, pants and dresses. All the garments and blankets Kit had for sale were being tossed outside.

What in hell were they up to? Tom wondered. It made no sense to him, no sense at all.

Then the front of the store grew bright with light, and seconds later a lit lantern sailed from the building and landed amid the pile near the front door. Another lit lantern was tossed from the window. Pistols cracked, and both lanterns burst into flames, which rapidly spread to the garments and the blankets. The horses whinnied and shied and frantically sought to pull loose from the posts and the hitch rail.

Tom still did not understand. Then smoke began to rise, lots and lots of smoke, screening the front of the emporium. "Son of a bitch."

To the east the prairie had grown a hump. Anyone gazing that way would mistake it for a mound of dirt. Or so Jed Adams hoped as he lay behind Hickory, the horse on its side, awaiting the dawn. It was an old cavalry trick. He had used it several times when he was on night patrol in enemy territory and had to take cover quickly.

His cavalry training was the key to their plan. Tom and Bret would draw the bandits out, and at the right moment, Jed would charge in and take Vasco Cruz and his men completely by surprise. If it worked, half the bandits would be dead before they could collect their wits, and the rest be put to rout.

A bandit stumbled from the store. Jed saw Bret knife him, saw another bandit emerge. Shots were exchanged, and the bandits started throwing clothes and blankets out. Mystified, he rose to his knees. When the first lantern was heaved from the building, he divined why.

"Up, boy!" Jed hollered, hauling on the reins and stepping into the stirrups as the horse rose. When it was fully erect, he was in the saddle, poised to ride.

A second lantern followed the first. Jed jabbed his spurs harder than he normally would and drew the Leech and Rigdon revolver Kit had given him. Smoke was rising from the clothes and blankets. Tom and Bret couldn't see the door or the window, which was exactly what Vasco Cruz intended.

Jed was still fifty feet out when the bandits spilled into the open, firing as they came. Eight of them. Four broke toward Tom, four toward the shed shielding Bret. A brilliant tactic. Jed could not help thinking that Vasco Cruz would have made a great military leader. But he wasn't there to admire the bandit's cleverness — he was there to kill, and kill he did, firing two shots into a bandit and scoring with both.

Tom Waldron was ready for the rush. He shot the first man to come through the smoke, then dropped the Sharps and drew his Starr Army revolver. He was no gunman but he could cock the revolver and shoot with some precision and he did so now, shooting a second bandit in the chest. But two of them were pouring lead at the shed and Tom had to crouch down or be riddled. The shed walls were too thin to stop the lead hail. His leg seared with pain and he flung himself to the left and fired even as another pain speared his ribs. Slugs smacked the ground around him as he worked the hammer and the trigger as rapidly as he was able.

Jed Adams let out with a Rebel yell. Three bandits were closing on Bret. His son had shot one of them but the man had not gone down, and now Bret was desperately trying to reload while the shed was being reduced to a bullet-punctured sieve. Then Jed slammed into them or, rather, Hickory did, and one of the bandits went flying. Jed snapped off a shot to the right and twisted and snapped off one to the left. Another bandit was firing back, and Jed winced as searing agony spiked his right arm. The next instant he was falling. He landed on his back and drew a spare revolver from his belt, a revolver he had taken from one of the dead bandits in the valley. A familiar face loomed, and Jed fired as Vasco Cruz fired, fired as Vasco Cruz swayed, fired as Vasco Cruz staggered back and pitched to his knees.

Tom was aware of a ringing in his ears, of the acrid scent of gunpowder. He swiped at tendrils of smoke and slowly sat up. Four bodies were sprawled in postures of violent death. He tried to stand and discovered he had a bullet hole in his right leg. He also had a deep furrow in his left side below his ribs and a wound in his shoulder. "Damn," he blurted. "I've been shot to pieces." A wave of dizziness afflicted him but it soon passed and Tom struggled to his feet. Moving stiffly, he limped past the shed.

Bret was on his knees next to his father, his face buried in his hands.

Tom's gut churned. "Is he . . . ?" he asked, but he could not finish the question. He saw Vasco Cruz; Cruz's face was blown half to hell. Tom smiled grimly. "At least he took that bastard with him."

"I'm not dead yet, you damned Yankee," Jed said. He wanted to rise but he was too weak. He had two holes in him and he was leaking blood.

Shuffling over, Tom grinned. "Didn't your captain ever tell you the general idea is *not* to be shot?"

"Look who's talkin'," Jed retorted. "I don't recollect that shirt of yours bein' red." To Bret he said, "Stop your cryin', son. You're a man now, and men do their bawlin' in private." He raised his right arm. "Help me up."

Gray tendrils swirled about them as they hobbled toward the emporium.

"Do you reckon you'll live, Yank?" Jed asked.

"I think so, Reb, yes," Tom said. As best as he could tell, none of his wounds were mortal. But, God, how they hurt.

"Then as soon as we mend, we'll brand our longhorns. Just think. We'll have the first ranch in these parts and —"

Bret suddenly stopped and pointed to the northwest. "Pa! More bandits! What do we do?"

Squinting at the far-off riders, Jed chuckled. "Look again. Unless bandits have taken to wearin' dresses, that's Kit and Constance and the rest."

"They were supposed to stay at the ranch house." Tom Waldron sighed. "Have you ever noticed how women never do what you ask them to do?"

"My grandpa used to say that females are born with their ears plugged with wax, and it just gets worse as they get older." Jed poked Bret with his revolver. "Take me inside, son. I want a drink before Kit puts me in bed and keeps me there until I'm fit enough to do cartwheels."

A bottle of whiskey had been left open on the bar. Tom filled a glass for himself and another for Jed. Dripping blood, so weak they could barely stand, they hoisted their glasses and clinked them together.

"To the North and the South," Tom Waldron toasted.

"Haven't you heard? The war's over." Jed Adams grinned. "To the Bar G!"